jules cassard

DIRT NAP RHAPSODY

HOPEWELL
MANHATTAN
PRESS

Copyright © 2014, 2015 by Jules Cassard, Hopewell Manhattan Press, Steven Guggenheimer. All Rights Reserved. No part of this publication may be reproduced, distributed, or transmitted in any form without the prior written permission of the publisher, except in the case of brief quotations embodied in critical reviews and certain other noncommercial uses permitted by copyright law.

For permission requests, contact the publisher at permissions@hopewellmanhattan.com.

Ordering Information: For details on Quantity sales, special discounts, or Orders by U.S. trade bookstores and wholesalers, contact the publisher at books@hopewellmanhattan.com.

This is a work of fiction. All names, places, events, and characters are products of the author's imagination or used fictitiously. Any resemblance to real persons, either living or dead, places, or events is purely coincidental.

Cover Design by Lynae Leblanc

ISBN-13: 978-0-9864178-0-1
ISBN-10: 0-9864178-0-7

First Edition, 2015

Printed in the United States of America

For Tierza, Natty, and Chloe

DIRT NAP RHAPSODY

PROLOGUE

CHAMBERS

First officer on the scene says it's a simple rear-ender, no fatalities or major injuries, but the force of the crash pops the front car's trunk open and, surprise surprise, also shakes up the fresh stiff they got hiding in there. The other driver is about to pull out his insurance information and beg the people he just hit to keep the cops out of it when he sees a human hand dangling out of the back of the car! He said it was even wearing some cheap costume jewelry that was reflecting the light off the street lamps and shining like the frickin' Star of Bethlehem! Everybody in a three mile radius could see it plain as day.

At this point you'd expect the perps in the first car to let a little bumper job slide under the circumstances and high-tail it out of there, but here's the best part: The perps almost hit the car in front of them, and the guy in that car got out to tell them watch it 'cause there's kids in his car. Man, I would have loved to see the look on his face when he found out what he was really dealing with. Well, to his credit he detained the perps while the rear-ender called the cops (who let him skate on the ticket by the way) and now here we are having happened upon one of the most open and shut cases in the history of the department. And I thought this was gonna' be just another dull Saturday night. Unbelievable.

So the perps are sitting on the side of the road all cuffed and ready to go when we get there. It's a husband and wife team, and Henderson's the first one to make a crack referring to them as Bonnie and Clyde. I'm sure one of the Uni's had made one before that, but they deferred to his seniority and laughed anyway. Bonnie looked cool as a cucumber, as if she hadn't been caught red-handed in a car with a corpse in the trunk. Clyde though, it was obvious he'd sing like a canary if we needed him to — he'd already sweat through his undershirt by the time I first saw him.

He also kept feeding the lamest excuses to anyone around who would listen: The car had been stolen and they'd just gotten it back, they never look in the trunk, he thinks the mob may have somehow been involved. The mob? Like the mob would steal a car, leave a body in it, then just leave it out in the open in good working condition for anyone to find. We all had a good laugh at that one. Bonnie kept nudging him, trying to get him to stay quiet. It was clear that she was the brains of the operation.

After we finished up at the scene we brought Bonnie and Clyde back to the station and stashed them in separate interrogation rooms. Our case was pretty strong already but it couldn't hurt to make it stronger, so we wanted to see if we could leverage the body in the trunk and turn it into a confession. We figured Bonnie would take a lot longer to break so we wanted to start wearing her down first, so Henderson and I got into character and went in to take a run at her. She greeted us with a warm smile. For a second I thought she might offer us coffee or something, but she just stared cheerfully. Alright then, I thought, let's see what this chick's made of.

"I don't know, Henderson, this one seems pretty open and shut."

"You got that right, Chambers. Talk about a run of bad luck."

"We got a fender bender with a stiff on its way to a dirt nap, body practically falls out of the trunk, dead only a few hours, caught red-handed, that about sum it up, Henderson?"

"It does for now, Chambers, but who knows what we'll find once we start digging."

"Hey, we could use the shovels we found in the trunk with the body!" I looked over at Henderson and we just busted out laughing.

Then Henderson got in on the fun, looking at Bonnie and asking, "Do you mind if we borrow 'em for a while?" I gotta admit, Henderson and I make a pretty good team.

"So the way I figure it, Henderson, there's two ways this can go."

"Yeah?"

"Yeah."

"What's the first way, Chambers?"

"The easy way."

"And what's the second way?"

"The hard way."

"Whoa, Chambers, that second way doesn't sound too pleasant."

"It's not, Henderson."

"I bet it's not, Chambers."

"Do you gentlemen want some privacy?" Bonnie interjected, "This seems like a personal matter." We both looked up at her in surprise. Aha! She speaks! But I think she was mocking us. Who does this lady think she is? She's the one facing 25 to life. No problem, stay cool, just keep her talking.

"What? No ma'am," I replied as politely as I could, "in fact it's quite the opposite, Henderson and I would love to hear your input on the matter."

"Well, okay then," she began, "I think that even though you may find the hard way less pleasant, in the long run you'll find it a much more worthwhile experience, because you didn't cut corners and you earned your achievements the old fashioned way: with good old blood, sweat, and tears... and a little bit of elbow grease thrown in for good measure." This lady, Jesus. Look at her smirking like she has the upper hand.

"See, but that's where you're wrong, Henderson and I love to cut corners. We don't feel slighted by it in the least."

"That's what I figured, but I don't want to be an enabler."

"An enabler, huh? An enabler of what?"

"Your chronic incompetence."

What did she just say to me? I tried to stay calm, "Is that right?"

"I'm sorry Detective, that was rude of me. Forget I said anything."

"No, please, speak, we're all friends here."

"Are you sure? I'm only trying to help."

"I think the lady's right, Chambers, we should move on and..."

"Uh-uh Henderson, I wanna hear what the lady has to say. Please, go on."

"Okay, well... I couldn't help but overhear you talking on the ride over about how unfair it is that this guy and that guy gets away with not doing this thing and that thing..."

"Okay…"

"And how you're the hardest working person here and nobody shows any appreciation for it…"

"And?"

"Then we get here and you spend about 45 minutes sipping coffee and shooting the breeze with the fellas before you process us in."

"Yeah?"

"Then you comment — out loud — about how many steps you're skipping in the report you're filing because they don't make any sense and you shouldn't have to do it…"

"So…"

"So, with respect, it seems to me like you're the dumbest one here."

Okay, that does it: "Listen you psychotic bi…"

"Chambers, Chambers, come on now, settle down."

"Don't you ever…"

"Chambers, cool it."

"I will cut you in two!"

"Chambers!"

Henderson had me in a bear hug. I'd lost my cool. He ushered me out of the room and told me to cool off, he'd take it from here. Dammit. Not only did she get me to lose my cool, but now she's got us playing good cop-bad cop — the ultimate interrogation cliche. I hate good cop-bad cop. It's predictable, it's boring, and it's old fashioned. And now Bonnie either thinks she got to me, or that I'm the type of cop who does good cop-bad cop. Shit, I don't know which one is worse.

Now Henderson, one of the only allies I have left at this point, thinks I'm a hothead. Great, what else can go wrong today?

"Chambers."

"You get anything, Henderson?"

"Nope, still playin' it cool."

"Listen Henderson, about before, I don't know what…"

"Hey, it's been a long day, don't worry about it, Chambers."

"No, you don't understand, that wasn't me in there, that's not how I operate."

"I know I know, we'll get 'em next time. Come on, let's go grab a beer, I'll buy."

"No thanks."

"What's this? You're turning down a free beer? *You*? Man, this chick really got to you, didn't she?"

"I think I want to take a run at the husband."

"Whoa whoa whoa Chambers, are you sure that's a good id…"

"I said I want to take a run at the husband."

"Okay okay, just be careful, I don't want to have to write any more reports tonight."

"I'll be careful." Yeah, I'll be careful alright.

I walked into Clyde's room and found him sitting there all peaceful and serene, like he just found out his mother got into heaven. Where was the nervous putz I met at the scene? He had to be in there somewhere, and all I had to do was find him: "So I gotta tell ya' buddy, it's not looking good for you and your Mrs. at the moment. I got a fender bender with a stiff on its way to a dirt nap, body practically falls out of the trunk, dead only a few hours, caught red-h…"

"I want to make a full confession," Clyde said. Excuse me? You what? "I did it. I did it all. By myself. No one else knew anything about it. And I'm not sorry. I'll tell you everything you need to know including how I did it, why, and where the others are buried. Now give me something to sign of my own free will."

Wow. Take that, Bonnie. Wait… did he say, "Others?"

MONDAY

TAG

I'm a slave to my own biology. I know they always tell you in public service announcements not to give up, but I feel like this might be an exception. Why can't I just throw my hands up and admit that I'm powerless to stop it? Alcoholics get to, why can't I? I've tried to fight it, but it's always there — poking its head around the corner, watching from afar, waiting to pounce. And there's nothing I can do because hormones can't be reasoned with.

It's scaring me because I don't know if I can bring myself to talk to Lori about this one. I know eventually it'll just come spilling out — I've never been good at holding back, at least not with her — and the worst part is that I know when it does she'll be totally understanding with me, just like always. I just don't know if I can listen to myself tell her that I'm afraid that my desire to mess around with every woman I see is eventually going to eat me alive. What's wrong with me? This was never a big problem before. Is there some magic spell that kicks in a few months after you say "I Do" that suddenly makes every other woman in the world irresistible? Is it the natural male biological instinct to spread my seed? Or is it the natural male emotional instinct to rebel against the idea of being with only one woman for the rest of my life? Well, I actually do want to be with only one woman for the rest of my life. At least my brain does. The rest of me craves variety. I hate biology.

I've even resorted to drastic measures to try and force myself to behave. For example, I hired the fifth best person for the job of secretar… uh, administrative assistant at the office solely because he was the only male that applied. I was pleasantly surprised at Dan's work ethic and ability to keep the appointment books the way I like them, but I'm ashamed that I trust myself so little that I feel like I can't risk letting another woman come anywhere near me. Not even an ugly one.

And lately it's been getting worse. This morning I almost got into a car accident because I was undressing a woman at the bus stop with my eyes. If it wasn't for my slightly better than average reaction time, I would have plowed right into the tan Corolla that was stopped in front of me. I knew I was moving too, but I needed to finish my little mini-fantasy at all costs. Even if that cost was my front bumper.

I arrived at work only to find out that Dan had gone and taken ill. Even worse, I had to learn about it from the knockout temp with the perky tits and the unbelievably bubbly personality that was “sooooo excited” that she was gonna be working with me for the next few days. Just kill me now.

Also, it didn't help that she kept batting her eyes at me and giggling, basically saying with her body language that I'd be doing her a huge favor if I just took her into the back room now and got it overwith. The end of the day couldn't come soon enough. All I had to do was concentrate on work until around three and then make it past the temp on my way out

— then I'd be home free. Okay, sounds like a plan.

"Mr. Harrison, can you put your chin on the line and look through this big Viewfinder-looking thing for me? Terrific. Now, do you see a pair of letters there?"

"Yes."

"Which one is easier to see, the one on the left or the one on the right?"

"Uh, the left."

"Okay, which one now? The one on the left or the one on the right?"

"Right."

"Okay, how about now?"

"Right."

"Now?"

"Left."

"And now?"

"Right."

"Great. Now, look at the green light for me. I'm going to shoot two tiny puffs of air at your eyeball, so keep still. Good. Mr. Harrison, you have glaucoma!"

At 2:48 I figured it was close enough and I retreated to my office to plan my escape. Okay Tag, remember, no eye contact, but be polite, keep moving, do not stop for any reason, head down, focus. Also, keep your wife's disappointed face in your mind for motivation.

"Callin' it a day?" she chirped in her unbelievably upbeat way as I passed by her desk. If she wasn't so damn alluring I'd find that unbearable.

"Yep."

"Then I guess I am too!"

"Okay, before you go though, could you set up everything

for tomorrow morning?" I asked, hoping to avoid an uncomfortable walking-together-to-our-cars situation.

"Done and doner! They don't call me Remarkable Whatevermynamewas for nothing!" Shit. She's good.

"Have you rotated the magazines yet?" Whatever that means.

"Rotated the... huh?" Her sincere confusion only made me want her more.

"Uh, yeah, I like to rotate the magazines in the lobby just so uh... people have a variety to choose from." Oh my God I hope she's stupid.

"But nobody who was here today is going to be here tomorrow too."

"Just..." Calm down, Tag, "Just do it... please."

"Um, okay," she said, attempting to smile but not quite getting there. I didn't want to be an ass, but her efficiency was ruining my escape plan. "Here," she said as I inched closer to the exit, "take my card just in case you need anything before tomorrow. I'm a full service assistant!" That wasn't what I needed to hear. Regardless of how she meant it, my mind went straight to the gutter. Look her in the eyes, Tag, look her in the eyes! Say good night, and get out! I must have looked as stressed as I felt because then she said, "Are you okay, Dr. Taggart?"

You're almost home-free, Tag, just say something vague and innocuous. "Uh, me? Yeah, I'm... I'm uh... it's just been one of those days, ya know?" Good one.

"Really?" Her concern was almost tangible. "Ooh! I just had an idea!" Wonderful! "My cousin is a licensed massage therapist and she's been showing me the ropes a little, you know, to see if it's a field I'd be interested in, and I'm, you know, like, kinda good now and, well, I've been looking for subjects to practice on and, well, you look like you could use a rubdown, so we could kill two birds with one… rubdown!"

What? Did she just offer me a rubdown? I responded with hesitation and, well, terror: "Oh I don't know, I really should be going and…"

"Come on, it'll only take a sec, sit." She patted the chair next to her and I sat dutifully, the cold touch of her small, dainty hand sending a shiver down my spine. Not really my spine. That was a euphemism. "Now listen to me," she cooed, "my soothing voice, feel my hands squeezing all of the tension out of your body." My eyes rolled up into the back of my head and I melted into a powerless puddle before her. "Take all of the troubles of the day and lock them up in a box and throw them into the ocean. Clear your mind and listen to your soul." I had no idea what that meant but I tried really hard to do it.

As I started to lean back and cede control to the hands of fate, I remembered the shame I felt looking at Lori after just thinking about a moment like this. The fear of an even deeper feeling of shame was just enough for me to regain some of my faculties. I violently shook my head and may have even slapped myself in the face a few times. It didn't change anything, but it was the crack in the bottom of an open window and I was barely, just barely, able to jump through it. I muttered some ridiculous excuse and sprinted all the way to my car.

On the drive home I kept staring at her card. Name, number, address, tiny photo. I couldn't take my eyes off of it. She said to call if I needed anything. Anything? I guess I wasn't out of the woods yet. I'd been saved by a distant feeling of shame and I was grateful for that, but who knows how long that was going to last. I had to do something, I just wasn't sure what. Then for the second time today I almost got in a car accident. The sound of screeching brakes followed by angry car horns jolted me out of my stupor, but it only caused me to stare at the card for most of the remainder of the drive rather than all of it. I've got to be more careful. Shame and a quick reaction time will only get me so far.

I got home and thanked the good Lord that Susan only gardens once a day and I could get into my house in peace. The events of the day had gotten me worked up into such a tizzy that I just needed a release. Maybe, I thought, if I could direct all of this frustrated sexual energy toward my wife, it would all work out in my favor in the end.

I screeched to a halt in the driveway and rushed into the house. "Lori?" I called out desperately. I searched the kitchen, the laundry room, the den, the downstairs guest room, the downstairs bathroom, the closet, the upstairs bathroom, the upstairs guest room, and the hallway closet, but I came up empty on every count.

I guess it's a testament to how foggy my brain was that the last place I thought to look was our own bedroom, but that's where I finally found her, half-dressed and putting on makeup. Perfect. I mean, she was clearly getting ready for something, but that could wait.

"Hey," she said to me with a smile.

"Hey," I replied as I walked toward her.

"How was work tod… oh!" Before she could finish her sentence, I grabbed her and kissed her passionately like men do in steamy romance novels. Of course women never react like they do in steamy romance novels — maybe that's because in steamy romance novels it's never the husband who's doing the grabbing. As I kissed her I could tell that she was trying to say something, but I hoped against all odds that if I just kept kissing her she'd figure it could wait. No such luck.

"Tag, Tag, Tag, hold on."

"Huh?" I said with a grunt.

"You can't get me all excited right now, I have a client I have to meet in like, ten minutes."

"Aw, honey no."

"I know I know, it bums me out too. Can I get a raincheck? Maybe tonight after the news?"

"Uh, yeah, sure, it's a date."

"I wish you would've come home an hour ago, but right now is just..."

"It's okay."

"Really? Are you sure?"

"Yeah, it's fine."

"Okay, thanks honey."

Later on Lori was true to her word and we got busy after the news, but it wasn't quite the same, the moment had already passed. It was a shame too, it would have been a minor mental victory for me to channel my lust for the temp back toward Lori, but that's not the way it worked out. I was just grateful that I made it through the day relatively unscathed.

As Lori dozed away in bed next to me, I stared at Marcie's business card: "Call me if you need anything." Anything. In a fit of desperation I tore up the card and threw it into the wastebasket. I stared at the tiny, tattered pieces and the frayed edges and exhaled, relieved that I was at least temporarily able to conquer my demons. I'll worry about tomorrow tomorrow.

MARCIE

Am I happy? My knee-jerk response to that question has always been an unhesitating yes, but I don't think I've ever really thought about it. I've always assumed that my quick response meant that my happiness was undebatable, but what if it really means that I'm answering quickly so that I don't have to think about it because if I think about it I'm afraid of what I might find?

My friends and loved ones always seem to be amazed by my optimistic (they call it "perky") outlook on life, no matter how good or bad things are going at a given time. I used to try to tell people that it's more complicated than that, that an optimistic and cheerful disposition doesn't necessarily mean that I'm always happy. I worry about things sometimes.

Tsunamis and knifings and pestilence and frowning, dirty people don't make me happy. I'm not trying to see the glass half full with that! When somebody's sad I don't always try to make them feel better, I know that sometimes it's appropriate to be sad. Goddammit sometimes I'm sad! I just firmly believe that whining is a dish best served rare. Nobody wants to listen to other people's problems all the time and I refuse to be a downer every time I have an issue. We've all got issues! Mine are no different from anyone else's. But instead of appreciating the fact that I'm not constantly dropping loads of discontent on everyone, I get, "Marcie, why are you always so perky?" I don't know, bitch, why are you always so pregnant? I know why, because being pregnant is a great excuse to whine about how miserable you are all the time and everybody has to listen because you're pregnant and they're not! Tracy!

Oh wow, I apologize for that, I don't know where it came from. Scratch that, I don't apologize, I had an emotion and I expressed it. It's a thing I want to start doing more often in the future. That said, I do hate how angry I get about things like this, and I hate even more that society has convinced me that it's all because of my lady hormones. No, I'm not on my period and fuck you for thinking it! And my ovaries are fine, thank you very much. I have a prescription for orthotricyclin and several mechanical doodads in the top drawer of my night-stand to prove it. I'm just sick of being condescended upon because I don't whine enough. That's supposed to be a good thing! Tracy!

So yes, I think I'm happy. Not always, and not in a way that anyone who knows me understands, but overall I am indeed a happy person. I guess the reason all of this is coming up is that I'm finding that I'm not very good at reading people. When I think a person is being sincere, sometimes they're not, and vice versa. It's gotten me wondering if sometimes I'm fooling myself as well. For example, my temp agency just placed me at an optometrist's office in the mall. I was told that it could be a long term situation and at this point I'll take anything that pays actual money, so I wanted to make sure I got off on the right foot. Well…

I was my usual perky, mmm, optimistic self from the start: "Good morning, Dr. Taggart!" He looked at me like he wanted to eat me.

"Oh, uh, good morning, uh, where's Dan?" was his confused reply. It's your office, buddy, why am I informing you of your employee's illness? Way to be on top of things.

"Well, apparently Dan hasn't been taking his vitamins, and now he's got himself a little case of the sniffles!" I've been trying to get away from the baby talk lately but it's proving to be a tough habit to break. It's usually my go-to voice when I'm nervous. Of course it also ends up causing drooling optometrists to drool even more. I hate myself.

Becoming self-conscious I tried to jettison the baby talk and get serious, but that didn't last: "Dan's sick today, I'm the temp, but don't worry I have plenty of experience." Tick tick tick, silence. Awkwardness rising! We're at Defcon 1, baby talk alert! "So you don't need to be a grumpy-wump, because we're gonna have lots of fun today!" Just kill me now.

"We are?" he asked with a stupid grin on his face. I know I said I didn't like whining and bothering others with my problems but as part of my attempt to turn over a new leaf, allow me to sound completely self-absorbed for a moment: I hate being pretty. Women who don't consider themselves attractive get very angry when they hear things like that, but I've had enough of it and I've got to say something. The grass isn't greener on the other side, it's brown on both sides! I know it's no fun not being attractive, but it's not one bit better actually being attractive. Not one little, itty bitty bit. It's just hard being a woman period. And fuck you for thinking that was a pun!

Have you ever looked into the eyes of a full-grown adult that you've just met and known that there's no chance of ever having a constructive conversation with him? Has this ever happened to you with your boss? Then you, my friend, are an attractive female. Because sexual desire in many heterosexual males is a layer of a person that they simply can't look past. And it really gets in the way of even the most common, every day aspects of human interaction. For example, I tried to be a shoulder for a guy to cry on once, and he tried to cop a feel mid-hug. He didn't even stop crying first.

It's not fun seeing a man go all googly-eyed and embarrass himself in front of you because he's decided he wants to impress you for one reason and one reason only. And it makes me really, truly, sincerely wish I was ugly. I've binge-eaten for the express purpose of trying to gain weight, honest-to-God. If you want to hate me for that reason, go right ahead. I'm just trying to play with the hand I was dealt.

So with my effort to turn over a new leaf being in its infancy, I ended up bouncing in and out of baby talk all day like a psycho ping pong ball. He didn't even notice. All that mattered to him was the fact that my V-neck blouse showed just the tiniest bit of the top of my cleavage. His efforts to stare stealthily were the most embarrassing thing of all. I tried my best to get back to business: "Your 9:30 is waiting for you in 2, and your 11:05 called and said he'd be running a little late, other than that, everything's A-OK! Okay?" There I go again. Forget what I said before, I'll just go ahead and kill myself.

Dr. Taggart took his time heading over to Room 2. He even pretended to forget something at the desk so he could come back for one more look — of course once he got back he didn't bother to pick anything up. He finally made his way over to his first appointment, leaving a trail of drool in his wake all the way to the door.

I would've left right then if I hadn't been so desperate for some real, steady employment. And besides, for most of the day he was so busy I barely had to look at him. I could probably get used to it. It was really just first thing in the morning and last thing in the afternoon — those were the only two times I had to have an extended conversation with him. But OH! Getting through those two times? No.

As he was leaving for the day he came by to ask me to do some ridiculous tasks and of course I responded in my typically overzealous "Must... impress!" fashion. Still, I told myself, I could put up with a few pointless, menial tasks and a little ogling from afar. At least he kept his hands to himself, which is more than I can say about my last boss. And it's more than I can say for myself as well. Yes, guilty! In my zeal to impress and prove game for anything I gave him a back rub. And I can't blame him for that one, it was kind of my idea. He just looked so tired and stressed and I wanted him to... Look, it wasn't sexual in any way. For me. I just... I didn't want to seem like a stick in the mud, and I want to stop working at that damn temp agency and... In retrospect it may have been a little bit overboard but...

Can't a girl give a guy a stress-reducing, clinically approved back rub without sexual connotations being implied? I would have given the same back rub to a female coworker or a male coworker or my dad. Still, I felt nothing but shame as he moaned in pleasure at the touch of my hand. And anger. I felt anger. If this is the worst of it, though, I think I can deal with it, I told myself, hoping desperately that I'd believe it.

I don't think I'm going back tomorrow.

SUSAN

In my opinion the lilac is the peasant of the flower kingdom. It says it right there in its science name — Syringa Vulgaris. It really is a vulgar runt of a flower and no garden of mine would be caught dead with it. For my money daffodils are the handsomest flower. Sure I love roses and daisies and tulips, but daffodils, Oh! Their science name is much more my style — Narcissus. Some people think narcissism is a negative characteristic in people and flowers, but me? I couldn't disagree more! If you can't obsessively admire yourself, no one else is going to do it for you, that's what I always say! I'm kidding of course, not about the narcissism but about the obsessing.

It's like what I always say about shrubbery: you can never have too much, unless you do. And that's not just how I tend my garden, it's how I live my life. Take our little neighborhood here for example. I've lived in this neighborhood for twenty-some-odd years and every single new neighbor gets a special welcome and a nice little housewarming gift from little old me. I guess I'm sort of the self-appointed, unofficial neighborhood welcoming committee in lieu of the non-existent one that the lazy heifers around here never got around to creating. Every new neighbor gets welcomed. And when I say my door is always open, my door is always open. And I consider their doors always open too. Until they're not. It doesn't matter who they are, black or white, red or brown, Chinese or other type of Asian, I welcome them all.

That said, I have to admit it's nicer when a new neighbor also happens to be a fine example of the best the human species has to offer. It's even better when it's two of them, and right next door to boot! And let me tell you, Tag and Lori are just about the cutest couple I've ever seen! They're like the couple on the top of the wedding cake — just perfect!

The other morning I was in the garden and Tag comes out in that clean white doctor's coat of his and Oh! I could just eat him up in that thing! Literally. (I'm kidding of course.) Anyway, he's heading for his car when he realizes he's forgotten his little doctor's bag, so he turns around and Boom! There she is holding it out for him! See what I mean? She's a saint! In fact I'm considering inviting her to become my unofficial deputy in my unofficial neighborhood welcoming committee. Unlike those other heifers I can tell that she possesses both of the two vital characteristics necessary to be a good welcomer: 1.) a cheerful disposition and 2.) a strong backbone of moral fortitude. Also, it doesn't hurt that she has good taste in men. That Tag, MMM MMM MMM, if I could smear him across a bagel and savor every little…

Now don't get the wrong idea, as a widow I am well past my prime and slightly unquenched in the nether regions, but I am not the type of woman to go around wrecking homes. I like a sip of wine here and there and, well, everywhere and I'm not what most of these heifers would call classy or dignified, and the reason for that is — well, I'll just come out and say it — I like to have fun! Is there something wrong with that? I don't think so, but those heifers...

You know how people always say their momma or their daddy told them this or that? Well, my mantra came from just the opposite: My momma and daddy always told me "Stop it Susan, that's undignified," or "That's not ladylike," and I hated it! So now I have my own golden rule: Never be dignified or ladylike in any way, shape, or form. And I'm not ashamed to shout it from the rooftops: I'd rather have fun than be included in any "classy" heifer book club or barbecue any day of the week and... where was I?

Oh yes! I am who I am. And who I am is someone who would never attempt to break up the perfect couple. It's enough to see the look in Tag's eyes when he comes out each morning in that clean, white coat. That look tells me all I need to know. It tells me, "Susan, you may be past your prime, but there's just something about you that... there's just something about you and... I'll never say it, and I'll never do anything about it. But I want you, baby." Just seeing that look is enough. I'm not in the business of breaking up marriages, but if circumstances were different...

Now look at me going and letting my baser instincts take over. My point is that Tag and Lori have been such a delight ever since they moved in next door about... well, almost a year ago, and it's been such a relief to have... Oh my goodness, did I say a year ago? It's been almost a year? I have to admit I'm a little embarrassed at the moment because after all that chatter about being the unofficial welcomer and all, I've just now realized that I have neglected to get Tag and Lori a housewarming gift!

Here I am talking about how I get every new neighbor that moves in a little something no matter what, and then I go and forget to give something to the nicest couple of neighbors I've ever had. No no no, Susan, unacceptable!

I will say in my defense that part of the reason I'm so late is because on several occasions I've put off getting something in the hopes that I could think of something a little extra special for such a nice couple. And next door to boot! It seems however that my neglect has now stretched out to almost a year. Unacceptable! I need to get them something this week. In fact, I'm gonna sit down right now and not move until I think of the perfect thing. Now let's see, what should it be?

TUESDAY

TAG

The funny thing about problems is that no matter how sure you are that you've gotten rid of them, you never know when one is going to pop out of the bushes and let you know that it was never really gone to begin with. Arriving at the office on Day Two of The Marcie Experiment, I realized that I hadn't conquered my problems at all. I'd just swept them under the rug to be revisited tomorrow. Now that tomorrow was here, I took one look at Marcie and almost melted with desire. I felt stupid for thinking everything might be better just because I was able to tear up a damn business card and resist the powerful urge to tape it back together. But as soon as I set eyes on that gorgeous porcelain skin, that flowing brunette hair, that impish grin, those dainty little hands that you just knew were freezing cold… I knew I didn't stand a chance.

She was just as perky as the previous day and her eyes looked just as inviting. I was growing weaker by the second — I had to do something fast. The last straw was when it turned out that Dan had come down with mono and he'd be out for a few weeks. A few weeks? I could barely hold out for a few days. Then Marcie started talking all sexy about mono being

"The Kissing Disease" and making kissy faces and I just couldn't take it anymore! So I fired her. Right then and there. I didn't have the luxury of planning out a strategy, I just came up with some lame excuse and got her out of there as soon as possible. A wrongful termination lawsuit would be tomorrow, but an illicit tryst on the examining table could have been minutes away.

I felt a different kind of shame as Marcie left sobbing. She hadn't done anything to deserve this. Sure, maybe she did flirt a little and egg me on, but in essence she was a sacrifice at the altar of my weaknesses. "Run Marcie! Run away!" I thought to myself as she disappeared into the early morning mall din, "This is for your own good." The temptation to call her back took hold immediately. Thank God I'd torn up her card.

It was obvious, though, that my issue had spiraled out of control and it was time to talk to Lori. It had always made me feel better before, but then again it had never been about *this* before. I knew I had no choice though, this wasn't going away, so it had to happen before I lost my mind. It had to happen today.

I rushed through the remainder of the day unable to calm my nerves, further confirming my belief that the sooner I got this overwith the better. But as I pulled in to the driveway and stared at the outside of my house, I realized that I still wasn't quite ready. I sat in the idling car for a long while, trying to find the courage just to walk through the door. Am I really about to do this? Is Lori going to react the way I think she is? Can she hear the car running from inside? Does she know how long I've been out here? Is she ever gonna look out the fucking window? Run away, Tag, run away!

No, stop it Tag, don't try to take the easy way out. Man up!

Go in there and tell her what's going on like you always do!

Or don't.

Really, how bad can it be? You haven't actually done anything wrong yet — quite the opposite in fact — you've shown admirable restraint. Just what is it that you're so afraid of? And what is it that you feel you need to tell her? That you're a human being who has weaknesses and who feels the bitter pangs of temptation now and then? Tag! She's just going to laugh at you and ask, "Is that all? That's what's been bothering you? Tag, relax." That's probably what she's going to say.

Unless it's not.

I guess she could get angry and ask me why she's not enough for me and why I'm treating her like this. The woman who I swore to love and honor and cherish 'til death do us part. The woman who will one day, God-willing, be the mother of my children, the grandmother of my grandchildren, the great-grandmother of my great grandchildren and so on and so forth. Why am I treating her like this? Why, Tag, why?

No. She won't say that. That's not her style. I'm sure she'll nod and give me that sympathetic face like she always does.

Unless she doesn't.

What if her nodding face instead betrays her true feelings? A twitch at the corner of her mouth, an awkwardly raised eyebrow, a quick glance at the ceiling revealing the oceans of hurt and disappointment that my admission has truly wrought? And what if I don't see it on her face? What if she's able to keep those oceans hidden behind her normal sympathetic visage? My God, if I tell her, how will I ever know how she truly feels about it deep down inside? No matter how she reacts there will always be some nagging doubt about how she really feels! That settles it, I won't say anything. It's the compassionate thing to do — to protect her feelings.

At least that's what I told myself as I finally got out of the car and entered the house, carefully taking off my shoes in order to avoid dirtying up the brand new rug. Last week that rug was protected by a thin sheet of plastic, and I really don't know why Lori took it off if she wasn't ready for it to get dirty yet. But there I was meekly tip-toeing up to her in my sock-feet, and there she was on the couch, calmly folding clothes and watching TV.

The moment I saw her I knew I had to tell her. Protecting her feelings was a great idea in theory, but going on another day with this weight on my chest was not an option. Telling her had to happen, I was a fool to think otherwise. The question was how could I tell her in the most roundabout way possible without feeling dishonest. I casually plopped onto the couch next to her.

"Hey," she said flatly.

"Hey," I returned. Then I waited for what felt like days. I know silence is supposed to be part of our little routine, but this was a different kind of silence. This was awkward silence.

"Something wrong?" She finally asked.

"No," Wait for it, wait for it, "Well…"

"What is it, honey?" She said, finally looking up.

"Nothing." This is the part of the routine where I usually go ahead and tell her what's wrong, but this time I just wasn't ready yet. I could tell she was a little surprised.

"Nothing? It doesn't look like nothing."

"Oh, it's really nothing."

"Oh, okay," She went back to her folding. We were in uncharted waters now, I wasn't sure if she was going to pursue it any further or not. I also wasn't sure whether or not I should wait for her to ask again. I hate going off script! Finally, much to my relief, she said, "Are you sure?" Come on, Tag, it's now or never!

"Well… I think I have a problem," I said as matter-of-factly as I possibly could.

"Oh?" Good, we're back on track.

"Yeah, I think I… Lori I have to tell you something," I said, looking up at the ceiling.

"What is it?" She looked more concerned than sympathetic. I tried my best not to panic.

"I uh, I… I… I… Ya' know how they say you can look but don't touch?"

"Like at an antique store?"

"No… well yes, but they also say it about other things. Like women." Subtle, Tag, real subtle.

"Who says it about women?"

"People."

"What kind of people?"

"Women people, Lori, women people say it about other women people. Women people who have husbands with testosterone pumping through their bodies at uncontrollable rates. Women people who have husbands with urges that they can't always control." Not exactly how I rehearsed it in my head, but it could have been worse.

"What are you saying, Tag?"

At this point either my patience or my desire to use any kind of finesse just wore out and I went even further off script: "What I'm saying is… uh, um, uh… I can't control my urges, Lori! I want to, like, so bad! But I can't! I am a horny motherfucker!" I wondered what motels were within walking distance.

"Tag, what are you..."

"I just fired a girl at work for no reason. No reason except that I was afraid I'd end up plugging her in the employee washroom if she stayed there looking all... yummy for one more second!" I hear the one on Grove is nice.

"Tag, I think you're..."

"I don't want to feel like this, Lori, I swear! I'm trying so hard, but sometimes it's all I can think about! I think I need help." I hoped desperately that I was finished, but I honestly didn't know. I'd lost control of my vocal cords somewhere around "horny motherfucker."

"Tag," she whispered, trying to calm me down, "It's okay."

"No, it's not okay."

"Yes, it is."

"Wh... What? How is it okay?"

"Everybody has feelings like that, honey," she said soothingly, "the fact that you're trying so hard just makes me love you more."

"It does?"

"It does."

It was true. I was trying hard. Really hard. I felt a giant wave of relief pass over my body, "Wow. Just... wow. That is such a relief to hear. I mean I thought I was... Wow!" I should have had more faith in her, I thought to myself. Not only was there not a hint of disappointment anywhere on her face, but she put me completely at ease that it wasn't anywhere under her face either. "But how am I gonna handle my... I mean, I have to unfire Marcie, there's no way I'd win *that* lawsuit."

"I can tell this is really bothering you," Lori replied, "but Tag, we're partners, and I want you to know that I'm here to help you. We're in this together, babe." She took my hand and I melted into a pile of mush. She could have asked me to eat mealworms and at that moment, I totally would have. I smiled giddily and kissed her passionately. I didn't think it was possible, but Lori had outdone herself.

I slept more peacefully that night than I had in months, maybe years. Normally I spend at least twenty to thirty minutes a night staring wide-eyed at the ceiling before getting to sleep, but not tonight. A freight train could have sped through our bedroom and I still would have... okay that probably would have woken me up, the point is I slept like a baby.

MARCIE

Mononucleosis is often referred to as the kissing disease. This is mainly due to the fact that that's the sexiest way you can get it, and sex sells — even in high school. Also, the popular retort of "Who you been kissin'?" in response to learning that someone has contracted the disease is not only obnoxious but also often factually incorrect. The truth is you can get it from several less sexy ways as well, like sharing a drinking cup or an eating utensil, or a lollipop, or doing mouth to mouth on a potential drowning victim. I know that last one is highly unlikely, but also technically possible. Believe me I know, that's how I got it. They say no good deed goes unpunished… yeah.

It was late August, I was a teenage lifeguard at the local country club and he was Rex Hutchinson IV, son of Rex Hutchinson III and scion to the Hutchinson family fortune. He was also in my third period Geometry class. So Rex Sr. and his wife got into a tense whisper-fight that the rest of the club pretended to be oblivious to and Rex Jr. decided to act out. He mimed shooting himself while falling into the pool and managed to bump his head for real on the way down. I actually made the paper for my semi-heroic role in saving the poor douche bag.

When I found out I had mono I knew exactly where it came from. I had never kissed a boy on the lips before and my status as a raging germaphobe pretty much ruled out any sort of dinnerware-related hanky-panky. Anyway, the next few weeks of solitude weren't so bad — I got an extended summer vacation while everyone else suffered through those awful first few weeks of tenth grade. It was actually pretty wonderful. The bad part didn't happen until I got better.

Upon returning to school I learned that Rex and I had become somewhat of an item. Rex's return had preceded mine by a couple of days and it seems that he had turned his bout with the disease into some sort of folk legend. Of the several departures from the truth that Rex was guilty of, however, the worst one had to be that I was the one who gave the mono to him. Before I knew it, a betting pool about which student had given me the kiss of death had become all the rage at lunch break and every free period. I'm not sure if anyone ever ended up winning, but I definitely know who lost. I quickly developed a reputation for being easy several years before I lost my virginity, and I earned myself a nickname that followed me throughout my high school career: they called me "The Kissing Whore." Well, at least they had fun with it.

All of that baggage had been residing comfortably in the past until the positive diagnosis of a man I've never met brought it all screaming back. Yesterday was Day Two working for strip mall optometrist (Yes I went back. *Of course* I went back), and on my way in the agency informed me of Dan's diagnosis and that now my potential long-term gig had become an indefinitely long-term gig. "Who's he been kissin'?" was Dr.

Taggart's uncomfortable attempt at humor when I told him (Apparently those two never communicated outside of the office and Dan handled everything except the eye charts.)

Who's he been kissing? For one thing, none of your business, and for two things, he probably wasn't kissing anybody! Asshole! So with the correct buttons being pushed, I simply had to say something, although knowing me I'm sure it came out as the most pleasant and helpful thing Dr. Taggart would hear all day: "Actually…" The motto of the insufferable know-it-all, "kissing is just one of several ways you can get it. You can also get it by sharing a drinking cup or an eating utensil, or a lollipop, or doing mouth to mouth on a potential drowning victim."

"Mouth to mouth?" he asked droolingly. Okay Marcie, unpack that baggage!

"Sure! Basically any time you're swapping spit."

"Swapping spit…" he stuttered, his mouth wide open and his glances at my cleavage no longer in any way covert. I mean, come on! I purposely chose the grossest way to describe it that I could think of and he *still* gets hot and bothered? That's it, I thought to myself, I'm definitely not coming back tomorrow. "Swapping spit… like kissing," he noted, looking like he wanted a demonstration.

"Sure, kissing is one of them, just not the only one, not really even the main one probably. I'm just saying, just because you come down with mono doesn't mean you're, like, a kissing whore or anything." Baggage unpacked.

Dr. Taggart's demeanor immediately changed — I wasn't even sure what I'd said to set him off. Did he resent the implication that he was being unfair to Dan? Was he disappointed that I apparently didn't approve of whores of any kind? Or did he just take it as a cruel rejection of his passive aggressive come-ons? I don't know, but the lever had been pulled and the train reversed course. Everything was different now.

"You know what, Marcie?" he said, uttering my actual name for the first time that I could remember. He grabbed the calendar off of the desk, "No no no no no! This is all wrong."

"What's all wrong?" I asked innocently, knowing that whatever it was, it had nothing to do with the schedule.

"The schedule," he said, "it's all wrong."

"But I did it just like you…"

"I specifically ask you to do it one way, and you go and do it the exact opposite way. Are you messing with me? I mean, is there any way that this was not on purpose?" He said, waving the schedule around recklessly.

"No! I'm telling you Dr. Taggart, I did it exactly the way you…"

"Look, look here, I told you to write down the patient's name, followed by the time, followed by the…"

"No, you want the time written first, then the name."

"Marcie, who do you think knows better what I want? You or me?" I knew better than to answer that, but he persisted, "You or me?"

"Uh…" I considered my words carefully, "Dan?"

"Well, yes, Dan definitely knows but…"

"I know, that's why I checked the old schedules before I started," I showed Dr. Taggart the evidence, "just to be sure." He looked at the old schedules and his face soured. Busted. He clearly hadn't thought this shabby excuse through. I mean, there were literally dozens of better scapegoats to cast his anger at me upon — bullshit ones, yes, but at least they would have stood up to some light scrutiny. But this, this one was bad and he knew it. He stared at the schedule for what felt like an eternity.

When he finally looked up, he glared at me as if I'd just told him I'd killed his puppy. With a hammer. On purpose. He tried in vain to sound professional as he hissed, "The thing is, I just don't think you and I are a good fit. It would probably be better for us both if we parted ways now — before things get too… yucky." Yes, he did indeed use the word "yucky."

I know I should have been relieved — I'd already decided not to come back, and now I'd been given an out. I wouldn't even have to be the one to break it off! Of course the way my dumb ass expressed that was to immediately burst into tears to the point of hyperventilating. Dr. Taggart even rushed to his office and returned with a brown paper bag for me to breathe into. The rest of the afternoon is kind of a blur, but I'm pretty sure in between paper bag puffs I asked him if this had anything to do with the rubdown from yesterday and I was sorry if I did anything inappropriate and I didn't mean anything by it and I'll never do anything like that again. That's right, this bitch apologized to him!

Somehow I made it back to my apartment before I broke down and spent the rest of the day chugging ice cream under a mound of used tissues. I know, sad *and* unoriginal. I think the thing that got to me the most was the fact that, even though I knew that both Dr. Taggart and I knew the truth, he still got to be the disappointed daddy and dictate all of the terms. It's not fair, the disappointed daddy always gets to be the one in charge, holding all the cards and calling all the shots, even though more times than not *he's* the pervert with the fragile ego and the poor understanding of the concept of boundaries. It was bad enough it was like that when I was younger, but now that I'm an adult… it's fucking maddening!

Anyway, if things go like they always seem to he'll probably call and apologize tomorrow morning, and I'd like to say that when he does I'll tell him to go fuck himself, but in all honesty I'll probably just cave and go back. I can't stand it when Disappointed Daddy becomes Disappointed-In-Himself Daddy, when he tries to cleanse his guilty conscience the next morning after yet again crossing the line. "I'm really sorry… I don't know what came over me… I'll never do it again… Please don't tell anyone!"

Whatever, I'll probably feel better after a good night's sleep anyway. Maybe I'm blowing this whole thing out of proportion. Maybe I did take it too far with the back rub. Maybe I was the one who gave Rex mono after all. Maybe regardless of how wrong he is, I just don't like disappointing daddy.

SUSAN

I once threw a gift card off the 23rd floor balcony of a five star hotel in Miami. I'm not proud of it now — mainly because I would have enjoyed using it — but certain things really get my goat. My Graham had taken me there for our 25th anniversary, he got down on one knee, and presented me with a small, square-shaped black box. Be still my beating heart! Is that what I think it is? It wasn't. I opened the box and lo and behold, a $500 Tiffany's gift card stared back at me. Now my Graham, God bless him, he didn't know any better, he just had no earthly idea what he was looking at in that store, so he figured I'd rather pick something out for myself than to have him roll the dice on some big shiny rock. I tell ya', men! I guess my Graham hadn't heard me the 325 times I'd said in the previous 25 years that my greatest pet peeve is gift cards. They're so impersonal!

I don't think I'll ever understand why it's socially unacceptable to give cash as a gift, but giving a gift card is totally fine. It's like saying, "Here, I didn't want to insult you by giving you this stuff that you can spend anywhere, so I'll just give you this thing that you can only spend in one place." It's madness! Nothing says, "I don't know a thing about you" like getting someone a gift card. Real, close relationships deserve a personal touch. That's why the more I think about it the less I regret tossing that gift card away. Whatever I ended up picking out, it just wouldn't have been as special knowing that my Graham hadn't seen it and immediately thought of me. I guess I'm just sentimental that way.

So here I stand in the middle of Howard's Big Buy wondering how I should go about housewarming the Taggarts. Let's see, what do I know about them? He's an eye doctor with great big hands and quite a muscular figure for a man that I never see out jogging and she's an adorable sweetheart who deserves every blessing she gets in this life and the next. I'd love to get them some wall art, their walls look so bare from what I can see through the windows. But I'm not much of an artist myself, nor am I in any way skilled at photography. Plus I don't believe in giving a piece of someone else's soul as a gift from me, it's disingenuous and impersonal. Either the Taggarts buy their own wall art or old Vinny Van Gogh will just have to give it to them himself! I want my gift to be from the heart.

Hm. If I want it to be from the heart, then maybe I should be asking questions about myself as well as questions about them. I already know all about myself, so I suppose the question is what part of myself would I like to share with them? Well, I know what part I'd like to share with him. I'm kidding of course! In theory. But seriously, I'm a top-notch gardener, but I don't really believe in gifts with expiration dates. It's like saying, "Here you go, enjoy, but use it quick before it rots!" To give away flowers you have to literally cut off their life supply: "Here you go, it's pretty now but it's rapidly dying and will decompose before your eyes." It's like giving someone a pet fish without the bowl — enjoy it while it lasts! No, that won't do. What else? A nice vase? Or should I say hospice for flowers? No. How about a cookbook? I like cooking. Does Lori cook? Does Tag cook? I don't know, too risky. Oh, how cute! Matching Ma and Pa Rooster salt and pepper shakers! I love it! Too garish? Yeah.

Maybe I could put together a little... wait... of course! Why didn't I think of that sooner? I know why, because those heifers are all gonna' have a good laugh if I... ya' know what? I don't care. Let 'em laugh, this is perfect and I'm gonna' do it. Heifers be damned!

WEDNESDAY

TAG

If you've only seen a dead body in a casket at a funeral, then you've never seen a real dead body. Believe me, I know, because recently I saw my first real dead body. At a funeral the body is made up and stuffed with all sorts of goop to the point where you barely recognize the person lying there. Seriously, why do those embalmers have to go so heavy on the makeup? Do they think it'll make it easier to get through if your recently deceased loved one looks like a statue from the wax museum?

Unlike casket bodies, real dead bodies look desperately disorganized. They lie in awkward positions, their eyes aren't always looking in the same direction, and their facial expressions are what I'd describe as inappropriately comical. In fact, overdoing it on the makeup aside, I have to admit it did make me appreciate the process of embalming quite a bit more, just for the artistry of it. Seeing a real dead body is a traumatic experience, especially if you're not expecting it. And to think yesterday at this time my worst problem was wanting to bang the temp. Wow. But I'm already getting ahead of myself.

I woke up this morning to find Lori in the kitchen cooking up a big breakfast as if nothing had happened. I beamed at her, unable to contain my excitement. She smiled back cheerfully and said, "Hey."

"Hey," I replied, "I want to thank you for last night, just knowing you're in my corner makes me feel like I can face anything the day has in store for me."

"Well, like I said, we're in this together."

"That we are."

"Oh, Tag, I almost forgot, could you drop these off at the dry cleaner's on your way to work?"

"Anything."

"Thanks, bye."

"Bye." I stood there for a second admiring her. She looked up with that mixture of confusion and glee that very well might be my favorite facial expression of hers. As I walked out the front door and inhaled the morning air, I found myself whistling a happy tune.

Even Susan's shrill greeting piercing through the peaceful morning wasn't going to kill my mood, "Morning Tag! How's my favorite neighbor today?" But it could get close.

"Morning, Susan."

"Oh look at you in that clean, white coat! I could just eat you up! Literally. I'm kidding of course. How's Lori?"

"She's f…"

"She is just too sweet. And you two make the cutest little couple! You're like the couple on the top of the wedding cake, just perfect!"

"Thanks Susan that's very…"

"Ya' know I have been meaning to come by with a little housewarming gift ever since, well ever since you two moved in! My my, where does the time go?" I think you spend most of it talking.

"I don't know," I responded. Honestly I was surprised I got the entire phrase out before she continued.

"Nothing fancy now, just a little something or other, a proper welcome to the neighborhood, as I am the unofficial neighborhood welcomer it is my duty!" The car is mere feet away. Must... Get... To... It!

Time to start wrapping it up, Tag, "Okay I'll let Lori know, anyway I've got to..."

"Lori! Oh Lori, your wife is a saint!" Dammit. "And you! You are just delectable! I'm kidding of course, well not really but I mean it in a playful way. Really playful. I'm kidding of course..." I'm not sure what came after that because I shut the door and turned the radio up loud. It's okay, she'll have forgotten by tomorrow morning.

I resumed my whistling in the car — now how about that, even Susan couldn't put a damper on my day! I gave a cursory glance to my friend at the bus stop but only to admire her beauty in an aesthetic way. Okay fine, I still wanted to bang her but that didn't bother me, because Lori and I were in this together! I whistled on over to the dry cleaner to drop off Lori's clothes, I whistled all the way to Starbuck's to treat myself to a mocha-latte-chino or whatever, and I whistled right on in to work.

In fact my whistling didn't stop until I saw the empty reception desk and remembered that I'd have to call Marcie. I felt kind of rotten about the way things happened. After all it wasn't her fault that she was attractive any more than it was mine. I felt confident that I could face the temptation head on with Lori by my side, so I sat down and began planning out what I was going to say to her.

After a minute I picked up the phone and began to dial

her... wait a minute, where was her number? I know I had it around here somewh... Oh yeah, I tore up her card, didn't I? Luckily enough, though, in her rush to escape without me seeing her cry yesterday, she left a whole stack of cards in the top drawer of the desk. This really was my day. I dialed the number and I guess I shouldn't have been surprised to get her voicemail. I couldn't blame her for screening my calls after yesterday, but that's okay, I'd just have to win her back with some of the old Tag Taggart charm:

> Hi Marcie, it's Dr. Taggart. Listen, I feel really bad about yesterday. You know, it was... I guess it was just one of those days. Anyway, I hope you can accept my apology and of course you're not fired. So if you would do me the great honor of coming in today, I promise, the Dr. Taggart you saw yesterday will be gone. No more! Dead and buried and replaced with a new, improved, and much more understanding version. So anyway, hope to see you soon. Bye.

That should do the trick. She'd be calling back or waltzing through those doors any minute now. I picked just the right tone: sullenly repentant but still authoritative and warm, the perfect ingredients to put her mind at ease that yesterday was just a one time thing, a blip on the radar, an anomaly. It was just one of those days.

The time passed by quicker than usual with me being my own secreta... administrative assistant for the day, in fact by around 11:30 I got to asking myself why I needed a secreta... administrative assistant at all. Then around noon I was reminded again why I needed one when about seven people walked in at the same time, and that's when it dawned on me that Marcie had neither called me back nor shown up for work yet. I retreated to my office and called her again. When the voicemail picked up this time, I began to entertain the possibility that she really was angry. Maybe she was already planning that lawsuit. Okay, time to work that magic:

> Marcie, hi, Dr. Taggart again, look, I don't blame you for not calling me back, I wouldn't call me back either. But I meant what I said. The me from yesterday is gone. I killed him and replaced him with a way more easy-going guy. Ya' know? Uh, but seriously, I don't know who that other guy was, but I promise you won't be seeing any more of him. So feel free to come on in whenever you can. See you soon, bye.

Hmm, that one didn't feel quite as smooth as the last one. My attempt at humor fell flat and I stuttered like a nervous teenager. Maybe the pressure was getting to me. "Don't let the pressure get to you, Tag," I told myself, "you have a teammate now. You and Lori are in this together. Stay strong!" I stayed strong until around 12:15 when another rush knocked the wind out of me and I began to resent the fact that my apologies were being rebuffed. I mean, I hadn't done anything *that* bad, right? Who does this Marcie girl think she is? This is a great opportunity for her! Is she really just gonna flush it all away because I raised my voice one time? How does she think she's gonna make it in the real world if she can't handle being yelled at one time? Does she really think she can sue me over this? Shit, I hope not.

Beep:

> Marcie come on, come back. Or at least answer the phone. Or call me back or… tell me something. Don't make me beg. But I will if I have to… Okay, please come back? I really, really meant what I said about uh… killing myself from yesterday and uh… just please come back. Or call. Or something. Bye.

I hung up the phone. I cracked the door to my office and spied on the line of people waiting at the front desk. I picked up the phone and dialed again:

> Marcie? Marcie? Marcie Marcie Marcie Marcie. Oh Marcie Marcie Marcie. Marcie Marcie Marcie? Marcie. Hey Marcie. Oh Marcie. Marcie Marcie Marcie. You there, Marcie? Please, Marcie. Marcie Marcie Marcie! Uh, Marcie? Marcie! Shit.

I slumped down in my chair, depressed and defeated. I allowed my thoughts to wander to scary subjects like subpoenas and settlements and having to take out a second mortgage on my relatively new house. I had to do something. I definitely couldn't check out people's eyes at a time like this. I looked at the address on Marcie's card. Beachwood. That's college town — a residential area. This is her home address! Oh sweet, adorable, naive little Marcie, there might be hope for us yet. Maybe she could resist the lilt of my voice, but she was guaranteed to crumble at the pout on my face. I decided to close up shop early.

On the way to Marcie's I felt the hope rising up again in my stomach. The bitter pangs of panic waned as my confidence grew. I was never that great on the phone anyway. I was always more of an in-the-room type of guy. I sped past rows and rows of apartment complexes and frat houses and off-campus dorms until I reached a more suburban stretch of real estate. I guessed that Marcie hadn't wanted to move too far away after finishing college, so she found a place only a couple of blocks away. Maybe she split the difference with a few of her old college buddies, or just one college buddy, or a boyfriend, or maybe she lived alone. I arrived at the modest little one story stand-alone apartment that matched the address on the card. Her car sat in the driveway. I reviewed my speech one last time in my head, took a deep breath, and headed for the door.

For some reason I chose that moment to do a little armpit check. I remember that because while looking around to make sure no one saw me, I marveled at my almost Pavlovian ability to do that in any situation without realizing it. Many a time Lori has walked off pretending not to know me as I thoughtlessly smelled my own armpits in the middle of the grocery store, or at her nephew's tenth birthday party, or at a funeral. Yes, all of those things happened, and now I could check "Approaching the home of a recently fired, smoking hot employee in a desperate attempt to make peace and avoid further disgrace" off the list as well.

On the positive side, though, I hadn't been sweating as much as I'd thought — thank heaven for little miracles. As I reached the front porch I noticed that the door was slightly ajar, a safety hazard if I'd ever seen one. In addition to that I thought about all the air conditioning that was escaping the house and the unnecessarily high electricity bill that she may or may not have realized that she was in store for. I suppose in retrospect the open door should have set off a few red flags, but at the time I just saw it as an opportunity to score some extra points by imparting a bit of wisdom to a naive young lady. Maybe I was the one who was naive.

I knocked on the door and called out for Marcie. No answer. I knew she was in there, I could see the TV on through the crack in the door. I called for her again, pushing the door open ever so slightly. Then I saw it. A pair of feet, one shoe on one shoe off, stretching out on the floor just behind the couch. My mind told me to get out of there, but I had to see it to make sure I wasn't dreaming. Also, I wasn't 100% positive that I had the right house. I crept in slowly, a dark sense of inevitability beginning to take over. I quickly peeked around the couch, and sure enough there was Marcie lying in a pool of blood, dead as the proverbial doornail.

STEINER

I wonder how long it takes to get a realtor's license. That seems like a nice gig — flexible hours and good pay would be an interesting change of pace, especially since I'm not feeling all that fulfilled by my pursuit of a higher calling anymore. The moment that started me on this long road to disillusionment didn't happen at a crime scene or a performance review, it happened one ordinary day as I drove down an ordinary street in an ordinary suburban neighborhood.

I must have been 27 or 28, my whole life was in front of me, I was ready to take the world by storm. Then for some reason a For Sale sign in front of a nice, two-story house caught my eye — not because I was looking to buy, but because of the picture on that sign. I instantly recognized Mr. Velasquez, my tenth grade guidance counselor and one of my all-time favorite teachers. He was more than a teacher in fact, for a lot of us he was a role model. I hadn't been all that great at keeping in touch so this was the first time in a couple of years that I'd seen his face. And under his face it said, "For Sale: Call Joseph Velasquez, Macdonald-Kent Realty" and then a phone number.

Unbelievable, after all the years of inspiring young men and women, he must have finally gotten tired of a teacher's pay and sold out. I couldn't blame him though. It's a tough living, day in and day out giving everything you have doing something you love only to struggle to make ends meet at home, living paycheck to paycheck, just barely getting by. I thought about calling the number on the sign. It would be nice to catch up with Mr. Velasquez, let him know the difference he made in at least one young man's life. But then I figured that would only make him feel worse for turning away from it, even if it probably was the right move for him and his family.

As I drove past the sign I thought about all the young me's that were now going to miss out on learning how to be a man from a truly good example of one. I thought about how much inspiring he could possibly manage while selling houses to grown-ups. I thought about the world we live in, and I asked myself why we don't place more value on the kind of work that Mr. Velasquez had devoted his life to.

I didn't hold his decision against him back then, but I understand it even more now. People usually choose a career because at least in some small way they want to do something that's worth doing. They want to make a difference, leave their mark, but eventually they realize how small they are in the grand scheme of things and accept that the best they can do is get by. So if real estate was good enough for Mr. Velasquez back then, it's good enough for me now. I stopped thinking I made a difference a long time ago.

Sure, I guess I make somewhat of a difference when the work I do leads to an arrest, but it's not like my skill set is any better than the next guy's. It's not like without me there, the murderer would have gotten away with it. My clearance rate is average, my work hours are above average, and my salary is below average. What it all adds up to is a case of the doldrums, and it's a case I'm having trouble solving.

I think if you add up everything that's happened in my entire career, you'd barely have enough excitement to fill one episode of your average cop show. In almost twenty years I've never had to use my gun, not even close. I've never even had to pull it out. In fact right now I'm not really sure if it's loaded. I'm not even sure if it works. Do guns go bad? Is there some maintenance process that needs to be repeated to prevent them from going bad? I know they teach you that stuff but I forget. I've never been in hot pursuit of a "perp" either. The reality is that most of my job is paperwork, and the rest isn't much more exciting. I wouldn't make a very good cop show.

Why? Well, your average suspect isn't exactly a criminal mastermind, and your average homicide is pretty much never a carefully planned avant grade art piece from a deranged genius who toys with the police for fun. It's usually the result of some dispute (domestic, drug-related, etc.) that got out of hand, and if there's a plan, it's usually a terrible one.

I remember one time a guy planned out his entire crime and made a checklist to keep himself on schedule. I have to give him credit too, the list was very thorough. It stopped just short of saying, "Kill my girlfriend on this date at this time." He even drew a helpful little diagram of her apartment. I appreciated the gesture. The truth is most people who commit crimes of passion don't consider themselves any different from you and me, and most career criminals aren't exactly Bonnie and Clyde. It's actually funny sometimes how easy they make it. Getting a confession out of a guilt-ridden husband or a junkie without all of his wits about him isn't exactly rocket science. And I'm glad, because if it was I'd have a much weaker record than I do right now.

Now that's not to say all criminals are idiots, it's just that the idiots are the ones we usually catch. The idiots are the ones we deal with day in and day out. The smarter ones? I usually don't get the privilege of meeting them because they're the ones who get away with it. And I don't mean smarter as in actually smart. I mean smarter as in smarter than those unbelievably dumb ones who leave glowing neon evidence trails in their wake everywhere they go.

Contrary to popular belief, you don't need to commit the perfect crime to get away with murder. All you really need to do is be semi-competent and not be married to the victim. It's not like we keep going and going until we get our guy. As long as it's not a high profile, media-saturated affair, just don't make it too obvious and we'll eventually turn our attention to something else. The old adage about the first 48 hours being the most important is true, and maybe the odds against you ever solving it after that period of time are exaggerated, but most cops still believe in it wholeheartedly. The colder a case gets, the more we begin to believe that we're wasting our time. It's not laziness, it's prioritizing. Every second we waste on a lost cause is a second we could have spent on a more hopeful one.

For example, tonight I caught a homicide in the Beachwood area, right around college town. Pretty girl, early to mid twenties, stabbed up right in her living room. The scene was fairly clean, no obvious piles of foreign D.N.A. lying around waiting for us to find, no mysterious prints jumping out at us. Now that doesn't necessarily mean that we were dealing with a stone cold professional, it just means that the intruder had the common sense to throw on a pair of gloves and possibly a shower cap before heading over to the house. In most cases the victim knows the perpetrator well and with apparently not much physical evidence to go on, I was counting on that being the situation here. If not, the odds of closing would get a lot longer.

So I talked to the victim's distraught parents and sister, several of her friends and co-workers, the neighbor that found her, the temp agency that she was working at, and nothing sounded out of the ordinary: no boyfriend, no torch-carriers, no nemesis, just real tears from genuinely shocked and devastated faces. Fuck. Even worse, there was no roommate and nobody else could tell me if anything valuable was missing, so I couldn't rule out random home invasion. Double fuck. Then the neighbor said she found her when she heard a ruckus and went over to check on it, she found a shattered front porch light and a half-opened door, but no fleeing suspects to identify. Triple fuck.

So there's still a chance some physical evidence could pop up. I'll double check the scene a little more meticulously tomorrow afternoon, and I'll swing by the doctor's office she'd been temping at while I'm at it, but this one's looking more and more like that random robbery I was afraid it might be. If that's the case, odds are we give it our best for a few more days, then another corpse will pop up to distract us. We'll do some follow up off and on for a week or two, but by a month from now I'll probably have forgotten it ever happened. Maybe twenty years ago I would have stayed on it longer, done a little free overtime and given the victim the effort she deserved, but honestly I just don't have it in me anymore.

Oh my God I've become a cliche. Here I am thinking I'm

telling it like it is — as opposed to all those glamorized Hollywood versions of cops that you see on TV — when what I'm really doing is sounding like every grizzled, seen-it-all cop with a week left before retiring and making pension that Hollywood has to offer. Well, I have a lot more than a week left before making pension, and I'm definitely not grizzled, anybody who knows me will tell you that. But I sure could use a change of pace. I wonder if Hollywood would be interested in a show about an ex-cop who gets his realtor's license.

SUSAN

There are few things that get better with age. Humans definitely don't, and don't let anybody tell you different. Getting old stinks, and nobody values the wisdom of experience over a smooth complexion and pain-free knees. The same goes for cars, milk, and panties: they never get any better than when they're new. I learned a long time ago to cherish that first day of owning something new, because it's never going to get any better than that. That's it. There are very few exceptions to this rule — in fact I can only think of two: caterpillars and grapes.

The caterpillar is a disgusting creature unworthy of empathy or pity. I never feel the slightest bit of regret for crushing one under my shoe when I'm working in the garden, and I never, ever consider the amount of suffering it's going through or the feelings of its extended family regarding its untimely demise. But whenever one of those revolting little critters manages to survive long enough to hit the pupa stage, the result is objectively and irrefutably better. I take great care to preserve the sanctity of any butterfly that chooses to grace my garden with its presence, and I've often prayed that one would stay perched on my windowsill long enough for me to get out the old camera and capture the moment. One day an errant butterfly even found its way inside the house and I spent the better part of an afternoon attempting to capture it in a plastic cup so I could safely release it back into the wild.

As for the grapes, well, I hate the way they taste, I hate the way they squish between my teeth when I chew them, I hate the way I can never tell which ones will be sweet and which ones will be sour, I just hate them. Fresh off the vine I find them disgusting — so disgusting I can barely stand to look at them. However, if you leave them out in the sun for about a month they become a far more tolerable, semi-sweet treat known as a raisin. But that's not all! The grape rewards a person's patience like no other substance on the planet. Leave that raisin out a bit longer and let a process known as fermentation take hold, and what you're left with is one of the finest delicacies on God's green Earth, commonly known as… (drumroll please)… Wine.

Wine. Oh! Nectar and ambrosia wish they could taste so sweet! This is going to sound terrible, but it's true: I drink wine with every meal — lunch, dinner, and *especially* breakfast! Nothing kicks off the morning like a good glass with some toast and a few orange slices. Don't judge me! Or do, I don't care. Everybody has a vice and at least mine isn't coffee or cigarettes. Some people drink mimosas in the morning and it doesn't make them alcoholics, so I resent the implication that my three glasses a day habit makes me one. Even if it did I wouldn't care. You can get addicted to anything.

I don't know why some substances are labelled "addictive" while others get away scot free. Everything in moderation, that's the best advice I've ever given or gotten. Anything can be poisonous if given in high enough doses, even water! We call things poison because they're poisonous at smaller doses than other things, but with the right dosage, everything is poison. That's a scientific fact. Did you know that there's arsenic in water? As far as I'm concerned, that means that there's poison in poison!

Anyway, I don't know why I'm getting so defensive, it's just that I hear the chatter around this neighborhood. Those heifers think they're being slick, but I hear it! Sitting on their front porch swings being all judgmental — as if I can't have a good glass of wine at 8 A.M. on my front porch swing without the gossip police calling out an all points bulletin! It's disgraceful. Speaking of poison, I'd like to invite a few of those heifers over for a nice, friendly bowl of Cream of Poison. I'm kidding of course.

It just gets me so aggravated that every time I want to talk about my passion for wine, I have to go and get paranoid that I'm being judged. I keep telling my brain that I'm not going to let it get to me, but apparently my heart isn't ready to comply. Oh well, any way you slice it, wine is a universal good.

As long as you use it in moderation.

See now? Why did I feel like I had to say that? It's true about everything, but I don't feel like I have to say it when I'm talking about scrapbooking. And it's just as important to be able to scrapbook in moderation. In fact, if you've got an alcoholic on one side and a rabid, obsessed scrapbooker on the other, which one would you say is crazier? And if you say the alcoholic, you know you're lying.

Anyway, the tragedy of it all is that wine makes the perfect gift, and here I am letting my paranoia get in the way of giving it. No matter, Tag and Lori aren't your typical neighbors, they're genuinely good people. I have no worries about them casting aspersions on me, and that's why for the first time I'm letting myself give the perfect housewarming gift!

Now the reason that wine makes the perfect gift is that there are so many types to choose from that you're guaranteed to find one that's ideal for any gifting need. There are wines that fit every type of personality and occasion, so you can personalize it like no other gift. A perfume is a perfume is a perfume, but each and every type of wine is its own unique and distinct experience.

Still, selecting the perfect type is more an art than a science, but there are a couple of general guidelines that should be followed. First, an obviously expensive or obviously cheap bottle can cause unnecessary tension, as with any other gift you have to spend the appropriate amount of money corresponding to the relationship you have with that person. You don't want to get a Vosne-Romanee for a distant cousin, and you definitely don't want to regale your lovely new bride with a ticket on the Night Train Express.

The safest way to go is a nice middle-of-the-road selection (there are plenty of moderately priced 5-star wines) with a sophisticated, classy design on the label. Presentation counts, people! As far as red wine vs. white, I personally love them both, but if someone held a gun to my head and I had to make a choice I... well, I still don't know if I could choose. I guess they'd just have to shoot me! I'm kidding of course. If you're not sure which kind to get, I suggest to err on the side of red. The red wine snobs are generally much more vicious than their white counterparts. Most white wine drinkers will take a red, but many reds scoff at the mere suggestion of a white. Beginners can't miss with a Cabernet Sauvignon — its taste is non-controversial and palatable to almost all levels of wine drinker. If you can find a Chilean one out of the Maipo Valley region, I'd say you've got yourself a winner.

Me? I think I'll go with a hearty syrah (you might know it as shiraz), maybe a Cave de Tain. Yes! That would be perfect for Tag. I've always said I like my wine like I like my men: manly. I'm kidding of course! No I'm not, I'm so bad! I'm sure Lori will like it too. I guess. Maybe I should ask just to make sure. Oh, but then it won't be a surprise! No, I'd better ask, just to make sure. Hmm, but then… no, I'd better ask.

TAG

"Okay, so I panicked," I thought to myself as I raced home frantically, veering in and out of lanes, running red lights, taking turns at 40 miles an hour. I guess all the cops were at a meeting that night because somehow I made it home unscathed. Avoiding a speeding ticket was the least of my worries though, I had just seen my first dead body. That girl seemed so sweet and innocent and sexy, I wondered what she could have possibly, uh... Wow, I just referred to a dead person as sexy. I don't think I've ever done that before. Creepy... Anyway, that girl seemed so sweet and innocent and... perky, I wondered what she could have possibly been into to get herself killed.

Temps don't exactly make a lot of money, was she supplementing her income with some light drug running? Did she suddenly grow a conscience and tell her pimp... that's not what drug dealers are called, is it? Oh my gosh, was she supplementing her income with some light prostitution? Did she suddenly grow a conscience and tell her pimp/drug dealer that she wanted out? Or worse, was the pimp/drug dealer her boyfriend, and did he suspect she was cheating on him? Did he hear the voicemails I left and think I was her lover? I *was* begging her to come back and saying this time I'd be different —just like a lover would. Shit, could he be after me next?

Okay breathe, Tag, breathe, you're making a lot of assumptions right now. Remember Occam's Razor, it's much more likely that she just had an abusive boyfriend who went too far. That happens all the time, I've read the statistics. But what if her abusive boyfriend suspected she was cheating on him? Could he be after me? What if he's a pimp or a drug dealer too? Okay breathe, Tag, breath. Remember what Lori told you about catastrophizing: how it's a vicious cycle where you use your overactive imagination to come up with ridiculous things that could maybe, possibly, potentially happen and then you go to town worrying about them. You need to stop it, Tag, you have enough real stuff to worry about at the moment.

The sound of the car knocking over all three trash cans as I skidded haphazardly into the driveway finally snapped me out of my stupor. I hopped out and rushed inside, trampling all kinds of debris onto the new rug in the process. By the time I reached Lori, who was calmly relaxing on the couch with a magazine, I was a sweaty, stuttering mess. "Hey," she said to me as I gasped for air, "something wrong?"

"I… I… I… I…" had to sit down before I passed out.

"Tag what's the matter?"

"We… we… we… well…"

"Tag?"

"Ma… ma… ma… ma…"

"Your what?"

"N… n… n… no…"

"Tag, you're not making any…"

"Marcie is uh, Marcie is… Marcie is… Marcie is d… Marcie

is murdered. Marcie is murdered." There, nailed it.

"Oh?" She asked in her typical way.

"Yes! She is a corpse! A real live corpse! Fuck!" I replied in my typical way.

"Okay calm down hon, just tell me what happened."

"Well," my mind was racing all over the place and it took me a minute to remember. "When she didn't return my calls I went over to her house — for business purposes only of course..."

"Of course."

"And when I got there she was lying on the floor like... like she'd fallen asleep playing Twister. And there was blood everywhere and a knife on the ground and she was wearing this really sexy nightie... not sexy sexy like she was trying to impress someone, more like cute sexy like she was..."

"Tag." Yes, Lori, please stop me.

"Huh?"

"Tag, it's okay."

"What kind of a person could do that to a... a... a... an innocent uh... uh... uh... and she was so young and uh... uh... uh... wearing that really cute..."

"Tag." Thanks again.

"I wonder if it was her boyfriend. Yeah, I bet it was her dirty, asshole boyfriend. I'll kill that son of a bitch!"

"Honey!" she said with a growing sense of urgency, "You need to calm down. Right now." She stared at me panting and realized that mere words just weren't going to cut it this time. She gently lowered my head into her lap and began running her fingers through my hair. Ahhhhhh. That feels nice. Why hadn't she thought of that before? The problems of the day were quickly fading away into the distance, never to be thought of again. "Good, good," she continued, "that's better. Relaaaaaaax… there, good. Now, we need to talk about evidence."

I sat up straight. The problems of the day came zooming back into focus. "Evi… evi… evi… What?"

"No no no honey, we're still relaxing, come on…" She tried to bring me back to her lap, but this time I resisted.

"What do you mean evidence?"

"Did you leave any evidence behind? At her place?" This was a question I hadn't even considered.

"What kind of question is that?" I asked.

"An important one."

"Hey, I'm kinda going through something here, I was hoping for a bit more, you know, emotional support."

She stared at me sternly. I could tell she was getting frustrated, but to her credit she kept it together. She grabbed my hands and squeezed them affectionately: "Honey, I'm here for you, you know I am, and you will get all the shoulders to cry on that you need, I promise. But first we have to make sure you're protected."

"Protected? Protected from what?"

"If the girl was murdered, theeeeeeennnn…"

"Oh my gosh, then whoever was after her could be after me now. Oh my gosh, what if they were after me in the first place? What if they killed her because she wouldn't tell them how to find me? Oh my gosh, honey, we have to get out of here! They could be on their way right now!"

"Tag!" Now she was frustrated, but she quickly caught herself and got back to business, "Calm down. You're catastrophizing." There's that word again.

"I am?"

"Yes, you are. You're not a drug dealer, you're not into organized crime, you don't have a huge gambling debt, no one is trying to kill you. And if they were they wouldn't need to torture your temp to find you. We're listed." This was all true. And obvious. "The most likely scenario is an abusive boyfriend or a burglar or something, so quit catastrophizing because the only danger you're in is if the authorities find evidence that you were there at the scene!"

"Right, because if they find evidence that I was there..."

"They'll wonder why you didn't call them and report it."

"Oh shit. I just fled the scene of a crime. I should call them and report it."

"No, no you shouldn't," she said.

"Why not? I have nothing to hide."

"You just sexually harassed her and fired her with no cause and now she's dead."

"I did *not* sexually harass her!"

"Do you know what sexually harassed means?"

"Uh... uh... yes!"

"This is beside the point. Firing her plus evidence you were at the scene equals prime suspect. Got it?" She's always been really good at putting things into perspective.

"Oh, right. Oh right! They're gonna think I did it! They're gonna think I did it! Shit. Shit shit shit, they're gonna think I did it!"

"Honey, you're not relaxing."

"No, I'm not relaxing, I'm freaking out!"

"Well, stop freaking out. Look at me, breathe. Breathe. Breathe." I repeated the words after her, imitating her rhythms as if I was learning how to breathe for the first time. Somehow I managed to regain my composure. "Better?" she asked.

"Yeah, better," I replied, "okay, so what now?"

"Now you have to go back there."

"Go back there! What? Why would I have to go back there?"

"Breathe. Breathe."

Repeating her words again I calmed down outwardly, but inwardly there was still a storm raging. Go back there? I'm barely hanging on as it is, does she want me to go completely off the rails? I tried to reason with her: "But I'm pretty sure I didn't touch anything while I was there."

"Pretty sure?"

"Almost positive."

"Not good enough," I figured it wasn't but I guess I needed to hear her say it, "and fingerprints aren't our only concern. Even one hair at the scene can link you to it. We have to be thorough. If we're lucky we'll get there before anybody else finds the body. Did she live alone?"

Hm. "I don't know," I said.

"We'll just have to be careful. Check out the place before you go in."

"Right. Are you coming with me?"

"Yes, but you have to go in by yourself," she said as I began to freak out outwardly once again, "honey I told you, we're in this together, and we're gonna get through this together. So relax, okay?"

I smiled at her as I reminded myself to breathe, it was true what I'd told her earlier about how knowing we were in it together was really all I needed to feel better. "What would I do without you?" I asked gratefully.

She allowed herself a fleeting, wry grin and what I could have sworn was a wink, then she replied, "Probably die." It was the most romantic reference to my potential death that I've ever heard.

Since I was still about two-thirds of a mess, Lori drove us out to Marcie's place. Every time I felt myself starting to relax I'd remember that I was on my way to a crime scene to tamper with evidence. I'd never done that before. I'm not the type of person who does things like that. Come to think of it, neither is Lori. She must really love me to be violating our principles like this in the name of saving my dumb ass. And I guess all those cop shows came in handy because she seemed to know exactly what needed to be done.

We swung by Howard's Big Buy on the way to pick up supplies: one black knit stocking cap, latex gloves, a hairnet, trash bags, Lysol disinfecting wipes, and one of those miniature broom and dustpan combos. I already had the black outfit covered head to toe, and Lori pulled one of those old-fashioned Dustbusters down from the attic.

Dustbusters. I forgot about those. I wonder why those things didn't catch on more. I mean, it seems like a great idea: a tiny handheld vacuum cleaner that you can easily use in tight spaces and on couches and chairs and whatnot. What's not to love about that? Sure, you can use the hose attachment on most larger modern vacuums for much of that these days, but this! This thing is portable! Lucky for us Lori saved her old one because I don't think they sell them anymore, except maybe on EBay, and I sure would have hated having to lug my giant Hoover to a crime scene.

As we neared Marcie's house, my mind began to race again. Am I really doing this? What makes me think I'm qualified to remove all traces of my D.N.A. from this place? What makes me think I'm qualified to remove all traces of my

D.N.A. from anyplace? I don't even know what D.N.A. looks like. How am I supposed to find it? Even if I'm able to find literally every hair on her living room carpet, how am I supposed to find my skin cells? Don't those things fall off anytime your skin rubs up on something? I heard that somewhere, what if it's true? No way I'm finding every skin cell I left in that house. Why am I risking being caught there when I know I'm not going to be able to find all the D.N.A? This is a fool's errand! Oh God I'm going to jail! Why'd she have to go and get herself killed right after I unfairly fired her? Why?

I didn't share my cold feet with Lori because I figured she'd seen me cry enough for one night, throw in last night's waterworks and the tears were starting to add up fast. Don't get me wrong, I'm not ashamed to show her my vulnerable side, and I know she doesn't think less of me because of it either. I just think there comes a point when even the most sensitive soul can't help but get fed up and say, "Enough already!" Plus, I knew I'd probably need some more consoling after I wet myself inside Marcie's house in a few minutes, and I just didn't want to push it too far.

Lori pulled up about three houses past our target and shut off the headlights. "Okay good," she said, "it looks like nobody's found the body yet. Now remember, anything you might have touched gets wiped down. Be sure to take all trash with you when you leave. Also, run the Dustbuster over any part of the floor that you might have contaminated. How close did you get to the body?"

"Not very."

"Good, don't get any closer this time. Now we still don't know if she has a roommate or not so make sure you…"

"What if the roommate's already inside?"

"The roommate's not inside."

"Okay… But what if she is?"

"She's not."

"How do you know that?"

"Because if the roommate was inside she would have noticed the dead person on the floor and called the police already."

"What if she's the one who did it?" I asked. The look on Lori's face made me think I finally may have stumped her. After a moment, she reached into her jacket and pulled out a… Christ, is that a gun? "Lori, where did you get that?"

"From the store."

"Uh, yes, I know it's from the store but, where uh… what uh… which store?"

"Howard's Big Buy."

"Howard's Big Buy?"

"Yeah, just now."

"Just now?"

"Yeah, just now."

"Isn't there a waiting period or something for that kind of purchase?"

"Ya' know, it's funny, I kind of thought so too. But apparently not."

"What the…"

"Tag, it's a gun. Lots of people have them. There's even an amendment to the Constitution specifically saying that we have the right to…"

"I'm familiar with the Constitution, Lori, but I don't think the Second Amendment covers the situation we're in right now."

"Okay, you don't have to take it, but you're the one who

said the roommate might be the killer waiting inside to kill again." She had a point. She always does. I took the gun and stuffed it into my waistband. That's where people put guns, right? So having resolved that issue, Lori continued with her instructions, "Now if there's any movement out here, I'll signal you. If you hear the signal, get out of there fast."

"Okay," I said, "What's the signal?"

She had to think about that one for a second, "I'll honk once, then wait, then honk two more times."

"Honk once, then wait, then two more times."

"Yes."

"How's that gonna sound?" I asked.

She had to think about that one for another second. Finally, she made the noise with her mouth: "Beeeeeeep… beep beep."

"Huh?"

She did it again: "Beeeeeeep… beep beep."

I knew there was no room for error and I wanted to be sure I had everything down like clockwork. I also knew that there were a few subtle differences between a mouth beep and a car beep. "Can I hear it with the actual horn? Just to make sure I've got it?"

"No." Huh? I thought we were on the same page here, Lori. She elaborated, "No unnecessary risks."

Oh right. Hearing the signal once isn't as likely to arouse suspicion as hearing it several times, but maybe just one test run was worth the risk, just so I'd know I had it. "How 'bout just once so I can make sure I…"

"No unnecessary risks. Once is risky enough."

"I know that but… can't ya' just do it real quiet?"

"You're not gonna have to pick the signal out of a lineup, if you hear it just come out."

"Okay," I said hesitantly, "well let me hear it one more time with your mouth."

"Beeeeeeeep… beep beep. Got it?"

"Yeah," I said, "I think so."

"Good. Well let's do this then."

"Yeah." I put on the gloves, the mask, and the hairnet, "How do I look?" I asked Lori.

"Like a cat burglar," was her reply. Great, just what I was hoping for. Once I was ready, it took me a few seconds just to get the courage to open the car door — then it took me a few more seconds to get out of the car. Once I was out of the car in the open air though, I felt unavoidably visible. If a jogger had happened by at that moment, I don't think there's any way I could have hidden the giant guilty sign I was wearing like a sandwich board. I sprinted toward the house and onto the front porch, only stopping to carefully push open the still ajar door.

I peaked my head into the house, "Hello? Marcie's roommate? Are you here? Do you exist?" There was no response to my inquiry. Still, as I poked my head in further, I couldn't shake the feeling that there might be a psychotic roommate killer lying in wait behind the door or in the hallway. "Hey," I whispered, testing the waters a bit. Still nothing. "Hey!" A little louder this time. "Hey!" I shouted, hoping to surprise any potential lurkers into revealing themselves, but all I succeeded in doing was startling myself.

After a quick look around to confirm that I was alone, I checked my pockets for the… shit. I forgot the wipes. I pictured Lori staring at the wipes in the car, judging me silently. Shit shit shit. I struggled to keep calm. Should I risk going back to the car and exposing myself further? Should I just try the old breathe and wipe with the shirt-sleeve trick to remove the prints? Does that even work? Think, Tag, think. Still thinking. Still thinking. Eventually something's going to come to me, right? It's bound to hap… ding! Got it. Disinfecting wipes are a household item, and this is a house, ergo I bet they have some wipes right here in the house! Okay, where's the most likely place to find disinfecting wipes in a house? Where are the disinfecting wipes in our house? Ding! Kitchen cabinet, under the sink.

I made my way to the kitchen and before I even had a chance to check the cabinet, Boom! I saw some baby wipes on the kitchen table. I didn't even have to go all the way into the kitchen! I grabbed them and went back to the den and began wiping down anything and everything I may have touched, being careful not to go any closer to the body than I had before.

The body. I barely had time to comprehend it before I ran out earlier, but now I had plenty of time. And silence. Being in close proximity to a lifeless corpse for an extended period of time is something I wouldn't recommend to anybody. It's downright ominous. I kept imagining the pale, bloodless remains that formerly belonged to Marcie sitting up and speaking to me as if nothing had changed. I found myself having hypothetical conversations with her in my head, feeling that somehow, somewhere, in some small way, she could hear what I was saying:

> Sorry this had to happen to you, Marcie, I wish I could have done something to prevent it. Sorry I fired you for no good reason on what turned out to be the last day of your life. In my defense though, I didn't know it was

> the last day of your life any more than you did. I guess we both would have done things differently if we had known. I wonder how much warning I'll have before the last day of my life. I wonder how much warning I'll want. Nobody wants to waste away in the hospital for months beforehand, but nobody wants to go out with absolutely no warning either. I don't know what I want yet, but I hope one day soon I'll figure it out. Sorry Marcie, I didn't mean to make this all about me. You probably feel like I'm rubbing all of this in your face, talking about how I want to go, with me being still alive and all. Anyway, if there's anything I can do, don't hesitate to… I don't know… tell a psychic to contact me with a message or something. If any of them are for real that is, if not, any old sign will do. Anyway, I hope you don't mind me messing with your crime scene a little bit, but you wouldn't want an innocent man to go down because of you, would you? That would be a very big burden to bear — even in the afterlife. Anyway, I uh… I hope you made it into Heaven I guess, or whatever comparable place your religion of choice would have you end up in. See you later, bye.

I ran the Dustbuster over the carpet and the couch and the easy chair, got up under the couch pretty thoroughly, and let myself out. When I heard that door shut behind me and looked around to see a distinct lack of S.W.A.T. teams surrounding the house, I realized that I'd done it. I'd actually done it. I leapt into the air and let out a loud "Woooooooooo!" as I ran back to the car to see a now furious Lori gesturing at me to shut up.

I got in the car and Lori sped off. "Sorry, I couldn't contain myself."

"We good?" She asked.

I was too exhilarated from my recent covert awesomeness to bother with the details quite yet: "Wow! That was incredible. I've never done anything like that before! I was like, in the room and sneaking around and being all stealthy…"

"Tag," Lori said, trying to bring me back down to Earth. I looked at her in awe.

"Lori, I don't know what to say, wow! How'd you know how to handle this so well? How'd you stay so calm? I mean… wow! You're my hero!"

"Tag, focus, are we good?" It's okay honey, I'll be down in a few seconds.

"Oh we're good. Woooooo!" Make that a few minutes.

"You forgot the wipes." Oh Lori! So organized! And that's why I love you!

"Yeah I know! And ya' know what? At first I panicked, I was like, 'No!' I didn't know if I should run back to the car and get them or… I was a mess. But then I did what you said, I breathed. I was like…" I showed off my incredible breathing skills for Lori, which had come a long way since earlier in the evening. She was about as impressed as you'd expect, but I was too amped up to slow down: "Then I told myself, 'Cool it Tag, you can do this.' And I fuckin' did it!"

"You did it."

"I fuckin' did it!"

"What did you use?"

"What did I use?"

"To wipe the place down."

"Oh, that's the best part! I was about to check the cabinet under the sink in the kitchen and..."

"You went into the kitchen?"

"No! That's the best part! There was a pack of baby wipes just sitting on the kitchen table! It was like... serendipity!"

"Baby wipes."

"Yeah, baby wipes."

"Plastic case or disposable baggie?"

"Huh?"

Lori repeated herself, this time more slowly, "Plastic case or disposable baggie?"

"Uh, disposable baggie?" I answered, more than a little perplexed.

"Good," Lori sighed in relief, "So you pocketed the baggie then?"

"Yes," I replied, "I pocket the baggie." Lori didn't look completely satisfied with my answer, but hey, I followed her instructions to the letter. Everything I used came out of that house with me, nothing went in the trash can. Still, she needed some reassurance, "Honey, relax, I was freakin' Macguyver in there."

She didn't seem to find that very reassuring either, "And you Dustbusted the floor."

"Lori, I appreciate your concern, but you don't have to worry. I handled it. I took care of business, baby!"

And that's when she looked at me out of the corner of her eye and dropped a bomb, "Where's your hairnet?" Where's my hairn... Dammit. Motherf... Godda... Son of a motherf... Are you kidding me? Everything went so right in that house, there was no way I did something stupid like leave my hairnet behi... I left my goddamn hairnet behind. I didn't have to look at Lori at all, I felt her white hot gaze as if laser beams were coming out of her eyes. My excitement vanished immediately. I tried to think of something to say, something to save some face, but no words came out. Lori wordlessly hung a U-turn and back to the house we went.

So I guess my time as a stone cold superspy was over, but it was a fun hour or so. As we passed all the familiar landmarks that we'd just seen a few minutes before, that same sense of dread crept back in. How would I ever live with myself if that stupid mistake is what ends up getting us caught? And not only me, but Lori too. That's a lot of stuff to have on my conscience. But there's still a chance, I thought to myself, don't freak out just yet, now is not the time to buckle under the pressure. Pull yourself together! This should be easy, you've already done it once, you're experienced now. Do you think James Bond never made a mistake? Of course he did! He just stayed cool and fixed it before anybody caught up to him. You can still be a stone cold superspy, Tag. You can do it!

Lori pulled into the same spot she was in before, "You know what to do, right?"

"I know, get the hairnet. In and out."

"No, you have to Dustbust again."

"I have to… what?"

"Without the hairnet you probably contaminated the scene all over again. Find the hairnet, put it back on, Dustbust. Got it?"

"Yeah, got it."

I guess I looked a little defeated after I said that because then she added, "I'm sorry if I'm being a little short with you, but we're up against the clock here, and we gotta get this done." It was all I needed to hear. I loved that she had my back like that. My smile came back and I leaned in to give her a big kiss — which I now realize wasn't the best use of my time. "Find the hairnet, put it back on, Dustbust," she repeated, rebuffing my advances.

I entered Marcie's house again, this time a wiser, humbler intruder. I searched carefully for the hairnet which I eventually found under the couch. I put the hairnet back on and Dustbusted the floor and under the couch again. When I exited the house I felt the same sense of relief that the S.W.A.T. team wasn't there waiting for me, but this time I chose to forgo the enthusiastic cheering in favor of the more subtle triumphant fist pump. This turned out to be far, far worse as my wildly swinging fist then swung the Dust buster right into the front porch light. Smash. Boom. Darkness. Yelp! I guess I sort of froze amid the haze of loud noises, sparks, and shards of glass raining down on me, and I didn't come to my senses until around the third time Lori sent out the signal.

Beeeeeeeeeep.... Beep Beep. Oh, so that's what it sounds like. I sprinted to the car even more humbled than before, and needless to say the ride home was uncomfortably silent. In fact for the rest of the evening I kind of kept to myself. I was still feeling a rush from the success of the mission, but I was ashamed at how my clumsiness could have exposed us. I wondered if Lori felt the same way, but I decided to give her a bit of space just in case she wasn't ready to talk about it yet.

As I climbed into bed next to Lori, I prepared myself for a rough couple of days of cold shoulders and the silent treatment. But as my head hit the pillow and my thoughts began to drift, a faint whisper reached my ears: "Hey," she said without opening her eyes.

"Hey," I responded.

"You did good tonight. I'm proud of you."

Those words sent my heart aflutter once again, "Really?"

"Yeah," she said with a slight smile on her face, "good night."

"Good night." What else could I say? She did it again. She saved my ass and put up with all my craziness while she did it, and she still had time for a nice confidence booster to cap the night off. That's why I married her. And now as I try to quell my excitement long enough to fall asleep, all I feel is relief. Relief that things went so relatively well, relief that we got through it in one piece, and most of all relief that the worst is behind us.

THURSDAY

STEINER

It just goes to show ya'. My gramps always used to say, "It just shows to go ya'." I didn't really understand what he was doing until I was eleven or twelve years old, and I still don't find it that funny. But for him, it never got old. For me, I'll just say it the regular way. It just goes to show ya'. Just when you think you've seen everything, something comes along and surprises you.

Here's how my day has gone so far: I wake up, the wife has cooked me breakfast. Sheila never cooks breakfast — cooking's not really her thing, I knew that when I married her. But today, breakfast is hot and waiting for me on the kitchen table. And not only breakfast, but a full classic, just like you see on those TV commercials that show you breakfast — all the way down to the glass of milk *and* the glass of orange juice. I never understood why anyone would want both a glass of milk and a glass of orange juice for breakfast, but now I get it. You do it because you can. Because you're the type of person who has a full goddamn breakfast in the morning. You either have the time to get up and make one or you have someone else who has the time to get up and make one for you (or you pay them to get up and make one). Any way you slice it, it's a luxury of the privileged few. I'd never had a full breakfast on a random Thursday, but I did today. Eggs, bacon, grits, toast, two pancakes, the glass of OJ, the glass of milk, and I finished it all.

It wasn't the most expertly cooked breakfast in the world, in fact it reminded me why I never complained about Sheila not cooking in the first place. But the fact that it was there, that it existed at all, was pretty exciting. While I was chowing down, I allowed myself to fantasize that this little surprise morning treat was her way of apologizing. We had a bit of a tiff last night, and while in my head I always convince myself that I'm right while we're arguing, I usually know deep down that I'm wrong, or at least that I'm losing the rhetorical battle that's taking place between us.

"Don't push my buttons," she always says.

"I'm trying!" I reply, "But you have a lot of buttons."

One time a few years back when our son Blake was still in high school, Sheila just casually mentioned how she regretted that we never had another kid because she'd always wanted a girl. Just casually. The same as if she were to say, "Weather's nice today," she mentions this to me. Obviously this took me by surprise. "And you're just saying this now?" I asked her.

"Just saying this now?" she said, "I've always said that." Well, no, she had not always said that — in fact she had never said that in all our years of marriage. Not even once. Not even a hint. How do I know that? Because that's something I would remember. Like, for sure. I'd 100% no doubt remember it for sure. If she ever even hinted at it in a roundabout way, I'd stop whatever it was I was doing and ask her to clarify. Do you want another kid? If so, when? If this one's not a girl, will we keep trying until we get one? Please be specific.

But I knew better than to come at her head on, at this point in our marriage I'm a pro at the carefully worded response: "Do you still say that now?"

"What? Now? Are you crazy? I'm 43 years old! Do you know how much the odds of complications go up every year after 40? Are you crazy? Why would you even suggest a thing like that? Do you want our two children to be 17 years apart in age? Do you want a baby right now? At your age? Are you crazy?" Her voice kept inching higher every time she asked me if I was crazy until she was at an all out yell. I figured I must have been crazy, thinking anything I was going to say at that point was going to get me out of what I had coming to me. It just goes to show ya', whenever you think you've got something figured out, think again. Also, don't ever expect to win an argument with Mrs. Steiner.

Last night though, last night was different. We had gotten to that point in the argument where it's no longer about what it started out being about, and in fact you can barely remember what it started out being about in the first place. You know, when one person says how hurtful what the other person just said was, and then the other person denies that they said that and why don't you listen closer next time? Well, this time I knew in my head and in my heart that I was right, and I could tell that Sheila knew she was losing. I also knew she wasn't going to come out and admit defeat, but I didn't blame her for that because I never really did either. It was enough for me to see the defeat on her face, and I went to bed happy because of it.

So I let my imagination get the best of me while I ate this breakfast fit for a king, and think for a split second that maybe, just maybe this was her way of apologizing. I don't think I really thought that, but I entertained the idea. So imagine my surprise when Sheila enters the kitchen and tells me that the breakfast *was* her way of apologizing. She told me she was wrong and she's sorry and she wanted to make it up to me, and she knows she doesn't cook that great but she gave it her best shot. I smiled and kissed her and said thank you, it's great, and I accept your apology.

At that moment you'd think I would be elated — triumphant even — possibly floating on cloud nine. Me too, but that's not what happened. I actually started to feel pretty rotten. All this time I thought it was our thing never to apologize, just let our arguments fizzle out, both of us tacitly knowing who was right and who was wrong and that being enough. But now, a new wrinkle had been introduced: the apology breakfast.

I started to wonder if all those times that we both knew I was wrong, I was supposed to do something to make up for it. Did Sheila expect that every time only to be constantly disappointed? Am I a terrible husband for not atoning for my wrongness on a regular basis? Is not cheating for eighteen straight years not enough to keep a marriage happy and healthy? All these thoughts began swirling around in my head, and believe it or not I started getting angry at Sheila. Really angry. I didn't say anything for fear of discouraging her from future delicious apologies, but I was furious.

I did my best to kiss her goodbye and get out of the house without her sensing my demeanor, and I'm pretty sure it worked. But then as I drove in to the office, that anger gave way to an unshakeable fear. What if I'm the bad guy? What if everything that's gone wrong in my life personally and professionally up to this point has been because of <u>me</u>? I know, everybody goes through the platitudes: "I'm not perfect, I make mistakes sometimes, I've got regrets," but that's never the whole story because most people don't think they're the main reason for their problems. There's always someone or something else to blame the big stuff on, and in some cases the big stuff very well might be someone or something else's fault. But for me, today was the first time I realized that I had my doubts.

I trudged through the first part of the day in a bit of a haze, lost in thought and concerned that I'd grow old having no one else to be bitter at for my sad state of affairs. I hardly remember a thing about the Beachwood crime scene I was supposed to be reviewing. I was there in body, but my mind was elsewhere. I went over to the mall to wrap up the interviews for the Beachwood case and ate... something... at the food court. Then I wandered aimlessly around the mall for about a half an hour before I could get my head clear enough to go over and talk to the optometrist that the victim was temping for at the time of her death.

I was planning on it being pretty routine. As I said before, I got nothing from the friends and neighbors and even less from the crime scene and it was looking more and more like a random smash and grab gone wrong. In fact I had already kind of accepted that this one was probably going to go cold and eventually be all but forgotten. Just a few quick C.Y.A. questions for the optometrist and then back into the rotation to catch a fresh one. But then I met the guy.

It's rare to be surprised by anything when you've been doing this for as long as I have, but this guy was... well, he was weird. How weird? Weird enough to jar me out of my haze and make me forget about the Breakfast of Atonement for the first time since it happened, I'll tell you that much.

The first thing I noticed when I walked into Eyecare Associates of the Mall was that the place was completely empty. Now that's using the old spidey sense, isn't it?

"Hey look, I'm all alone."

"Good work, detective."

I searched for some sort of bell on the receptionist's desk for about a minute before I noticed the Beachwood victim's business cards on the desk. Oh right, the receptionist is dead. Some spidey sense, asshole. I wondered if the eye doctor even knew what had happened yet. Great, just what I needed, now I might have to break the news to this guy who only knew her for a few days and he'll have to pretend he's devastated out of some misplaced sense of propriety.

The optometrist, one Dr. Thomas Taggart, eventually returned and greeted me cheerfully, "Oh, sorry sir, just grabbing a little lunch, we're a bit short-handed today. Are you a walk-in or do you have an appointment?"

"Neither," I said in a much harsher tone than I'd intended. I guess those cop shows have finally gotten to me. I tried to make up for it by showing him my badge in as non-threatening a fashion as I could possibly muster, "I'm Detective Steiner, Homicide. Are you Dr. Taggart?"

"Detective?" he asked.

"Yes, Detective," I confirmed, "are you Dr. Taggart?"

"Detective?" Oh Jesus.

"Yes, Detective. Would it help if I put on a trench coat or something?" Fuck you, TV cop shows.

"Trench coa... no no no, I'm sorry, I'm just uh... confused... uh... is something wrong?" He's nervous. Really nervous. But not much out of the ordinary about that — in fact I see it a lot.

Most people instinctively tense up at the flash of the badge. The whole "To protect and to serve" thing isn't exactly the first thing that comes to mind when confronted by a police officer. Usually it's "What's this guy want? Did I do something?" It's okay though, it doesn't hurt my feelings that much anymore. Hell, at this point in my career it's become almost endearing. Poor guy thinks he looks like he's got something to hide, so then he tries to hide that and ends up acting even more strange.

"Well, I am from homicide so you're probably thinking that somebody died."

"Did somebody die?"

"Yes."

"Who?" he asked, starting to freak out. I pulled out my notepad and asked him if he knew a Marcie Tucker. "Marcie? Hm, Marcie, it doesn't ring a bell but... Oh yeah, the temp who's filling in while my regular assistant is out, I think her name is Marcie. In fact, she was supposed to be here today. I was actually starting to worry that... Wait. Is she..."

"Unfortunately yes," I said, "Marcie was found in her apartment late last night uh... no longer alive." My bedside manner has never been my strong suit.

Dr. Taggart looked distressed and began to ramble incoherently for a minute. I let him work through it though, I figured it was his way of grieving. I wouldn't have even paid attention to it except for the fact that it was kind of goofily, ineptly... well, poignant:

> Oh, uh, Oh my God. That's terrible. I uh... I hope she didn't have any family. I mean, I don't hope she didn't have any family, what I mean is, if she uh... if she

> didn't have any family then there would be nobody to get all bummed out about this and uh... you know, when something like this happens, you always think about the poor, heartbroken family, so uh... if she doesn't have any family then uh... the bright side would be that nobody would, you know, have to be all bummed out.

Hm. I guess I never thought of it that way. Awkward wording aside, he's kind of got a point there. People need their loved ones when they're alive, but after they're dead you kind of wish no one had to go through that whole "missing them" part. Having just had my mind blown, I quickly realized I had created a rather uncomfortable silence, which Dr. Taggart clearly felt the need to obliterate: "So uh... uh... uh... do you have any leads? Ya' think maybe it was a psycho boyfriend or something?" I wish.

"We're still trying to figure that out, did you notice anything out of the ordinary in the days Ms. Tucker was here? Any bizarre behavior, suspicious visitors, anything like that?"

"Uh, no, I don't think so," he said, the first of many beads of sweat appearing on his forehead.

"Any little things you may have shrugged off at the time but now in retrospect seem more significant?"

"Hmmmmmmm," he began after wiping sweat bead number two off of his forehead, "no, she seemed really peppy while she was here. Super peppy. And cheerful."

"Peppy *and* cheerful? I thought those kinda' meant the same thing."

"There are subtle differences," he replied. Okay.

"So she didn't seem overly worried or conflicted about anything?"

"Nope, peppy and cheerful!" he said after wiping away sweat bead number three, "She cried a little after I fired her, but not overly so."

Wait, What? I immediately perked up at this information and he immediately regretted sharing it. Almost on cue sweat beads four through maybe thirty appeared.

He tried to clarify: "It was a normal amount of crying. Under the circumstances."

"So you fired her."

"Well, technically…"

"But you said she was supposed to come in today."

"Yes, well… yes," he said as I lost count of the number of sweat beads pouring down his face, "I did fire her but uh… then I thought better of it and uh… then I called her up and unfired her."

"And what did she say when you told her she was unfired?"

"She said uh… she said that she really appreciated the second chance and uh… thank you Dr. Taggart and uh… I won't let you down again Dr. Taggart and uh… she was really grateful and peppy and cheerful and uh… full of life at the time. Very full of life as I remember, the last time I saw, um, spoke to her." Who knew the human body was capable of producing that much perspiration?

"Mm hmm, and what was your reason for terminating Ms. Tucker?"

"Terminating?"

"Of employment," I clarified, but now I was getting suspicious.

"Oh yes, of employment. Well uh... because of uh... certain irregularities of uh..."

"Irregularities?"

"Not of behavior or anything like that, more of the bookkeeping variety."

"Irregularities of bookkeeping."

"Yes," he said, knowing full well that we both knew he was hiding something. Now that doesn't necessarily mean he did it, he might have been having an affair with the girl or committed a less serious crime like embezzlement that he's afraid will come out in the investigation or... well, he probably did it. On the cop shows he would've done it. So I let him finish digging his grave: "Look, she would write down the time of the appointment, then the name, then the date when I specifically asked her to... it didn't make any sense! It threw me off and it... it... it... it may seem like a trivial thing to a layman like yourself, but in the medical profession these things are crucial!"

"Dr. Taggart, if it's not too much trouble I'd like to take a look at your books, see if I can tell what..." and that's when he snapped.

"Ya' got a warrant?" he shouted.

Play it cool, detective: "A warrant," I said flatly, "Dr. Taggart, I didn't think a warrant would be necessary, I just wanted to..."

"Then no! You can't see my books! Ya' think I'm stupid, Detective? Ya' think I'm an idiot?" Well...

"No sir, I uh... well I didn't think it was that strange of a request, I uh... I apologize if I was rude I... I'm sorry, thank you for your time." I nodded sheepishly at him and turned to go. I'm pretty sure I was able to hide my excitement until my back was turned to him, but once I cleared his field of vision I skipped all the way out to the parking lot. It's not every day that a guy practically falls out of the sky and presents himself as the lead suspect in a case that previously had no promising leads.

As I drove home, I thought about how my visit with Dr. Taggart had gone from a routine interview to the highlight of my day. I even giggled at myself a little because of the way I toyed with him there at the end. It's funny, I woke up this morning thinking I had nothing left in life to look forward to, and now I've got a newly agreeable wife at home and the world's dumbest criminal to deal with at work. It just goes to show ya', life never stops being full of little surprises. And now, for the first time in a long time, I'm excited about tomorrow!

I'm not saying I've changed my overall feelings about my career or the way my life is going, but that doesn't matter because tomorrow I get to have some cop show fun! First, I'm gonna go back to that crime scene and do a thorough once over and catch all the things I didn't care enough to notice the first two times around. Then, I'll do some follow up interviews to see if any of the family or friends recognizes this Dr. Taggart character. Then I go back to the mall for the dramatic follow up with the doctor himself! If I'm lucky I might even get to play a little cat and mouse game with him! Hey, maybe this is the jolt I need to get me out of my rut after all. Who knows? I might even wake up early and cook Sheila breakfast.

SUSAN

Quick, what's six times seven? I don't know either… at least I don't know off the top of my head. How is it that I spent six months in college as a Math major and I still have such a hard time remembering my times tables? I know how: it's because in all those calculus and trig classes I got to use one of those scientific calculators. I spent so much time figuring out equations and derivatives and logarithms and a hundred other things I've completely forgotten that I couldn't be bothered with the basic building blocks.

Come to think of it I don't think I ever got those times tables down in the first place. In first grade I — and this was a hundred years ago — but in first grade I was such a little beast! I wouldn't study no matter how much my momma tried to bribe me. I'd go without cake, candy, toys, friends, anything to get out of studying. I think I would have preferred boxed wine over a night of studying. I'm kidding of course. I can't believe I just said that, I don't prefer boxed wine over anything. Anyway, I suppose my aversion to studying carried on throughout the rest of my academic career, hence only the six months as a Math major.

But I guess that's all beside the point, the reason I'm on this tear is because I'm trying to figure out if I'm coming down with Alzheimer's. Now I admit I'm a bit of a hypochondriac, but it's like my therapist always says… or maybe she just said it once. No, she said it at least twice, but I don't believe it would be accurate to say she always said it. It's like my therapist said on occasion: "Even hypochondriacs get sick for real sometimes." I'm paraphrasing of course. She said it much more eloquently than that.

So I'm at the store this morning perusing the wine section, making a couple of choice selections for the weekend, checking out, loading up the car, and it's not until I'm making the turn up Pineview that it dawns on me that I completely forgot about the syrah for Tag and Lori! I've already been slacking on the housewarming gifts and now I go and forget about it while I'm staring at rows and rows of bottles. I thought I was going insane!

That's when the hypochondria kicked in and I got it in my head that I must be coming down with Alzheimer's. I mean, I don't think I'm at the age to get Alzheimer's yet, but I must be approaching the age to get early onset Alzheimer's at least. I wonder if they have a specific age for early onset Alzheimer's or if they just call it that because it comes before the specific age they have for regular onset Alzheimer's. I wonder if I used to know the answer to that but I forgot it because of my Alzheimer's.

Oh there I go with the hypochondria again. I wonder if a hypochondriac can have hypochondria about being a hypochondriac. No, that seems a bit too… 42! I literally just thought of it now. That's how bad I am. It took all that time for me to remember what six times seven was. Wait, it is 42, right? Oh, now I'm not sure... Should I Google it? No, that would defeat the purpose.

Oh yes! The purpose. So I'm sitting there parked in my driveway trying to decide whether to go back to the store for the syrah or to just spend the rest of the day wondering if I have Alzheimer's or not, when I come up with a brilliant idea. I'll just ask myself several questions that I should know the answer to, and if I still know the answers to them, then I don't have Alzheimer's. Seems simple enough, doesn't it? Well, it wasn't. First I asked myself the capital of Louisiana and I chose New Orleans as my answer. I was 100% sure of that until just for giggles I looked it up and found out that it was Baton Rouge. Now did I always mistakenly think the capital of Louisiana was New Orleans or did I forget about Baton Rouge because of my Alzheimer's?

So I decided to go with a simpler question. Who am I? I am Susan Connelly. But is that really who I am? I am a woman. I am a widow. I am a former aerobics instructor. I am a collector of porcelain figurines. I am a gardening hobbyist. I am a wine connoisseur. I am a person with Alzheimer's. No! That's what I'm trying to figure out... Well that question turned out to be too philosophical, so I kept on searching for the perfect Alzheimer's test question.

The most recent one is what's six times seven, but I don't know if it should count either since a.) I didn't study my times tables when I was younger and b.) I got the right answer but it took me a few minutes to remember it. So I'm going to continue trying to think of the right question. I sure hope I think of it fast though, because I still have to go to the store to get the syrah. Maybe I'll just go pick it up tomorrow, because you know what they say: there's nothing more important than your health. Yes, that settles it, I'd better keep thinking.

It would be a shame if I got sick at this point in my life, with all the things I still want to do. I was hoping to meet and marry some eligible 50-something bachelor who I can get along fantastically with and who by some wild coincidence also happens to be a billionaire. I was hoping to see the world with him from my perch in his hot air balloon and perhaps join the mile high club while I'm up there too. Do hot air balloons go a mile up? Fine, the kilometer high club is good enough for me, I'm not too picky! I'm kidding of course. I'm very picky.

Anyway, where was I? Oh yes, the syrah. Hey, ya' know what? I just thought of something. I remembered about the syrah this morning, and I also remembered that I wanted to ask Tag and Lori about it, and I did ask Tag and Lori about it! Would someone with Alzheimer's remember all that? Let's see, I was in the garden when Tag came out and I played with him just like usual. I was like, "Will ya' look at that coat? I tell ya', I just love a man in uniform," and he blushed and smiled which usually means he's in a good mood and I can play some more, so I went further: "Sure some people prefer police and firemen, but I say give me a doctor any day of the week. Ya' know if you came out in scrubs one morning, I might get pregnant just looking at you! I'm kidding of course. I can't get pregnant anymore." Actually I didn't say that last part, about not being able to get pregnant anymore, that might have been a bit much.

But then I remember distinctly asking him about the housewarming gift and whether he and Lori preferred red or white wine. He said something about asking Lori because he doesn't really drink too much, but I told him I'd make it a special occasion. A very special occasion. I'm kidding of course! Not about telling him that, about the other... oh forget it. The point is that I asked him about the wine and he basically said they didn't care, so syrah it is! See there, Susan? You're still sharp as a tack. You even remembered that little detail about not being able to get pregnant anymore. Would someone with Alzheimer's remember that? Of course not!

Wait, but didn't I say that I didn't say that part out loud? Did I say that part out loud? Oh my gosh I can't remember. I'm almost certain I didn't say it out loud but... I do think I remember him looking at me in shock after I said it. Maybe I told myself I shouldn't have said it out loud after I saw that look on his face. No, no no no, I definitely didn't say it out loud... Unless I did. Oh no, it's starting. I hope I don't forget that I never drink boxed wine.

TAG

The worst is not behind us. The worst is not even close to behind us. The worst is right in front of us, blocking out the highway on either side and the sun right along with it. The worst peeks around the corner while I'm eating lunch and sucks away my appetite. It bounces on my stomach when I lay down to sleep. Lori says that this isn't the worst, that this is what we expected and that all I have to do is keep my cool and we'll be fine, but in all honesty I think she has too much faith in me. That's not to say I'm completely inept, I'm just not great under pressure. Lori says I'm not giving myself enough credit, and then she brings up the O.A.T.

The O.A.T. (also known as the Optometry Admission Test) is the test you take to get into optometry school. When I found out that the test was administered by the American Dental Association (which is true, look it up), I freaked out. On the night before the test, I was so nervous that there would be some surprise teeth questions thrown in that I almost threw up. Lori told me that was ridiculous and that I needed to calm down, and I said I was trying to calm down but I'm not good under pressure. She told me I'd be fine, and sure enough when I took the test, I was in the zone. I aced it with flying colors.

But the O.A.T. was about what I know. The O.A.T. was about eyes. Eyes I know. I know I know eyes. I get them. Eyes are easy. This? I don't think I can do this. Dammit, and things looked so bright this morning. I don't remember a morning where I woke up in a better mood than this morning. After getting dressed, I peeked into the kitchen to grab a bagel and kiss Lori goodbye, and she asked me why I was leaving for work so early.

“Well,” I replied cheerfully with a mouth full of bagel, “I figured I'd get a head start this morning since I've gotta pull double duty until they send in a replacement for Marcie.”

“A replacement for Marcie?” Lori asked, puzzled.

I was in such a good mood that I felt comfortable joking around about the dead: “Well, I don't think she's gonna be able to make it in today.” Rimshot. Then I'm pretty sure I winked at her.

“How do you know that?”

“Uh, did we not just go over there last night and…”

“Did we?” She interrupted.

“Yeah. Me and you. We… oooooooooohhhhhh.”

“Yeah.”

“I don't know that she's dead yet because we weren't there last night because I wasn't there yesterday so as far as I know she's still alive and coming in to work today!”

“Yes,” Lori replied with a hint of a smile, a valiant but failed attempt to hide her exasperation. I appreciated it.

“You are an amazing woman,” I beamed at her, “never let me forget that, okay?” She nodded as I kissed her goodbye and left the house. Lori's continued amazingness had put me in an even better mood. In fact I was in such a good mood that

I genuinely didn't mind having small talk with Susan as I headed toward my car. She babbled away about wanting to see me in scrubs and getting us a housewarming gift even though we've lived there for almost a year now. You know, same old stuff. Of course when the subject of what kind of wine I liked came up, it did get a little awkward. Apparently Susan is a wine expert, so it was a little dicey trying to get across to her that I don't drink wine.

I'm not a recovering alcoholic or anything, I just hate the taste of the stuff. I'm not much of a drinker at all really. Ever since that first time I succumbed to peer pressure and partook of an alcoholic beverage, just the thought of it has been enough to make me nauseous. The peer pressure came from my sister. I was five, she was eight and a half. She brought me behind the bar in our old house and produced a key from her right front pocket. She seemed so excited at the prospect of opening up this big wooden case that I couldn't help but feel it too. She pulled out a bottle of something or other — I remember it was reddish — and told me if I drank a few sips of this magic liquid I'd be able to fly.

Well, flying was my dream. Not on an airplane mind you, but unassisted — that's the way I wanted to go. I was constantly pretending I was Superman or Green Lantern or some guy I made up flying through the air, wind in my hair, ready for anything. In retrospect I really ignored many of Superman's way cooler powers because I was so obsessed with flying. He had laser eyes for Christ's sake! I don't think I ever used those in my fantasies. I remember one Halloween I was furious because my mom got me a Batman costume and my sister got to be Wonder Woman. I didn't care that she was a girl, Wonder Woman flew and Batman didn't, so I fought tooth and nail because I wanted to be Wonder Woman. Long story short, my sister knew my Achilles heel was flying and she exploited that weakness masterfully.

I grabbed that bottle and chugged down as many gulps of that nasty shit as I could. I don't remember how many, but it was enough to land me in the hospital and get Stacy grounded. I'll never forget the awful feeling I had after drinking that stuff, just talking about it now brings it back a little. So as far as wine or any other alcoholic beverage goes, I don't think I could touch the stuff if I wanted to. And I don't.

Whatever, I'm not even sure if Susan was listening to the answers to her questions, because before I got one all the way out, she'd be on to the next one. I wonder if that's what happens when one spouse dies after a long marriage. Do they try to fit a day's worth of talk into every conversation because they're not sure when they're gonna get a chance to talk again? It must be hard after having someone to talk to for however many years to just suddenly… not. I hope that doesn't happen to Lori if I die first. I don't think it will. I can't imagine Susan was anything like Lori even when her husband was alive. After I felt like I'd listened for a polite length of time, I waited for her next pause to take a breath and jumped in my car. I waved goodbye and drove off, watching in the rearview mirror as she finished off her thought for no one in particular.

My spirits were still up on the way to work, but as I walked through the mall a distant sense of darkness felt like it was getting nearer and nearer. I couldn't put my finger on what it was at first, but it hit me pretty hard the moment I set eyes on that reception desk. It was empty. I knew it was going to be empty, but it still shook me to see it that way. It was weird because it had been empty all day yesterday too, but yesterday I still thought Marcie was alive. I wondered when it happened… was she still alive as I sat right there leaving a message on her voice mail? Was she screening my calls or was she just a bit too dead to pick up? What was I doing at the very moment that it happened? I shook those macabre thoughts out of my head and tried to press on, but that desk kept bringing it all back.

What was it about that desk? It wasn't even her desk. It was Dan's desk. Still, the thought that less than two days ago I was staring lustfully at the tits of a living, breathing human who now could live and breathe no more was a little too much for me to handle. I sleepwalked through the day, pulling double duty was tough but at least it kept me busy.

I wanted to call Lori and have her talk me out of this madness I was feeling, but I felt that I'd already given her enough cause to worry about me and I didn't want to give her any more. But I knew that I wasn't going to get through the day at this rate and I could feel my will slipping away. It was only a matter of time before I broke down and called her. I only hoped that I wouldn't break down and cry until after I hung up.

I set a goal for myself that I'd make it past noon before letting myself make that call, and at 11:48 I was feeling pretty good about my chances. At 11:52 I started to get restless though, and I realized that it's harder to wait to make a call when all you're doing is staring at the phone. My mom always used to say, "A watch pot never boils," and I never knew if that really was something people used to say or if she just made it up, but I understood it either way. I needed to get busy quick before I drove myself crazy waiting.

Then, just when I was getting up to go rearrange the plants

on the wall or something, the phone rang. It was Lori. Perfect! Now it wouldn't seem as pitiful when I talked to her because she's the one who called. That's the way it works, right? I answered the phone excitedly, “Hey.”

“Hey,” she replied, and before I could get any whining out of my system, she continued, “I was thinking maybe you better call the people at the temp agency and ask them why the girl hasn't shown up yet. She wasn't there yesterday either, right?”

“Right, I should probably do that so it seems like I expected her to come in today.”

“You do expect her to come in today.”

“No, I d… Oh! Yeah, we probably shouldn't talk like that over the phone, huh?”

“Talk like what?” she replied, serious as a heart attack.

“Talk like we know she's not coming to…”

“Tag, what are you talking about?”

“I'm talking about the reason we shouldn't… Oh! Right! Nothing. I'm talking about nothing.” Wink wink.

“Okay, bye,” she said and then hung up the phone. I was so relieved to have finally caught her drift that I completely forgot to bring up my impending nervous breakdown, and now I had a new task to help speed up the process. Does she really expect me to call the temp agency? She's seen me under pressure, doesn't she realize that I can't pull that off? I'm not that great at using the phone on regular days (hence Marcie's voicemails), how am I supposed to use it now? Okay, okay, calm down. I can't think about that right now, I'll worry about it after lunch.

With that little panic attack out of the way, I headed over to the food court. Halfway through my meatball sub I looked up to see a spectacular strawberry blonde trying her best to make her flirty glances seem covert. It's funny, with all the activity of the past few days, I realized that I'd hardly thought about sexing it up with other women at all. It was the only time I felt grateful for having walked in on a dead body. But now, watching this aspiring supermodel across the food court, it all came rushing back pretty quick. I found myself instinctively playing her game: she'd look at me until I looked up, then she'd quickly look away in a fit of pretend bashfulness. Then we'd play the roles in reverse — back and forth we'd go in a silent, flirtatious tango.

I was only vaguely aware of the dangerous waters I was wading into as this was happening, in fact it all felt so natural that I don't think I became consciously aware of it until after I'd already started participating. Our gazes eventually met, as they were doomed to do from the start, and we both shared a giggle. Apparently she took that as the invitation she was waiting for, because then she started walking over with that look in her eyes like she was a tiger who'd just captured her dinner.

That's when reality hit me. I realized sex was coming, and it was coming fast. I had to do something quick, so I did the first thing that popped into my head. I jumped up and started shouting "No! No!" like a maniac, then I ran away, leaving the other half of the meatball sub on the table, uneaten.

It was a drastic measure, but also a necessary one. I couldn't chance that sexy siren coming even an inch closer to me. Not now at least, not when I was at my most vulnerable. I hoped my shouting and arm-flailing had prevented her from wanting to follow me, but just in case I planned to lock myself up in the office for at least a half hour. Better safe than sorry.

Of course that plan never happened due to the tall, serious-looking man who was lurking around the reception desk upon my return. He had one of those faces, not like a dentist, but close. Maybe a cross between a dentist and a delivery man of some sort. Regardless, I know exactly what he didn't look like: a detective. But that's what he was. A goddamn detective.

The worst part is I know I should have been expecting it — I was one of the last people to see Marcie alive — so it stands to reason that the police would want to talk to me about her. I probably wasn't even a suspect, but that's not was I was thinking at the time. When he flashed that badge all I could think was "They got me. I'm going to jail for the rest of my life. If I'm lucky. I can't handle jail! People like me don't do well in jail! Oh my God I'm gonna die in jail!" It wasn't my finest hour. I was a stuttering, sweaty mess — even during the routine questions. I don't remember most of what he said to me, but I knew I hadn't made a very good impression because eventually I just started shouting at him. As he left I sensed a slight, almost imperceptible grin cross his face. I could tell I was making it easy for him, and I knew he'd be back. So needless to say I panicked.

I gave the Detective five minutes to clear the parking lot and then I closed down the store without explanation and ran to my car in a full sprint. I gasped for air as I sped home, ignoring all traffic signals and regulations. The only time I stopped on the way home was when I had to avoid plowing into the back of a blue Mercedes going half the speed limit. The sound of screeching brakes and honking horns was starting to get a little too familiar for me this week. I needed to calm down, but that wasn't going to happen until after I talked to Lori. I parked in the driveway and stumbled out of the car, calling out Lori's name before I even reached the front door.

"Lori!" I called out desperately as I entered the house, "Lori!"

"In here!" She called out from the laundry room.

I ran to her and got right to the point: "We gotta pack! We gotta go! We gotta pack we gotta go! We gotta get out of here!"

"Tag, slow down. What?"

"They're onto us!"

"Who's onto us?"

"They are," I said carefully, as if uttering their names would make them appear right in front of us.

"Who?" Lori persisted.

"The cops," I whispered.

"The cops?"

"Shhhhh!"

"Tag, what's the problem?"

"What's the problem? A detective... a homicide detective came to see me today. He asked a lot of questions."

"And did you answer?"

"No!" I replied emphatically.

"Why not?" she countered.

"Because I didn't have any answers!"

"Why didn't you have any answers?"

"Because... because uh... I uh..."

"Because you didn't do it," she said matter-of-factly.

"Because I didn't do it. Yeah, that's right. It's because I didn't do it."

"So then you have nothing to worry about."

I didn't? Well, I was sure I could think of something: "But what about the..."

Lori cut me off before I could go any further. "Honey, you

don't know anything, you were never at her house, and most of all, you really, truly didn't do it. So why would you worry about a homicide detective?"

For the first time in about forty minutes, I exhaled: "I guess I wouldn't." Wow. This was very comforting. I knew Lori could do it.

Still, she could sense I wasn't all the way convinced, so she pulled out an oldie but goodie. She put her hands on my shoulders, looked me dead in the eye, and broke it down for me: "Tag, you didn't do it."

"I didn't do it," I repeated zombie-like.

"You don't know anything."

"I don't know anything."

"You were never at her house."

"I was never at her house."

"So what's the problem?"

"I guess there isn't any."

"That's right," she grinned, "there isn't any. We knew a detective would probably visit you, the girl was working with you on the day she died. That's why I wanted you to call the temp agency."

"The temp agency. Shit, I forgot to call the temp agency. The detective showed up before I could call the temp agency. Shit shit shit, I'm screwed."

"No Tag, you're not screwed, you didn't call the temp agency because a detective came and told you what happened."

"Right. That's right."

"I know that's right, Tag, now stop worrying, relax, we're gonna get through this. Why?"

"Uh..."

"Because you didn't do it."

"Because I didn't do it."

"Because you didn't do it." Her words were a soothing balm on my wounded soul. I felt a thousand times better as I exited the laundry room. Her gentle touch and unwillingness to show exasperation, no matter how exasperated she was in reality, were a real godsend. I must be the luckiest guy in the world, I thought to myself. I felt an almost tangible sense of euphoria as I walked through the house, repeating those magic words to myself softly: "You didn't do it."

As I made my way to the bedroom and prepared to shower off the troubles of the day, I felt better about handling Detective Stevens or whatever his name was. I realized that I didn't owe him any plausible explanations at all. In fact, I didn't owe him anything. I didn't even have to talk to him. He could call me a suspect all he wanted, if there was no evidence then there was no case, and the only way he could get evidence was to break me down mentally. I wasn't going to let that happen again, so poor Detective Stevens was out of luck. I looked forward to another peaceful night's sleep as I undressed and started to run the bathwater.

I wanted to express my appreciation to Lori in so many ways, but I decided to keep it simple for now. As I showered I composed a sweet little note in my head that I'd leave for her to find when she woke up in the morning. I'd put it in the top drawer of her night table so she'd find it when she went in there to grab her wedding ring. Damn Tag, you are romantic. I hopped out of the shower and composed the note:

Dearest Lori-Bear,

Hey.

Throughout all the tough times
and all the hard days,
You're special to me in so many
great ways.

You wipe off my tears when I'm
down and depressed,
You sew up my buttons when
I can't get dressed.

But the greatest of all of your
numerous sides,
Is how you can find me when I
want to hide.

You bring me the truth when I
need it the most,
And that's even sweeter than
your sweet French toast.

I want you to know that no matter
the year,
I'll always adore you and love you
my dear,

Love,
Taggy-Bear

Suck on that, Hallmark! Sure it's corny, but I believe that the concept of corny was invented by someone who had a hard time expressing himself emotionally. Saying something's corny is a way to avoid appearing vulnerable and admitting to someone else how much you need them. Well, I need Lori and I wanted her to know it, so call me corny! I folded up the letter and placed it beneath her wedding ring in the drawer. This one's going to score me some major points! Not that points are why you do something for your wife, but points are always good to have, especially when you're in a situation like... what's this?

I saw a familiar object poking out from underneath some envelopes in Lori's drawer. Now I'm not one to go snooping, but that thing looked familiar and my curiosity wasn't going to be quenched until I knew what it was. I gently nudged it a little further out into the open and... wait. What's Marcie's business card doing in Lori's top drawer? Didn't I tear that up and throw it away? I picked it up and inspected it, and to my utter confusion I saw that the card had been meticulously taped and glued back together as if it were some kind of makeshift jigsaw puzzle. What the... what the... why would... is this a... I ruefully kissed my peaceful night's sleep goodbye.

FRIDAY

SUSAN

I have an appointment today with Dr. Mack… laruse? Was that his name? Or McElroy? No, that doesn't sound right. Mackle… rose? Whatever his name is I've heard good things and besides, it's time to make a change. I no longer believe in Dr. Bruce's ability to be objective with me. It's not like I'm an actual, honest-to-goodness, real life hypochondriac! I don't go see him every week complaining about one mystery ailment after the next, I see him periodically. Often months go by between visits. Still, every time I've gone to visit him recently I've seen that same look on his face when I describe my symptoms. I think he's tuning me out altogether now!

So I made an appointment with Dr. Macken… russen? I made an appointment with him because this one is really important. This one *really* could be for real. Take that, Dr. Bruce! Now you've lost a patient because of your attitude. I only hope that doctors don't have some sort of secret underground brotherhood where they gossip with each other about patients the way we used to talk to each other about professors in college: "Don't take calculus with Professor Thompson, I hear he takes attendance!"

And don't even get me started about H.I.P.A.A., I don't think doctors and nurses worry about that at all. And why should they? It's not like we can do anything to them if they get caught violating our privacy, all they'd have to say is "Fine then, if we can't talk about patients then we just won't fix anybody." Yeah, we'd cave real quick. Say what you want about the medical profession, but we literally can't live without them. So if there's a doctors' poker night that both of them are a part of, I'm up the proverbial creek without the proverbial paddle. Maybe I should find a doctor like they select juries:

"Do you have any knowledge of this patient whatsoever?"

"Yes."

"Thank you, you're dismissed."

I have to be careful not to taint Dr. Mackensacken's observations because I've got to get to the bottom of my Alzheimer's situation immediately. I'm beginning to doubt all my memories now. It doesn't matter how clearly I remember something, now that the possibility of Alzheimer's has crept into my brain, I'm doubting everything! I need an exam from an objective, impartial, non-judgmental, neutral, unbiased physician or I fear I'll never trust a memory again. Yesterday I spent the whole day testing myself. And the whole night. I got so distracted by my self tests that when I finally looked up I realized it was two in the morning! Needless to say I didn't get the syrah yesterday. No matter, I'll stop by the store on the way back from the doctor. If I remember to, that is.

Gosh, I better get crackin' on that too, who knows how long my mind's gonna last if I do have Alzheimer's, and it would be such a shame if I lose my mind and Tag and Lori never get properly welcomed to the neighborhood. Lord knows those heifers won't do it. Well, that's one positive to getting Alzheimer's at least, I won't just forget about the good stuff, the bad stuff will disappear right along with it. It almost makes it seem worth it. I'm kidding of course.

Oh! How awful would that be if there was a disease that only took away good memories? Every day would be a living hell. I guess I should thank the Lord that at least I'm not going to get that one. Where was I? Oh yes, the heifers. It would, I must admit, be a special kind of Heaven to be blissfully unaware of those heifers and their poison tongues, always whispering and tittering at each other while looking in my general direction. They think they're being clever by casually glancing then quickly looking away as they gossip, but I know what's going on! I'm no fool.

I won't miss those memories when my Alzheimer's kicks in, but there will be things it'll be a shame I can't hold onto. First and foremost my Graham. He's only been gone for two years and sometimes I still wake up in the morning expecting to turn over and see him there, snoring away like a foghorn. I'd be ready to shake him awake because he overslept again and watch him bound about the house furiously getting dressed for work, yelling "Aw heck" repeatedly as he did it. Just once I wanted to hear a "Sonuvabitch" or a "Goddammit" come out of his mouth, but I never did. And now he's gone. It's funny the things you miss when you lose someone. I never would have thought I would have missed his oversleeping and his "Aw hecks" at all, but I think that might be what I miss the most. Besides the snoring of course.

I can't ever, ever let myself fall asleep on the couch because when I wake up on the couch I'm taken right back to the only reason I ever woke up on the couch for 32 years. My Graham snored like a megaphone. I'd hit him, I'd kick him, I'd scream at him, I'd even pretend I was having sexy dreams and call out other men's names — nothing would stop him. He slept like a brick and snored like a freight train. I'd go sleep on the couch and still hear it loud enough to keep me awake. It drove me crazy, and I miss it like hell. I'll miss the memories of it even more. They may cause me pain, but it's a comforting pain.

Oh my gosh, will you look at me now? Going on about my silly problems and bringing down the mood like that. It's the reason I made an appointment with Dr. McCracken today: I just can't be my regular old chipper self with all of these worries on my mind. And it's more than just the Alzheimer's itself, without my Graham around, who's going to take care of me when my mind goes? I can't live in a home, I don't think I'm old enough. Plus I need my garden. And my house needs to be kept up — I can't sell it, too many memories. Although I guess once my Alzheimer's gets going those won't be much of an issue anymore anyway.

Oh, but I can't have people coming and going through my room as they please, I can't stand the thought of someone watching me sleep! Always waking up with drool on my face, mouth hanging open like a fool, I even slept with my back to my Graham most of the time because I didn't want him to see me that way. I can't have people going through my stuff either. I need everything just so and I can't have anyone rooting around and mucking up the grand order of it all. No! No rest home. I will stay here, at this home.

But who will take care of me? The heifers won't, and I wouldn't want them to anyway, they already whisper about the outside of my house, I won't have them whispering about the inside too. Oh! Ya' know what would be perfect? Tag and Lori live right next door! I could live at home, and they could come check in on me periodically to help me with my daily activities and whatnot. Lori is just a dear, I'm sure she'd be happy to help me with my more feminine needs, and I just know she wouldn't whisper either! I bet I'd even feel comfortable with her seeing me sleep.

And Tag could do the more physically challenging tasks like carpentry and heavy-lifting and sponge baths. I'm kidding of c... Actually, I'm not kidding at all. Why can't a man help out a poor, ailing woman with an oh-so-soothing sponge bath? It's not like he's cheating on his wife, in fact I bet Lori wouldn't mind it one little bit. And if Tag were to get a little personal enjoyment out of it, what's wrong with that? I know I'd get a lot of personal enjoyment out of it myself. Ooh, I bet he does massages too — he is a doctor after all. That would be just perfect! It would be the ultimate bright side of having a terrible disease.

That settles it, but I won't bring it up just yet, that might be a bit creepy. I'm sure I have a little time before things get dire anyway. I'll add it to my last will and testament just in case. I wonder if Alzheimer's makes you forget things that are happening that day. I have to look that up because it would be a shame to forget the sponge baths. But I won't bring that up today, however it's even more important than ever to get the syrah taken care of. You know, to butter them up for when the time comes. I'll definitely pick it up after the doctor and bring it over tonight. Like a friend would do. Oh, I'm so excited I can hardly stand it!

STEINER

I think I'm due for a new hairstyle. It's probably been about fifteen years, that's a long time to go with just one. I mean, no one ever complained about it so I always figured I shouldn't mess with success. It's also very low maintenance — which is a huge plus because I hate fussing over myself in the mirror. My looks are just about average in every possible way so it just feels like the height of vanity to spend any extra time primping. And believe me I'm not fishing for compliments when I say that. I am completely, 100% A-okay with my averageness. I might even go so far as to say I love it. I met Sheila at a young age and married her soon after, so looks would have never brought me anything but trouble anyway.

Of course if I'm being honest I get plain sick of looking at her sometimes and yes, there are times when I wonder if we'll ever have sex again, but that's even more reason to be grateful for my mediocre looks. If it was in any way easy for me to have a one night stand I'm almost certain I would have had several already. And while we argue a lot and in general sometimes hate each other's guts, I've grown too accustomed to the lifestyle we have to want to give it up. If I cheated on Sheila and she left me, I'd be like a bear in the woods having to find my own nourishment and… never showering or cooking or cleaning. I'd probably hibernate too. So please, don't pity me for my average looks.

That said, it could be time for a change. I've gotten so used to being miserable that I think part of me is afraid to be happy. When you're miserable, the stakes are low — everything has already gone wrong, so there's no need to worry about your day getting ruined. If something else goes wrong, it's just one more thing that's gone wrong. Who cares? Just another drop in the ocean. No expectations, no worry, just misery. When you're happy though, at least for me, it's such a high-wire balancing act trying to keep everything together. What if this goes wrong, what if that goes wrong? It's so unbelievably stressful trying to keep everything together and stay happy that it makes you miserable. So I've pretty much steered clear of happiness for a good long while now, considering myself perfectly happy being miserable. But everything gets old eventually, and it's been just long enough since the last time I tried it for me to have forgotten how disastrous it was, so I'm considering giving happiness one more try. What can I say, I'm an optimist at heart.

If you're thinking I'm a strong candidate for a mid-life crisis, you're wrong. I think this is just the opposite — I'm going through a mid-life renaissance! I'm on a two day hot streak mood-wise, which is rare for me these days, and I want to get a few things done before I sink back into my pit of misery again. So maybe I'll grow the hair out a bit, maybe I'll buy a trench coat, maybe I'll start smoking a pipe too. The sky's the limit for the next week or so.

And yes, I did make breakfast for Sheila this morning. It

felt like sort of a cheap imitation while I was doing it because she had just done it for me yesterday morning, and I was afraid it would be plainly obvious to her that that's what it was, but I went ahead and gave it a try anyway. So what if I hadn't cooked anything more complicated than toast in about 20 years, it's the thought that counts, right? Eh.

While I was scrambling the eggs, I kept thinking they looked too runny. I didn't want my wife to get salmonella poisoning the first time I ever cooked for her, so I waited until I was sure it was edible before I turned off the stove. If you think you can see where this one's going, you're right: that egg was so rubbery and impenetrable I probably would've felt comfortable wearing it instead of my kevlar.

Luckily for me my wife doesn't have much of a sweet tooth so I was able to forgo the traditional pancakes, waffles, french toast, and the like. The bacon was of the microwave variety and the orange juice was a simple pour and serve job, so that left the coffee and the good old Southern grits like they make back in Memphis (that's where Sheila's from). The coffee came along well enough considering I've been known to partake of the beverage myself on a somewhat regular basis, and the grits were a little bit burnt but not as much as I feared they would be after the egg debacle, so I considered it an overall above average performance — for my skill level, at least.

After I was done I gazed upon my creation with a feeling approaching pride, but as I said it felt a little disingenuous doing it the day after she did it for me. Still, I was riding high and excited about the day ahead of me so I just said screw it. That feeling lasted until about three seconds before Sheila entered the kitchen when it suddenly occurred to me how badly this could backfire. I could potentially get a "Oh, so I cooked you breakfast and you just had to outdo me!" speech and be thrown unceremoniously into the doghouse where my good mood would die a slow, painful death. That might even be what I deserved. Oh well, too late to worry about that now, "Surprise!"

Okay, I want to preface what I'm about to say by acknowledging the role luck played in all of this. I grant you that not every woman would react positively under these circumstances. In fact even Sheila herself may have given me the old "You just had to outdo me" speech on any number of other days. I don't know if she just got up on the right side of the bed today or what, but she took one look at my mediocre breakfast and started to cry. Good cry. Happy cry. Tears of joy cry. It turns out she didn't care how unoriginal my gesture was, she didn't care about the timing, she didn't care about who won last night's argument, she just cared about getting some sort of indication that I still cared. Hm. Okay.

I sat there and watched her eat every morsel of that breakfast, chewing each bite of scrambled egg at least a thousand times, wincing a bit at the burnt parts of the grits, and drinking every last drop of that black coffee, even though later on I remembered that she preferred tea. She even insisted on doing the dishes afterward, and she did them exuberantly rather than begrudgingly like most mornings. It was a magical start to the day, and my good mood week was quickly turning into a great mood week!

I kissed Sheila goodbye and I'm pretty sure she slipped me a little tongue for the first time in a good decade. That was interesting. A little roll in the hay tonight is virtually guaranteed, but first I have to go and pull a rabbit out of a hat on Beachwood. My superiors at the office aren't expecting much from it, and I've been letting them go right on not expecting it. Hey, a win is a win in homicide, but everybody gets wins. If you want to get those silent, awe-filled stares as you walk to and from your desk, you gotta take a dead end case and pull a rabbit out of a hat. See, I haven't mentioned our sweaty doctor friend to anyone yet, and I'm not going to until I can bring him in in the palm of my hand — which shouldn't be too long at this rate.

On my return visit to the crime scene I'd found some pretty interesting stuff, and I planned on sharing it all with the good doctor in the most dramatic way I could think of. First, I set up shop on a bench in the mall with a good view of the eye place. Then, I called the new temp girl to ask about an appointment and, surprise surprise, Dr. Taggart had an opening that day. Right after lunch! Perfect. I waited for the good doctor to head on over to the food court before showing up for my appointment.

"Right this way," she said as she led me to an exam room at the end of a fairly short hallway, "Dr. Taggart will be with you shortly."

"Thanks," I said as she shut the door behind her. I looked around the exam room at the various types of equipment, diagrams, and eye charts. It seemed like your typical exam room, probably not much different from what you'd find in most doctor's offices. I looked at his diploma hanging on the wall:

By the authority of the Trustees of this University and upon the recommendation of its Faculty, the University does hereby confer upon:

Thomas Thaddeus Cornelius Taggart
The Degree of
Doctor Of Optometry

Those colleges sure know how to put things fancy. I remember my diploma saying something similar. I also remember wondering if they used all those fancy words with the fancy handwriting more to make me feel important or to make themselves feel important. Maybe it was a little of both, but it still confirmed for me my suspicions about those university types. How they want more than just to be smart, they want to feel smarter than everybody else. Because nobody talks like that unless they're trying to make something seem more important than it is. Now don't get me wrong, I'm not some hillbilly who thinks that academia is poisoning the minds of our youth with "thinkin' words and commie speak," but I do think they take themselves a bit too seriously. For one thing, those gowns look ridiculous! And the higher the degree, the more ridiculous they look. Have you seen those atrocities that they make the PHD's wear? I wonder if Dr. Taggart looked as dumb at his graduation as he did when I talked to him yesterday. I doubt it.

Next to the diploma was a nice picture of the doctor with a woman who I assumed to be his wife. Pretty girl, I wonder if he deserves her. Probably not. I wonder how many of his secrets she knows. She can't know them all. I bet when she finds out about the philandering she'll think it's the worst news she could ever hear in her whole life! Oh, just you wait Mrs. Taggart, there's more. Lots more. Your husband has been a very bad boy and he's not exactly the type to be able to hide it. He's also not the type that lasts very long in prison. No matter, I don't expect you'll be paying him too many visits once you find out the extent of his extracurricular activities. So don't worry, you don't know it yet, but I'm doing you a favor.

I could hear Dr. Taggart talking to the temp up front, so I got into position. Okay, so it was a bit dramatic, but only a bit. Hey, just once I wanted it to feel like it did on the cop shows, so sue me. I turned my back to the door, peered through the lenses of the eye machine, and waited. When the doctor entered I imagined the tense music building to a crescendo as I turned around to see the defeated look on his face: "Hello, Dr. Taggart."

"Goddammit." he muttered. Not quite as dramatic as I was hoping for, but he was definitely surprised.

"How'd you sleep?" I asked politely.

"What do you want?" he muttered again. He seemed to be trying to say as little as possible. Hm, I thought, this isn't the Dr. Taggart I met yesterday — I wonder if he's been coached. But coached by who? Does he have a cop friend? Am I thinking too much like a cop show now? Probably.

"Well, I want a bigger house for starters. And a pool would be nice." Attaboy, Detective, disarm him with your charm.

"I don't know," he muttered. Definitely coached.

Okay now hang back, don't get too cocky: "I have a confession to make. I'm not here for an eye test."

"Really?" he asked facetiously. Good, let's start to bring him out of his shell.

"But I do have a few more questions and, well, I didn't think you'd talk to me by choice after yesterday, so…"

"I have nothing to hide, Detective, I'll be happy to answer your questions." Hm, not only was he coached, but he was coached well.

"Oh, great," I said as I pulled out my notepad and got down to business. I wondered if this wasn't going to be as easy as I'd first thought, "I found a few things I'd like some clarification on and..."

"Unfortunately, it's gonna have to wait, I'm actually pretty swamped this morning, so if you're not here for an exam then I'm gonna have to ask you to leave." Ha! A zebra doesn't change its stripes! He can paint them so he looks like a horse, but he can't change them altogether. The good doctor could play it cool as long as he had his script to go by, but wear him down and he'll be stuttering and sweating again in no time!

"I'll take an eye test if I have to. I did pay for one," I told him. Your move, Taggart.

"Uh... okay then."

"Great."

Looking defeated, he swung that funny looking machine around so it faced me as he muttered out his instructions: "Put your forehead up against the black bar and tell me which of the two images looks more clear, the one on the left or the one on the right." He turned a knob and I saw two identical letter W's pop into place. It occurred to me how funny it would be if this is how I found out I needed glasses.

What hadn't yet occurred to me was the fact that in all likelihood I was talking to a murderer, alone, and in a very vulnerable position. What was to stop him from stabbing me with a broken lens or something? I guess that would have been a bit harder to get away with though. Still, thinking back it may have been a little reckless, but hey, so is driving with impaired vision. Growing impatient, he repeated his question, "One on the left or the one on the right?"

"Left. so I looked into Ms. Tucker's employment history..."

“Left or right?” he continued, turning that large knob again.

“Left,” I guessed, “And it turned out she had a perfect record...”

“Left or right?”

“Right. At least she did before...”

“Left or right?” he was getting flustered already. Goodie!

“...before she came here. Left. Everyone else gave her high marks.”

“Left or right?”

“Right. I also learned that...”

“Left... or right.”

“...that you were a busy little bee in the hours before her body turned up. Left.”

He stopped turning the knob and wheeled backwards slightly in his rolling chair. I instinctively looked up at him and could tell that the exam was over, “Busy bee?” he asked.

“I figured that would get your attention. You left some messages on Ms. Tucker's voicemail earlier that day. Somewhere right around her approximate time of death.” Trump card... played.

“I told you, Detective, I asked her to come back.”

“ 'Asked' is one way to put it. 'Practically begged' would be another.”

“Begged? Come on,” he said, more like a petulant child than like a poker faced pro.

I smirked at him as I opened my notebook and read his own words back to him: “Marcie come on, come back, don't make me beg, but I will if I have to. Okay, please come back?”

“Okay, okay but...” he was on the ropes now.

“That doesn't sound like a call to a co-worker.”

"But that wasn't..."

"Sounds like more of a call to a lover if you ask me."

"Lover?" he barked desperately, "No that's not... see, you don't understand. It isn't what it sounds like..."

I referred back to my notes, "I meant what I said about killing myself from yesterday."

"Okay that's out of context," he said. Tell it to the judge.

"Hmm, let's see, threatening to kill yourself if she doesn't come back. Sounds like a lover to me." Those cop shows are right, this is fun.

"That's not what I meant."

"Not what you meant? It's what you said."

"If... if... if... if," he began, his stutters sounding like music to my ears, "If you listened to the messages I left before that you'd... you'd... you'd... you'd know I was saying that I'd killed the mean me from yesterday and uh... uh... uh... uh... replaced him with a nicer me today. I uh... I didn't mean that I was gonna, uh... kill the nicer me today if she didn't come back. If... if... if... if you listen to all the messages it's obvious!"

Okay, time to bring it down a bit. Call it the calm before the storm: "Dr. Taggart, I heard all the messages, and frankly, they don't paint the most flattering picture of you. Now I don't want to come off as rude or inappropriate in any way, but I think we both know it's in your best interest to come clean now."

"Come clean about what?" the good doctor shouted.

Time to go in for the kill: "Now I'm not saying you killed her on purpose..."

"I didn't kill her at all!"

"It might have been an accident..."

“It wasn't an accident!”

“It wasn't an accident? Dr. Taggart…”

“No! I mean, it wasn't my accident. It might have been someone else's accident, I don't know because I wasn't there! I… I'm telling you the truth!”

“Dr. Taggart, please, you're yelling again.”

“I'm yelling because you're making… spurious accusations!”

“I was hoping we could have a nice, polite conversation about this, but…”

“Polite conversation! You come in here and accuse me and…”

“Clearly you're not interested in being civilized, doctor, so…”

“Civilized? You're talking about being civilized?” It was a fair question, and in fairness he was right. I was not interested in a polite, civilized conversation — I was interested in a conversation, well, like this one. Thank you, Dr. Taggart.

And now it was time to go in for the second kill: “I approached you at your office because it's a sensitive situation involving uh… illicit sexual activity and…”

“Wait…” he said, a furious rage bubbling up, crushing all traces of his former nervousness.

I blazed on, needing to get it all out before he stopped me: “…and the last thing I want to do is get your wife involved but…”

“You son of a…”

“I will if you make me…”

“Goddammit!” he raged, and I swear the force of his voice made his diploma shake a little bit. He stared at me with hate and fear dancing just behind his eyes. He soon became aware of how fast he was breathing and tried to calm down, "Look, I'm innocent. I didn't do anything. So you can investigate all you want, but leave my wife out of it."

"Nothing would please me more, Dr. Taggart, but if you force my hand I..."

"Get out," he said forcefully.

"I'd prefer to finish my..."

"Get. The fuck. Out."

Whoa. The F-word. To an officer of the law! I could tell I wouldn't need to push him much further, but the rest of the pushing needed to happen with witnesses, one witness in particular. I sheepishly put on my hat and said, "I see I've overstayed my welcome. Thank you for the exam." And with that I bid him adieu. For now.

Needless to say that was probably the most fun I've ever had on the job. Ever. I'm still kind of on a high about it now. I'm also excited to get home and reap the rewards of this morning's breakfast, I'm sure Sheila will be waiting, possibly fully nude, but she'll still be there in an hour. I have one more stop to make. Okay, the truth is that toying with Dr. Taggart was so exhilarating that I don't want the moment to end, so rather than let him stew overnight I think I'm going to go see the wife right now. I have the address here and it's kind of on the way home, so why not? Maybe I'll even close this up today. Look out world, I'm back! God, I really hope she's home. That would suck if she wasn't home. Please please please be home...

SUSAN

Human waste, I tell you. Nothing but human waste! Smelly, dirty, disgusting human waste! Good for nothing until they're dead and packed down nice and tight inside Mother Earth to aid in the growth of her clothing: the grass, plants, bushes, flowers, and trees. That's all they're good for, doctors. The arrogance of it all! Some accredited institution gives you a piece of paper and a funny-looking hat and all of a sudden you think you're God! Well, you're not God. You're just an imperfect, fallible, unreliable public servant! That's right, you're supposed to serve *my* needs! Driving around in your expensive midlife crisis, windows down, waving at all the ladies, snorting cocaine, playing golf all day, drunk during surgery, malpractice jackass! I bet that beard covers up a severe case of Rosacea, and you deserve it!

You think you're so much smarter than everyone else because you have letters behind your name and a diploma on your wall. My Graham had a diploma but he never hung it on the wall! And you know why? Because he was humble! He didn't need everybody else to know how smart he was or how rich he was or how special he was, he knew it and that was good enough for him! I guess you feel pretty good about yourself with all that power: the power to heal, the power to comfort, the power to prescribe, the power to diagnose. Well, just because you've done some good in your life doesn't give you the right to be an ass about it! I would think a mere thank you would be enough, but no! You've got to let it go to your head!

The world doesn't owe you anything just because you incurred all kinds of debt going to medical school and are certified to legally open up a body and dig around inside it. That doesn't mean you can just treat people any old way. We're still people! You don't even have the common decency to write legibly: "Oh I'm a big bad doctor, I can scribble any old bunch of curvy lines on a piece of paper, it's you peons' responsibility to figure out what it says." No! Not on my watch, it's not.

Dr. Mackler, what kind of a name is Mackler anyway? I bet your real name is something longer like Mackleberg or Macklerinski or Macklerov or Mackellini, but you cut it short because you're ashamed of your heritage! What kind of man is ashamed of his own heritage? What would your parents think, Dr. Mackler? If only they were alive to see this! "Oh, my boy, he makes me so proud, going to America, becoming a doctor, a real success story! Then he breaks my heart and chops our family name in half. My boy, what's wrong with your family? Is your family not good enough for America?"

Do you know that bastard "doctor" had the gall to giggle at me? He tried to hide it, but he couldn't hide it from me. I said that I may be experiencing symptoms of early onset Alzheimer's and he *giggled*! I went through each and every symptom: I told him about the syrah, I told him about the thing I may or may not have actually said, I even told him about the times tables! And he giggled! Sure, he turned around and took a second and when he turned back he had found his serious face, but I'm no fool, I know what was going on. He talked to me all calm and professional and said, "I wouldn't worry about that kind of thing, ma'am, those types of things are normal for a woman your age." A woman *my* age? Correct me if I'm wrong, "Doctor," but if I'm old enough to be "A woman my age," aren't I also old enough to have Alzheimer's too? Idiot.

Then at the end when I said that maybe we should just do a few tests to be on the safe side, he smiled all condescendingly and said, "Oh, I don't think you'd want that. I couldn't justify it to your insurance company and you'd probably have to pay out of pocket have a nice day." He said it so quick he was gone before I could respond! What does he know about my insurance company? And how does he know I wouldn't come out of pocket? I'm a widow! I have income! I thought I was supposed to be the one making the decision! Then the nurse ushered me out with another "Have a nice day" and before I could get my wits about me I was on my way home. Now if I want the test I have to make another appointment!

I wonder if he talked to Dr. Bruce… he had to have! I tell ya', the medical industrial complex is such a sham, all they care about is the almighty dollar. I bet those doctors have a secret deal where they trade patients back and forth so they can all make some fast cash before they tell you what disease you have. Damn that Dr. Bruce! But I'm smarter than he gives me credit for. You know what they say, fool me once shame on you, fool me twice shame on me. Well, I won't be fooled again, Dr. Bruce! No way! The next appointment I make, I'm making out of state. Try and reach me there!

I only hope I can get my Alzheimer's diagnosis before my

Alzheimer's sets in all the way, because I tell you what, I'm looking forward to walking into that Dr. Mackler's office and waving that positive diagnosis right in his face! That'll show him. Maybe he'll be so surprised that he'll drop dead of a heart attack right in front of me. Well, a gal can dream, can't she? I'm kidding of course. At least I'm trying to be kidding, I'd rather not wish death on anyone if I can help it... but if I can't help it I wish death on Dr. Bruce and Dr. Mackler! If they only knew how much stuff I forgot today alone, they'd change their tunes. But that's the problem with the medical profession these days, they don't listen. And why would they, they already know everything there is to know, at least in their own damn minds.

They're not gonna get the best of me, though, tomorrow I'll make myself an appointment far, far away, where nobody knows me and I don't know them either. I'll even make the appointment under an assumed name, yeah! I'll pay out of pocket and tell them I just moved in from some country that's not on friendly terms with the U.S.A. so I'll have no medical records for them to worry about, but I'm allergic to tetracycline, penicillin, and leather. I'll state my symptoms in a flat, emotionless manner and not suggest that I already know what the diagnosis is, and when he tells me I'll act like I'm shocked because that's the last thing I was expecting. Maybe I'll even start crying!

Then we'll discuss the next step and he'll give me a prescription and I'll hug him and thank him and tell him he's the best doctor I've ever had. I won't mention that that last part's not a very high hurdle to clear, I'll just let him feel that much more special. I hope I haven't wasted too much time arguing with these useless doctors already — I'd better get a move on!

Well, I probably can't call for an appointment until Monday anyway, so that gives me the whole weekend to do my research and find the perfect out-of-state physician.

In the meantime I have to go see my potential future caregivers tonight and surprise them with a belated housewarming gift. At least there's some fun to be had today. I wonder how much fun I have left. Oh! What a depressing thing to have to think about, how much fun you have left for the rest of your life! It's especially depressing when it seems like the answer is "not much." Well, I guess I'd better make the most of it then. Starting tonight.

TAG

I spent half the night staring at that card. I did tear it up, right? That wasn't a hallucination. Of course I tore it up, that's why it's been expertly repaired with Scotch tape and possibly a little glue. The question is why has it been repaired? And why was it in Lori's drawer? I know what I would be thinking right now if I were an impartial observer, but an impartial observer wouldn't have access to all the information that I have access to. Although an impartial observer also wouldn't be blinded to certain realities that I may be blinded to. Hmm.

Am I missing something here? Or rather, have I been missing something? Something that should have been as plain to see as the nose on my face, but I couldn't see it because my eyes are located directly above my nose and therefore at an inconvenient angle for the purpose of seeing it? No, that's ridiculous. I'm catastrophizing again. But it's the only reasonable explanation for why... no, it's the only explanation I can think of. Just because you can't think of a reasonable explanation for something doesn't mean one doesn't exist. The problem is, I can't think of any other explanation for why this card was pieced back together and in Lori's drawer. Not even an unreasonable one.

No, I'm sure there is one. I just have to think harder. After all, why would she have left the card in her drawer if she was going to… That's funny, not only can I not say it out loud, I can't even think it out… quiet. But it's true, why would she leave it in her drawer if she was going to… I mean she could have easily thrown it away. Unless that was her way of telling me without telling me, so I could know without either one of us ever breathing a word about it to each other. But we'd both know we knew, and we would communicate that we knew in tiny, furtive glances and half-smiles.

No.

There's got to be some other explanation that I'm missing. And I'd better think of it fast, before I embarrass myself again. I may have to find a new dry cleaner after this morning. I'd gotten up early both to pick up the dry cleaning and to avoid having to look Lori in the eyes, but the only thing that was really on my mind was that card. I couldn't take my eyes off of it. In fact I had to slam on my brakes outside the store just to avoid hitting some woman crossing the street. I really have to watch that.

As I walked in I noticed the dry cleaning guy glaring the moment he saw me. I smiled awkwardly and said, "Hi, I need to pick up an order for…"

"I know who you are," he interrupted.

"Excuse me?"

"I know who you are," he repeated. How did he know who I was? Was I on the news? Had that Detective already figured me out and I was the last one to know? "You said no special instructions." Uh…

"I uh… I did?"

"You're lucky I found it before I started."

"Found what?"

"Found this," he said as he held up a woman's garment.

I stared at the garment for a while, wondering if it was possible to hallucinate that something *wasn't* there, because I didn't see a thing. The dry cleaner had paused for effect, so I decided to bite: "What are we looking at?"

"Big red splotch," he said as he pointed to the garment, "right here." What? A big red splotch on Lori's outfit? The outfit she sent me to get cleaned the night after Marcie... No. No no no no no. I'm catastrophizing. There's got to be an explanation for that, I just haven't thought of it yet. I mean come on! Why would she send me to the dry cleaner's with something like that if she... Another way of telling me without telling me? No, she's more careful than that. Especially after the other night at Marcie's apartment... Right? She is more careful than that, isn't she? Yes, she's definitely more careful than that. I think.

As I silently freaked out, the dry cleaner continued his stern lecture: "A big red splotch requires special instructions. You said no special instructions."

"Oh, uh, I'm uh... I'm sorry."

"Don't apologize," he snapped, "next time give special instructions when special instructions are required."

"Absolutely, I'm sorry."

"Don't apologize."

"I'm sor... uh, okay. So you got the uh... special instructions out then?"

"Of course I got it out! It wasn't easy, but if it was you could have done it yourself." Fair point.

"Do you know what it was?" I asked hesitantly, unsure if I

actually wanted to hear the answer.

"Do I know what it was?"

"The big red splotch, do you know what it was made of?"

"Do I know what it was made of?"

Now I was at the point of no return. If I went there now, then it would be out in the universe that I have my suspicions about... that thing I can't bring myself to mention. It took a second but I finally blurted out, "Was it uh... was it... was it... was it... blood?"

"Was it blood?" he asked incredulously, "No, blood stains are easy. It wasn't blood."

"Oh good," I exhaled in relief. Then I felt bad for suspecting that... well, for suspecting anything. Of course it wasn't blood! That would be ridiculous! Tag, stop worrying, there's an explanation for everything! "So what was it?"

"It tasted like barbecue sauce."

"You tasted it?"

"Did I taste it, listen to this guy," he said, "of course I tasted it, how else would I know what it was and how to get it out?" Another fair point. Two for two.

"Oh, of course."

"It's not liked you gave me any special instructions to help me out now, did you?"

"Yeah, sorry about th..."

"Don't apologize. Next time give special instructions." With that I nodded sheepishly and left with my laundry. I felt bad for even allowing myself to go there, to think that Lori might have... you know. Of course when I got back in the car I saw the taped-up card again and remembered why I allowed myself to go there in the first place. And just like that I was back. Why else would that card be... no, stop it, put it away —

you have to get to work without staring at it or you're gonna cause a twelve car pile-up. I put it in the glove compartment and pulled into traffic, but all that did was get me to stare at the glove compartment.

I needed to find some way to feel better about this whole thing without coming straight out and asking her about it. I probably couldn't have brought myself to say it out loud to ask her anyway. Maybe I could play charades. No, I needed some other way to find out. I brought every one of my issues to Lori, the worst thing I could do was insult her with ridiculous questions about her character. Of course there were problems with not telling her too: for one thing, once I got home there was no way I was going to be able to hide my misgivings from her. I needed to figure this out today. If not I'd have to find some way to avoid going home until I did. Maybe I could get into a car accident.

That was a distinct possibility anyway if I didn't get my eyes off of the glove compartment. Come on, Tag, focus! Wait, you are focusing, you're just focusing on the wrong thing. Come on, Tag, stop focusing! Now, you know Lori better than you know anyone else in the world. You've known everything about her since grade school. You were the first one she told about getting her period in ninth grade — her mom didn't even find out until the next day. You were the only one who knew about her private alone time place in the alley behind the donut shop. There may be some things you don't know about her, but one thing's for sure: none of them are big. At least none of them are this big. Believe me, you'd know if she was capable of… of… well, believe me, you'd know.

By the time I got to work I was just happy to still be in one piece, there were so many things on my mind that I completely forgot about the new temp that was starting today.

"Hi!" said the Marcie look-alike at the front desk.

"My God, they must hire you in bulk," I'm pretty sure I said out loud.

"Huh?" Marcie Two asked.

"Huh? Oh, nothing. So you must be the new…"

"Yes! It is such a shame about Marcie, terrible. Terrible! When I heard I cried for like, three days. I know, it hasn't been three days but it feels like it, don't ya' think? O.M.G. And you worked with her, like up close and stuff, on the day that it all like, happened and stuff. You must've taken it pretty hard."

"Yeah?" I replied, trying hard to look her in the eyes. Man, they really don't make sweaters like they used to.

"Aw, poor baby, you look like you need a hug!" I did not need a hug. In fact, a hug was the last thing in the world that I needed. Still, a hug is what I got. I also got a really up close whiff of that perfume — she smelled delicious. Remember Tag, stop focusing. "I'm Becky by the way," she said mid-hug, her face buried in my neck.

"I'm Dr. Taggart, but you can call me…"

"Tag! I know, I do my research," she chirped, "So anyway, Tag, we are gonna have so much fun today!" I could feel my jaw literally drop. I wanted to tear that sweater off right then and there. It's funny how suspecting that your wife perhaps possibly maybe might be a… be a… be a… it's funny how suspecting that of your wife does nothing to stop you from being drawn to the siren-songs of young, naive assistants that smell like desire and almost definitely taste like… stop it, Tag, stop it!

"There's just one thing I need you to know before we get started," she said, "I am a lesbian, so if you have any problems with my lifestyle, which by the way I did not choose, you need to speak now or forever hold your peace, okay?" Yes! Hell yes! That was exciting news. I'd still want to bang her non-stop, but the knowledge that she's not interested in my type of plumbing should probably be enough to hold me off for a while. Thank Heaven for little miracles!

"That is great," I told her, "that's just… Oh thank God."

"Well, that is so refreshing to hear," she said happily, "I knew you were a sweetie, Marcie told me so the other day, God rest her soul." Her voice trailed off as she looked up in silence for a few seconds, and then she got right down to business: "So no appointments before lunch but you do have a walk-in waiting in 1, if you need anything else you know where I'll be!"

"Thanks."

"Welks!" I stared at her for one last moment before proceeding to begin my day. Sometimes I wish that all women were lesbians. It would make things so much easier for me. I struggled through the morning and decided to take an early lunch, and when I emerged from the back hall Becky hadn't seemed to have lost any of her perkiness: "Goin' to lunch?"

"Yeah, you want any…"

"No no no no! Don't worry about me, I'm a brown bagger. You know what they say, 'All work and no play makes Becky a great employee!'" Wow, she's actually pretty great. I wonder if Marcie was that good too and I was just too blinded by wanting her naked on top of my desk to notice it. If Dan ever quits, or if his strain of mono turns out to be terminal, I think Becky would make a great replacement.

"See you in an hour," I said.

"Okay! But don't be late, you have a 12:55 today!"

"Got it."

At the food court I was on the lookout for anybody trying to exchange flirty glances. I scowled menacingly as I looked around lest someone mistake my return glance as a flirt as well. The coast seemed pretty clear, but just in case I put my head down and chewed with my mouth open for the rest of my sandwich. I got back to the office at around 12:45 and was actually able to greet Becky cheerfully: "I'm back!"

"Great, your 12:55 is waiting in 1."

"Hm, got here early."

"Yeah, I showed him in, I hope you don't mind."

"No, that's fine, I'll just let him sweat it out for a few minutes. That'll teach him to be early!" Oh my gosh, I was even joking around. Becky even laughed. And it seemed genuine. My spirits were picking up! On my way to the back hall, I caught myself whistling! I figured something deep down inside was telling me that everything was going to be okay. I skipped into Exam Room 1 and… Goddammit!

Detective Steiner was my 12:55, what a spectacular way to ruin the day. All of my previous good feelings vanished in an instant. I could feel my sweat glands jumping to attention as if a fire alarm had gone off inside of my body. Don't panic, Tag, don't panic. Focus, focus, focus, just remember what Lori said: You didn't do it. You have nothing to worry about because you didn't do it. You don't even have to lie… that much. Don't act like you're guilty because you're not. You're really, really not. You didn't do it. Some other person did it. So you'd be doing all of society a service by acting cool so the Detective moves on to find the real, actual killer. Unless the real, actual killer is… no, it's not. It can't be. Okay relax, Tag, relax! Everything is still okay. Just breathe. Breathe. Breathe!

My head was pounding, I struggled to keep it together as the Detective grilled me. Then to make it worse, he had me give him an eye exam while he spoke so I had to concentrate on that too. He was trying to break me and I was holding on for dear life. Then he brought up Lori. Fuck, he knows. Wait, what does he know? There's nothing to know. But what if... no, he doesn't know, because there's nothing to know! Right? Right? Either way when he threatened to go see Lori I lost it and made myself look like a man with something to hide, and once I started I couldn't stop. I was digging the hole deeper and deeper until finally I just tapped out and begged him to leave. He did, but he did it with the biggest shit-eating grin I've ever seen on his face. Goddammit.

After he was gone I quietly freaked out for a few seconds before running to the mens' room and splashing water on my face until I calmed down. And by calmed down I mean go from Defcon 1 major freak out down to Defcon 3 minor-major freak out. Okay think, Tag, think, you haven't lost control of this yet, but these next few hours are critical. What to do first? I know, call Lori and warn her that Steiner might be coming by.

I shouldn't worry about that, though, Lori can keep it together better than I can. But can she keep it together under intense scrutiny from a professional? I don't know, I don't think she's ever been questioned by the police before. Either way I'd better warn her.

I called the house and got no answer, so I tried Lori's cell and got her voice mail: "Lori, it's Tag, don't panic but a Detective may be coming to see you today, it's alright just don't panic. I'm panicking enough for the both of us." Okay, what should I do now? Oh shit, what if he figures it out? Or at least figures it out enough to pin it on us. What if he's one of those dirty cops from the TV shows who isn't above planting a little evidence to ensure a conviction for someone he thinks he knows is guilty anyway? I'm pretty sure he thinks he knows I'm guilty right now. We're gonna have to skip town! I'm not ready to skip town! I have to pack! Oh my God Lori has to pack! That could take hours! I have to get out of here!

"Takin' a half day?" Becky chirped at me as I hurried past her. Somehow her perkiness wasn't quite as amusing anymore.

"Yep!" I called out as I blazed by, not giving her a chance to ask for an explanation. As I raced home in a panic, I was actually kind of proud of myself for only having to stop short to avoid the car in front of me once. Thank Heaven for yet another little miracle. Now I only need about twelve more to get myself out of this mess in one piece. Well, there's one more: Lori's home. I'm starting to get used to peeling into the driveway and frantically running into the house. Maybe one day I'll try it when I'm not in breathless mortal terror.

"Lori! Lori! Come on Lori we gotta' go!" I said as I busted through the front door.

And then, a familiar yet very unwelcome voice chimed in from the living room: "She's in the kitchen fixing me an ice cold beverage. I told her no thank you, but she insisted."

"Hello Detective." Shit.

STEINER

I really like this place. I didn't know what to expect when I pulled into the neighborhood, but this place has exceeded my expectations. I mean, he's a doctor so you'd think he probably has a nice house, but then again he's a doctor who works in a mall. But this is nice, I'm impressed. It's certainly out of my price range. Of course we had a honeymoon baby, so we never had the chance to save up for a place like this. If the Taggarts ever decide to start a family — well, if they do conjugal visits wherever he's going, that is — I think they might find the money situation tightening up real quick. Isn't that ironic? As soon as you start building a family and needing the extra space, that's when you stop being able to afford it. All those childless couples living in giant mansions must be infuriating to that family of seven crammed up in a three bedroom apartment.

That Lori, though, she is impressive. Pretty, polite, easy-going, welcoming, everything her husband isn't. Talks a little too much, but I'm not one to nitpick — overall, she's a hell of a woman. I wonder what she sees in him. Well, whatever she sees in him, she won't be seeing it for long. She's sweet as can be, but she can't hide that dark streak lurking right underneath the surface. She might be able to hide it from the good doctor, but she can't hide it from me — and I'm gonna use that dark streak to my full advantage in a few minutes. She'll turn on him like a hungry lion when she finds out what he's been up to, and I'm gonna sit back and enjoy the show. I should have asked for popcorn.

Oh, speak of the devil, here he is now. What's the deal, doc, it's only quarter after two, did you take a half day or something? Not feeling well? Guilty conscience?

“Lori! Lori! Come on Lori, we gotta go!”

“She's in the kitchen fixing me an ice cold beverage. I told her no thank you, but she insisted.”

“Hello Detective.” Funny, you don't seem happy to see me, Doc.

“Hello… Tag.”

“Don't call me that.”

“Well, what would you like me to call you?”

“Nothing! I'd like you to get out. I told you to leave my wife out of this.”

“And I implored you not to force my hand. But now here we are, so we might as well make the best of it.”

“You…”

“Well, hello again Mrs. Taggart,” I say as she comes back into the room.

“Here you go,” she says as she hands me my ice cold beverage, “and please, call me Lori.”

“Thank you so much, Lori.”

“Honey, what's the Detective doing here?” Tag interjects, spoiling our fun.

“Tag, you never told me Wayne was so funny!”

"Wayne?"

"That's me. Most detectives also have first names."

Tag immediately goes into damage control mode: "Well whatever Wayne said to you, it's..."

"Oh, don't worry," Lori interrupts, "it's all been good. So far." Then Lori and I share a good laugh. Tag is being such a stick in the mud.

"Yeah," I say, "I was just getting to the part about the voicemails you left on Ms. Tucker's phone. But before I go on, is there anything you'd like to talk about privately, Tag?" I can see the fire in his eyes, he'd like to reach out and strangle me right now. He knows I've got him and there's nothing he can do it about it. This is so much fun!

After a moment Lori breaks the tension, "Nope, you don't even have to say it, I know guy talk when I hear it, I'm gonna go..."

"No!" Come on, Tag, let her go, "No secrets between us, I don't mind if she stays."

"It's alright," Lori replies, "I have a feeling I'm not gonna want to hear what this is about anyway. Especially if what's on those voicemails is of a... sexual nature." Wow. This woman is amazing. Maybe I underestimated her. Maybe she's one of those cool wives who doesn't mind her husband messing around as long as she doesn't have to hear about it. I've heard about them before, I've just never seen one up close.

"What? That's ridiculous!" Tag says, "Come on honey, stick around, it's the twenty-first century, we don't send the women away like they did in the old days." What? What's with this guy?

Maybe I should insist: "Ya' know Tag, maybe it would be in your best interest to talk to me alone for a minute."

"Wayne's right, Tag, this is between you two. And don't worry, I don't feel discriminated against." Thank you Lori. It's a shame, there are so many victims in a homicide, not the least of which being the loved ones of the accused. The spouse is usually the last one to realize that their ostensible soulmate is a cold-blooded killer, assuming that they're not the victim. Even in cases like this where it's plainly obvious, you can't blame them for being completely in the dark, it's amazing what people can manage to hide from the people closest to them. It's also amazing what people can fool themselves into not seeing.

Now with Lori in the next room, let's see if we can make this easy on the both of us: "Amazing woman you have there. Top notch in every category. I'd say you'd have to be completely insane to go running around on her."

"I didn't go running around on her."

"Listen Tag, I'm a reasonable guy, but you gotta help me out here. I got you firing the victim without cause, screaming, shouting, tears shed, harassing phone calls, all on the day of. It's not enough to bring you in… yet, but it's definitely enough to get the higher ups to let me dig a little deeper. And what do you think I'm gonna find when I dig a little deeper, Tag? What do you think I'm gonna find?"

"I didn't do it."

"I'm not saying you did, but I know you know more than you're telling me, so why don't you just tell me the rest? Either that or I'm gonna have to go and figure it out for myself. But at that point, I won't be able to help you anymore." Bravo, Detective, nice speech — you definitely got the good doctor's attention. Look at that face! He looks like his cat just died. No, he looks like his cat just killed his dog and then killed itself in some bizarre murder suicide situation. We're in the home stretch now! I just might get home in time for a little fun time with Sheila after all. Sure, she might be a little miffed, but I think I built up enough romantic capital this morning with that breakfast to talk her down. But first thing's first, now that Dr. Taggart is good and ready, it's time to go in for the k…

TAG

What the... Who the... Why the... How the... Holy... Oh my... Jesus H... Son of a... Motherf...

I must have blacked out because all of a sudden I opened my eyes and there was Lori staring at me full of concern. At first I breathed a sigh of relief, thinking it was all a bad dream, but then I sat up and saw the corpse lying face down with a knife in his back on our brand new rug. I must have blacked out again because the next thing I knew I was opening my eyes to Lori's concerned look for the second time tonight.

"Honey, are you okay?" Am I okay? Am I okay? I just witnessed my lovely, angelic wife plunge a knife into a man's back with cold, remorseless efficiency. I am definitely not okay. I am the opposite of okay. I am unokay. In fact I am downright terrible. Of course none of that came out because my face was frozen in silent terror. Lori finally grew impatient and repeated herself: "Honey, are you okay?"

"You!"

"Now Tag, give me a chance to..."

"You!"

"Tag, calm down, relax..."

"It was you." I took the pieced-together business card out of my pocket and showed it to her. She looked at it stoically and shook her head.

"See? This is why I hoped you wouldn't have to find out, I was afraid you'd act like this."

"What the... what the... what the..."

"But the poem was really nice, I loved it. My favorite part was 'You bring me the truth when I need it the most, And that's even sweeter than your great French toast.' I laughed out loud at that part. In a good way."

"Honey..."

"I even wrote you a poem back, it's in your..."

"Honey!"

"I know, I know, I should have told you, but you see how you're acting? I just wanted to avoid this. You understand, right?"

"Understand?"

"I actually blame myself, I should have known you'd crumble under the pressure of law enforcement. But I'm sorry you had to find out like this."

"Like this?" I asked, my initial shock turning into anger, "Like how? By putting a dead man on our floor? Bleeding out on our brand new rug?"

"Oh no," Lori said gently, "not on the rug, I put the plastic back down when I saw him coming. You know, just in case." I looked down and sure enough there was that thin, clear sheet of plastic covering up the new rug just like it had been last week. I hadn't even noticed it until she pointed it out to me. Man, Lori never throws anything away. I guess the Detective didn't think anything of it either — maybe his wife is a neat freak too. Or maybe we men just don't notice anything.

"Wow, you thought of everything," I said in amazement.

"Tag, sit down, relax, let's talk about this, just like always."

"Are you some kind of psycho or something?"

"No, I'm not a psycho. Psychos do things for no reason."

"So you had a reason."

"Yes, a good one."

"And what was that?"

"You."

"Oh no, don't put this on me, don't you put this on..."

"I'm not putting it on you, Tag, believe me, I'm not. It was all me, but I did it for you!"

"Who are you?"

"It's still me, Tag. The same person you've known since we were kids. The same person you fell in love with. You asked for help and I wanted to give it to you..."

"I asked for help? Well, yes I did, but an extra quickie or two was closer to what I had in mind."

"That would have been a Band-Aid," Lori insisted, "it wouldn't have actually solved the problem."

"Well, for future reference, I'd prefer a Band-Aid over a stab wound."

She inched closer to me and for the first time I can remember, I instinctively inched backwards. She reached out and put a hand on my shoulder: "Tag, I saw that you were hurting, and it hurt me to see you that way. I wanted to make the hurt go away so bad I... I... Believe me, if there was any other way I would have... You have to understand. Please tell me you understand."

I sat down and tried to catch my breath. This was a lot. Sure, I appreciated the sentiment, and I had to admit that I was more than a little flattered that anyone would risk capital punishment for my sake, but still... two dead people? A romantic gesture, yes, but not the kind that I could totally get behind. But what could I do? I couldn't turn her in, she was still my wife. But how would I ever look at her the same? How could I ever hold her hand again without thinking that that hand had once buried a kitchen knife into the back of a relatively innocent man? I needed some time to think.

Unfortunately, time wasn't something we had a lot of at the moment, not if we wanted to get out of this mess intact. Lori carefully prodded: "Tag?"

"Huh?"

"You do understand why I did it, right?"

"Uh, yeah, right."

"Good," she said with a small amount of relief, "now come on, help me move this body." Shit.

We cleaned up the scene, packed the evidence into a duffle bag, and put it in the trunk of my car just as night was beginning to fall. We wrapped the body in the plastic sheet, then wrapped a few black trash bags around that. We waited for it to get totally dark outside before Lori pulled the car into the garage and shut the door. Man, she really seemed like she knew what she was doing, and I wasn't sure if that was a good thing or a bad thing. Probably a little bit of both. When she got back inside it was time to move the body.

Just a few short days ago I had never seen a real dead body, now I was touching one. And I'm sure this one was much heavier than Marcie. Struggling to maneuver around the corners of the living room, I was a jittery, sweaty mess. I looked at the limp, lifeless body of the detective and once again felt like I needed to say a few things. Hopefully wherever he was he could hear me:

> See, Detective? I really didn't do it. I guess you know that now. Sorry you had to go and get murdered to find out the truth. I really, honestly didn't see that coming. I could tell by the look in your eyes that you didn't either, and now I'm hoping you're the one who doesn't have any family to miss you. And sorry about covering up the crime too. I know that means you may never get the cosmic justice you need to fully rest in peace, and now you may be doomed to walk the Earth as a ghost for eternity, but what am I supposed to do? What would you do if it was your wife? You'd help cover it up, wouldn't you? You might not like it, but come on! You'd have to protect your soulmate, the love of your life, the apple of your eye, the mother of your current or future children. I know you get it. But I want you to know, if you *are* a ghost doomed to walk the Earth for eternity, I totally understand if you want to haunt me. I know I deserve it, and I'm prepared to accept the consequences. It's only fair. And once again — sorry.

After getting that off my chest, I turned my thoughts to Lori. The sad thing is that she'd handled this like she'd handled everything else: calmly and compassionately. She knew just what to say and how to say it, but somehow it wasn't the same. I guess that'll happen when you see a person forcefully snuff the life out of someone without hesitation. I think what bothered me most was how stoic she seemed about the whole thing. I know, it was the same attitude that allowed her to help me through a lot in the past few days, but that was back when I thought we were both innocent.

I mean, she said a lot of nice things after murdering that human being, but none of them conveyed any regret or sorrow or even inner conflict. She didn't even finish that, "If there was any other way…" comment. If there was any other way what? It wouldn't have been as fun? It would have been just a Band Aid? I was looking at Lori in a whole new light and it scared me that I may never see her in the old light again. She denied being a psychopath, but she had to at least be a sociopath, right? Can I be married to a sociopath 'til death do us part? Especially when making death happen doesn't seem to be that big of a deal to one of us.

After stuffing the body into the trunk, I sullenly crumpled into the passenger seat as Lori got behind the wheel to drive us to who knows where. In the car the hypnotic rhythm of the road beneath us put me into a trance-like state. I felt as if I was hovering over my body, only vaguely aware of what was going on around me. I was lost inside a giant, misshapen cloud of thoughts and fears, trying desperately to convince myself that everything was going to be okay, despite the fact that a very dead officer of the law was in the trunk and it was my sweet, sweet Lori who had made him that way.

From beneath this haze I could hear tiny, bite-sized snippets of what must have been a larger monologue Lori was reciting to me, trying to gently talk me off of the ledge: "I really wanted to tell you, but I just couldn't… I mean look at the way you're acting now… Just imagine what would have happened if I didn't… We're in this together…" But nothing was going to get me out of it, my brain had a lot to process and it wasn't exactly prepared for the extra workload.

My condition still hadn't changed as Lori pulled off the road and found a nice, quiet little open field hidden from the highway by a thick layer of trees. She shined the headlights on one particular patch of dirt and got out of the car. When she noticed that I still wasn't moving, she looked back at me: "Tag, are you coming? I might need a little help with the... Tag?" But still nothing.

With a loud sigh she went to the trunk and began to awkwardly drag the body through the dirt. After eventually getting the body to the edge of the field, she returned and pulled two shovels out of the trunk. I didn't even know we had two shovels. In fact, I'm pretty sure we don't.

"Tag? Ya' wanna come out? Help me dig? I have two shovels," she said, treading lightly, as if she was afraid she might break me if she said the wrong thing. I didn't budge, so my dainty little wife dug the hole, dropped the body in, and refilled it all by herself. She had taken the tarp off the body and stripped it bare before burying it, and now she was wrapping the detective's clothes and her gloves and other evidence in it. Then she set it all on fire. "Tag, come on out... please? We can make S'Mores!" She was probably joking. Then again that might be something a sociopath would do, so who knows?

After disposing of the ashes and putting the shovels back in the trunk, a very sweaty and dirty Lori got back in the driver's seat and we were off. It was as if we were never there. Once again, she seemed to have known exactly what to do. Oh my God, there's only one way someone knows exactly what to do in a situation like this: practice. Has she done this before? Is she, like, a serial killer? But I've known her all of our lives, I see her every day, when could she find the time? Wait a minute, how heavy a sleeper am I? Is she a night stalker? Holy shit, am I married to a night stalker?

I wanted to ask her all of these questions but I couldn't.

Maybe I was afraid to. Maybe I didn't want to hear the answers. Maybe I already knew the answers. I wondered how long my catatonia was going to last. Was it permanent? Part of me hoped that it was, then I wouldn't have to deal with any of this. I could live out my days in peace knowing that there's nothing I could do about it. Oh, to be catatonic forever! Wow, I never thought I'd hear myself say that, but it certainly sounded like the best option at the moment.

At some point on the drive back I once again became aware of my surroundings, and it turned out that Lori had resumed her one-sided conversation with me: “And don't worry, I'm not angry that you didn't help back there. I realize this is a lot for you to handle, and I want you to know that I'll be here for you as you try to get through it.” Well, that was a nice place to regain consciousness. Maybe I was a little hasty in questioning our entire lives together. Or maybe I'm just trying to fool myself for the sake of my sanity.

She still hasn't expressed any remorse, but that doesn't mean she doesn't feel any. Not everybody expresses remorse by wailing and pounding the earth with their fists. She's had to be the strong one these past few days and maybe she's just too concerned about my well-being to break down in front of me. If I look at it that way, her behavior is downright admirable. If only I could get past that whole murder thing. Well, it's not like I have a choice, I can't turn her in and I'm not going to leave, so I should probably try and make the best of it.

I looked over at her and managed to squeak out a little “Thank you.” As soon as I said it her face brightened up and I immediately knew that everything was going to be alright. Eventually. I'd still need some time, but at least I was finally able to see the light at the end of the tunnel. I felt optimistic that things could get back to normal, but I needed to make a few things clear before moving on.

When we got home I sat Lori down and launched into a speech of my own, one that I'd been preparing in my head during the last leg of the ride: "Lori, I get that you were trying to help, and I really do appreciate it. I mean, I knew it before, but now I'm even more sure that you'd do literally anything for me," she nodded enthusiastically at that, not exactly the reaction I was hoping for. I pressed on, "But you can't help me like that anymore."

She stood up and asked, "What do you mean?"

"Lori... uh... how should I put this? You can't just go around stabbing my problems away."

"Tag, you know that..."

"Please?"

"You know that I was only trying to..."

"I know. Please."

She thought it over for a second then shot me a wry grin, "Okay."

"You promise?"

"I promise. No more stabbing your problems away."

"Great," I said as I flopped down on the couch with a feeling approaching relief. Lori sat next to me and we shared a glorious moment of comfortable silence. We could have stayed like that all night, both because it was a wonderful moment and because we were too exhausted to move. But then the sound of the doorbell pierced through that moment like a mortar shell. Who could that be? We're not expecting anyone. Did the detective have a partner? Is the detective's partner looking for him? Are we completely busted?

Relax, Tag, try to stay calm. Lori cleaned up the scene and

she's cool as ice under pressure. Besides, if anything goes wrong she could just... wait, what am I saying? Did I just go there? Am I losing it already? It's been, like, ten minutes. The doorbell rang again. Please don't be Detective Steiner's partner, please! Despite the thoughts running through my head I managed to keep the veneer of a sane man as I matter-of-factly asked, "Hm, who could that be? You expecting anyone?"

"Nope," Lori said, seeing my calmness and raising me an air of apathy.

"Should we get it?" And I call.

"Mmmm... okay." She got up to answer the door. I couldn't believe how unworried she was acting. I mean, I was acting the same way, but let's be honest, I wasn't fooling anyone. I definitely wasn't fooling Lori because right before opening the door she turned to me and gently said, "It's okay, nothing's wrong, we're fine." Okay, that helped. A little.

Then she opened the door and in came Susan like a freight train, bottle of wine in hand: "Hi! No worries, just your friendly next door neighbor! I hope it's not too late."

"Well we wer..."

"Yes, I know, of course it's not, a young couple like yourselves? I bet you're up all night doing your business and such. Lori, look at you! Aren't you precious?" And dirty, she's also sweaty and dirty, Susan. Fun fact: my wife just single-handedly dragged and buried a dead person in a hole, isn't that interesting? Are you listening, Susan? Of course you're not because I'll never have a chance to say it. Do you even breathe when you're talking? "Oh my stars!" she continued, "This place is gorgeous! Ya' know we've been neighbors for almost a year now and I don't think I've ever seen the inside of your house. But now that I have, I must say, it is majestic!"

"Thank you Susan, Tag and I are very…"

"There he is! How's my little Taggie today?"

"Hi Su…"

"And could it be that you look even more scrumptious without your doctor's coat? Mm Mm Mm! Makes a girl wonder how you'd look without your doctor's pants! Ha! I'm kidding of course!" Then she looked right at me and loudly whispered, "But not really." Her obnoxious laughter filled the room, snuffing out all signs of peace and quiet as it went. "No, I'm kidding, I'm so naughty! Now let's see, where should I put this? Just a little housewarming gift, nothing major. I picked out a wonderful red Syrah, you may know it as Shiraz but the real vintners call it Syrah. This one's a Cave de Tain from the Rhone Valley in France, widely known as the birthplace of Syrah. This one's right up your alley, Tag. Its taste is powerful and full-bodied, like you I imagine. Oh! I'm so bad, I'm only kidding!"

"Of course," Lori said impatiently.

Susan plopped the wine onto the coffee table and made herself at home. Lori and I looked at each other incredulously — okay, I guess we're hosting tonight. I was speechless so Lori went ahead with the pleasantries: "That's very nice of you, Susan, thank you."

"So let's pop it open and have a toast, shall we?" She picked the bottle right back up and began pacing the floor, "Lori sweetheart, can you be a princess and break out the corkscrew? Oh I just love that word. It's got two of my favorite activities right inside of it — popping corks… and screwing! And we can do at least one of those things right now, ready Tag?" She laughed even more obnoxiously as I went white and Lori giggled politely. Susan seemed oblivious to the awkwardness, "I'm kidding of course. Lori, the corkscrew please."

Lori looked at me and I shook my head, she grasped for the words to tell her: "Um, well, actually, um… and we do appreciate the gift very much but… honestly I don't drink that much and Tag doesn't drink at all. So I don't think we even have a corkscrew. Honey?"

Don't look at me. "Uh, I'm pretty sure we don't." Oh good, words. At least I'm not catatonic again.

"Oh no," Susan began in astonishment, "No! Well, I wish someone had told me before…" Someone had told you before you crazy b… breathe, Tag, breathe.

Lori graciously filled the silence: "But we really do appreciate…"

"No matter," Susan interrupted, "I'm sure we can find something to do with it, use it in a recipe or to christen a boat or something!"

She put the wine back on the coffee table, and suddenly my need for her to leave usurped my inability to communicate: "Yes, thank you Susan, I'm sure we can find something to do with…"

"Absolutely, and next time I'll…"

"Susan," Lori politely interjected.

"…be sure to assume nothing when I…"

"Susan…"

"…pop in for a visit with…"

"Susan!" Lori's impatience echoed through the room, jarring not only for its bluntness but also because of how out of character it was. I'd seen her remain unfazed through much worse, but this one eccentric neighbor was able to get Lori to break. Susan snapped to shocked attention and stayed silent for at least ten seconds. Lori, to her credit, immediately reined herself in and politely said, "Thank you very much for the gift, really, but as you can probably see, it's been kind of a long day."

Lori and I watched, unsure if Susan was about to pass out or cry or throw something. Finally a switch must have clicked on and Susan was off again, "Oh of course! Silly me, overstaying my welcome."

"No, it's not that, it's just..."

"Well, I'm going to get out of your hair now, Lori you stay sweet, Tag... see you around," she looked at me, growling lustily, I looked away as quickly as I could.

"Thank you, Susan," Lori said, "it was very nice to see you."

"Anytime dear, anytime at all!" We said our goodbyes as Susan left and Lori shut the door behind her. She leaned against the door with a pensive look on her face, an uncomfortable silence building in the room. I'm not accustomed to our silences being uncomfortable, so I tried to figure out what was going on. I looked at Lori's face, deep into her eyes, into her soul. I thought about all that had just transpired: Susan barging in at the worst possible time, bringing the least apropos gift possible for the two of us, treating me like a piece of meat, then causing Lori to uncharacteristically lose her temper. The unnamed fear growing inside of me as I tried to decipher the look on her face suddenly swung into focus.

"No."

"What?" Lori asked innocently.

"No," I repeated.

"What?"

"She didn't mean it."

"Didn't mean what?"

"And I'm not uh... I'm not uh... attracted to her in any way. At all."

"I know that."

"No no no, I need to know you're with me on this. She is a harmless woman who I am not attracted to. In any way. At all."

Lori looked at me like I was crazy, "I know."

"She may be a little inappropriate at times, but she is not, repeat not, an issue for me."

"I know."

"But do you really know or are you just saying that?"

"I know."

"So I don't need any help in this area."

"I know."

"Nothing is wrong."

"I know."

"Will you quit saying I know, for Chrissake, Lori?"

"What do you want me to say? You asked me if I knew, and I'm telling you yes, I do." She began walking around the house straightening up this and that, but I wasn't done with her yet, "And remember, you promised."

"Tag, I know. How many times do I have to say it? I know, I know, I know, I know."

"I just want to make sure we're crystal clear."

"You're acting like you don't trust me."

"I trust you, I do, but sometimes I think you try to give me what you think I need rather than what you think I think I want. But in this case, that's not necessary because what I want and what I need are the exact same thing. Which is nothing."

"Okay, Tag."

"I need absolutely nothing."

"Okay."

"I need nothing because nothing is wrong with me. I'm not struggling with my desires or anything else for that matter. I'm 100% okay."

Lori stopped and put her hands on my shoulders and said, "Tag, I know. I'm not worried about Susan. All I care about is us. Now I made a promise and I intend to keep it. Okay?"

"No matter what?"

"No matter what," she smiled and ran her fingers through my hair. I sighed heavily and reluctantly nodded my approval. "Great," she continued, "now I'm gonna hop in the shower, but don't get too comfortable 'cause when I get out... sexy-time!" She disappeared upstairs and I slowly followed her into the bedroom. I sat on the edge of the bed and stared at the bathroom door.

She didn't have to worry about me getting too comfortable, I was as uncomfortable as I'd ever been. I saw no point in badgering her further, but her reassurances were leaving me with a rotten taste in my mouth. Come on, Tag, you've always trusted Lori implicitly, why are you having such a tough time with it now? Gee, I don't know, maybe because now I know that my wife is not afraid to literally get blood on her hands to defend her territory. Before I could claim ignorance, but now... I'm an accessory after the fact. Oh God, I'm an accessory after the fact! And worse, I'm gonna be an accessory before the fact for anything that happens after this. Shit.

But Tag, you know Susan is just kidding around, and Lori knows it too. Why are you worrying about the ramblings of a crazy widow? I know I know, but it was never about her, it was always about me not being able to control my impulses. But Tag, Lori knows you better than you know yourself, don't you think she's well aware that Susan isn't a real temptation for you? Maybe, but now that I know her secret, I'm afraid she thinks I'd tell her that either way.

I didn't like the feelings I was having as I laid back on the bed and tried to relax. They were feelings I knew I wasn't going to be able to shake. I mean, how is this going to end other than with a dead neighbor? Every day she's still alive brings along with it the lingering possibility that tomorrow might be the day. Until sooner or later when she eventually dies — she is a widow with her best years behind her after all — and I'm left to wonder exactly how accidental her heart attack or "stage four cancer" really was. It's not like she's going to stop making saucy comments to me, not unless I tell her to watch out or my wife might kill you — and I know I can't do that.

The worst part is that in reality Lori probably knows that Susan isn't a real problem for me, but how will I convince myself that she knows that? Every time I say, "Hi Susan, good morning," I'm gonna be paranoid that it looks like I'm flirting with her, and that in turn will make me act nervous which will make it look even more like I really am flirting with her. Shit. How can I make extra certain that Lori knows I don't want to… you know… with Susan?

I mean, it's not like she's unattractive, she's just past her prime. I'm sure in her heyday I would have found her very alluring. I'm sure some guys with certain proclivities would even call her a… Wait. What the hell am I doing? Am I doing what I think I'm doing? How is it even possible that I'm doing what I think I'm doing when all I'm trying to do is not do what I think I'm doing? And more importantly, how do I stop doing what I think I'm doing when the more I try to stop, the more I do what I think I'm doing? What am I doing?

I know what I'm doing. I'm panicking. The first thing I should do is stop panicking. But that's not a thing to do, that's a thing to stop doing. Hey, maybe that's why I'm getting all worked up. I've been putting way too much emphasis on what I should be doing when often the real question has been what should I *stop* doing. So the first thing I should stop doing is asking the wrong questions. The second thing I should stop doing is panicking. Good. What else? What else should I stop doing? Well, I should stop cowering at the enormity of all the different possibilities because it's causing me to start panicking. And I should stop doing that.

But how? I have to concentrate on the short term. What can I do right now? And what can I stop doing right now? Because that's all I have control over right now. I can't control what happens later until later becomes right now, and then I can handle that the same way I'm handling this. Right now. Wow, this just might work. So how can I handle this right now?

I suppose I could start by trying really hard not to say Susan's name during sex. I know, I would never have done that otherwise, but now with the power of suggestion I'm sure it'll be in my head. So I have to concentrate really hard on not saying her name while Lori and I are... Do you think that's why Lori wants to have sex tonight? She usually doesn't announce her intentions like that, we both like to keep it spontaneous. No, she isn't into tricking you, she wouldn't do that. But maybe she wants to give it to you really good because she feels like now she has some competition. No, that's not her style, she's totally secure. But maybe she... enough, Tag, I thought we were going to stop doing that. Stop doing what? Thinking? How can I stop thinking? Maybe I should just try to think about something else.

I wonder if accessory before the fact is a lot worse than accessory after the fact. Are they both felonies or… Shit, I should stop thinking about that too. Let's think about something safe, like puppies or flowers or… baseball. I hate baseball. Then think about football. Or soccer. Think about how in the rest of the world soccer is football and football is American football, but in America, American football is football and football is soccer. Okay, now what? Think about how rugby seems kind of like football plus soccer, or American football plus football. Just like how cricket is kind of like baseball plus golf, and badminton is kind of like tennis plus volleyball. No, that doesn't explain the shuttlecock. Think about how amazing the shuttlecock is. First of all, it's called a shuttlecock. Second, it looks like a ping pong ball wearing a skirt. Third… well I don't think I have a third but…

Thankfully Lori came out of the shower before I descended any deeper into the shuttlecock wormhole and my time to stew was over. For now. Now, don't say Susan, don't say Susan, don't say Susan… "Oh Lori." She gave me a funny look. That's when I remembered that I generally don't call out names during sex at all. Dammit I knew I'd screw that up, but it could have been worse. After everyone was good and satisfied we retired to our corners and turned out the lights.

"Hey," Lori said.

"Hey."

"Don't worry, everything's going to work out fine. I promise."

"I know."

"Good night."

"Good night." It's been a long, long, long day and I'm tired as I've ever been, but I don't expect sleep to come easily tonight. And for the first time in a long time, it's not just me that I'm worried about.

SATURDAY

SUSAN

I just don't understand it. Why don't people like to be neighborly anymore? Here we are on this ball of confusion for such a short time, and everybody's so busy they don't want to stop and smell the roses. Stop and smell the roses — I know that's just a saying and it's not to be taken literally — but sometimes it's good to take things literally. If I hadn't taken it literally after my Graham passed, I may have never discovered my green thumb!

Now I'm not saying that everyone should take up gardening, but they should stop long enough to find their own version of smelling the roses. And for God's sake, we're all neighbors, can we take a second to get to know each other? We spend so much of our time getting sick of our spouses and hating our bosses that we never have a chance to just sit down and chat with someone we still like.

I admit that I'm tragically unaware of the social norms regarding visiting hours and when it's time to make my exit, but it's only because I'm so fond of human connection. And what's so terrible about being fond of human connection anyway? It's literally the most important thing we have in life. On our dying beds we won't remember all the business deals we've done or the high score we got in some video game or the time we went to bed early on a Friday night, we'll remember our connections: husbands, wives, sons, daughters, sisters, brothers, cousins, aunts, uncles, grandkids, childhood friends, high school friends, college friends, work friends, in-laws, and neighbors! They may not be your closest friends, but they are your "closest" friends. They're literally right next door!

Now I don't want to sound like a harpy or anything, but since my Graham and I couldn't have kids, my list of connections isn't quite as large as some people's. I know that's not those heifers' faults, but you'd think people would want to make connections with the people who live around them too. I mean, who are you gonna call when you need a cup of sugar or your house is on fire? Not your cousin in Poughkeepsie, that's for sure. You're gonna call your neighbor, that's who!

Oh well, I guess all the heifers would just call each other. And I thought I could call Lori — and maybe I still can, I don't want to read too much into one encounter — I just didn't think Lori had that in her. I tell ya', ya' live next to somebody for almost a year and you think you know them, but I guess you never really, truly know anybody.

Except for my Graham. I knew everything about him — except for how to get him to quit it with that smoking. If I had a dime for every time over the years that I begged him to quit, well, I'd have a lot of dimes. I tried everything: threatening, pleading, bartering sexual favors, and nothing worked. It must have weighed heavily on my poor Graham, knowing how much he loved me and also knowing he was powerless in the face of his addiction.

Plus he had to deal with the fact that I didn't understand

addictions very well at all. I just figured it was as simple as making a decision that you're going to stop and sticking to it. It wasn't until after he was gone that I learned the truth. There's not many things I regret in my life, but I sure wish I had a do-over on that one. I would have treated my Graham a lot differently if I'd known exactly what he was up against, and I wouldn't have taken his addiction so personally. I wonder why I waited so long to find out about it.

After he was gone, I even tried to pick up smoking myself, I'm still not sure why. Maybe it was a way to hold onto him now that he was gone, maybe it was a way to speed up the process of joining him in Heaven, maybe it was that I wanted to feel that smoking feeling that he craved so much that he chose a shorter life over quitting. Oh! Shame on me for thinking of it like that, I know it wasn't that simple.

I just get so angry sometimes! Whatever the reason, try as I may I couldn't stick with it. I hear that it's an acquired taste, and I guess once you get to be my age, your penchant for acquiring new tastes is long gone. So I coughed and wheezed and suffered through each and every one until I couldn't take it anymore. It lasted about a week.

The point is unless you sleep in the same bed with someone, you can never be truly sure how well you know them. Actually I very rarely slept in the bed with my Graham due to his horrible snoring, but I did it enough to know who the man was through and through. Of course in my younger years I spent time in plenty of beds with plenty of men, none of whom I got to know at all... so I uh... what was I trying to say? Oh yes, Lori. I just didn't think she had that in her. But ya' know what? Maybe I should give her the benefit of the doubt. I saw her this morning and she was perfectly cordial, maybe last night was just a momentary lapse. Of course she didn't apologize to me when I saw her, so maybe she doesn't regret what happened. At least I don't think she apologized. Let's see...

I was out in the garden and she came out of the house and said good morning. Then I launched into a big "I'm so sorry about last night. If I had known about the wine I would have gotten something else and so on and so forth..."

Then she said, "It's okay Susan, it was a very nice gesture."

"I hope I wasn't intruding," I replied, "I have a tendency to not realize when I'm intruding. Oh, if I was intruding I'll feel just awful!"

Then she said, "You weren't intruding, it was nice of you to come by and..."

Then I jumped in and said, "Oh good, and I know you said you don't do a lot of drinking yourselves, Heaven knows it's a habit I wish I hadn't picked up so early... and often." I do love my little jokes. "But it's a good thing to have, you know, in case you ever have company over or... Well it's just a good thing to have. Just in case."

"Thank you Susan," she replied, "it was very thoughtful, but I have to go and blah blah blah..." Nope, no apology there! I don't think she was sorry. That heif... No, I can't do that, I can't write her off just yet, she's the only friendly face I have left in this neighborhood. I should give her the benefit of the doubt — even if she doesn't necessarily deserve it. But you'd think she'd at least throw in a, "Hey, sorry if I was short with you last night, it's been a crazy day, I chipped my nail right after a manicure and it just put me in the worst mood," or whatever her excuse is. Saying nothing, expressing no remorse whatsoever, well, it's a tough thing to get past. Ya' know what?

I don't think I'm gonna give her the benefit of the doubt. How hard is it to express a little regret that you gave an old widow a heart palpitation with your tone? It's just rude.

But what about my Alzheimer's? Is it worth removing my top candidates to take care of me when I'm incapable of taking care of myself over this? And what about Tag? It would be wrong to punish him for someone else's transgression. That settles it, I'm gonna go ahead and give her the benefit of the doubt. We all have bad days and I'd hate to have someone judge me by my worst day. Wait, what am I saying, I have several people who judge me by my worst days, that's why I call them heifers. That settles it even more, I don't want to be like the heifers so I won't judge Lori because of one unfortunate incident. If it happens again though…

I just hope poor Tag doesn't have to deal with that temper of hers on a regular basis, that would be such a crying shame. I hope she appreciates that man the way he deserves to be appreciated, he reminds me so much of my Graham — the strong, silent type. I bet he's a riot in the sack — and I mean that. But I don't think there's enough time for the two of them to get divorced before my Alzheimer's sets in, so I guess I'll never know. Oh, look at me going on saying terrible things, I don't want the two of them to get divorced, that's just terrible, I shouldn't say things like that.

It's just that it's hard not to dream of one last little fling before my mind goes and I don't remember… anything. Oh my gosh, I won't remember anything. I won't remember anything! Why am I holding so fast and true to my standards when soon I won't have the mental capacity to feel bad about violating them? It's like having a get out of guilt free card! For Heaven's sake, Susan, hasn't life thrown you enough rotten luck for you to deserve one final blaze of glory? Besides, Lori probably wouldn't even mind under the circumstances. Who would begrudge an ailing widow one last hurrah? Especially if soon she won't even remember it anyway. Oh! And I know just how I'll do it!

They say no good deed goes unpunished, but I don't believe that. I believe that no good deed goes unrewarded, and I did a good deed today. I know that Tag and Lori don't drink a lot (at least now I know), but I believe that there are several basic household items that should be in every home — regardless of how little they're used — just in case. These include but are not limited to a blender, a microwave, salt and pepper shakers, a coffee maker, a spatula, a whisk, oven mitts, assorted large cooking spoons, a can opener, a bottle opener, and last but certainly not least: a corkscrew!

You know what they say, a fine bottle of wine is absolutely worthless without a corkscrew to open it up. And if they don't say it, they darn well should. So this morning at the store I picked one up for the Taggarts. I didn't exactly have the luxury of checking on how many of the other items they had in their kitchen what with Lori's rudeness and all, and I figured it might be a tad bit inappropriate to get them any of the big ticket items so soon after the housewarming gift, but I did try to cover my bases by getting them a handy can opener/bottle opener/corkscrew combination.

I even mentioned that I was going to bring it over to Lori this morning. She said she was going into the office, and I didn't even know she had a job! It really is funny how much you don't know about people. Anyway, she should be gone for at least another couple of hours, so… oh my gosh! It's like the stars have aligned and the good Lord is rolling out a red carpet from my door to his. I'd be crazy *not* to take it!

But what about my new doctor? I haven't even started researching yet. Oh well, I'll have all of tonight and the whole day tomorrow to do that while I'm basking in the afterglow. It shouldn't take that long anyway, I have several states to choose from after all. That's a big pool of doctors, there's bound to be several that match my needs. It'll be like looking for a needle in a big pile of needles! Besides, right now this is what I need, so I'd better go get ready.

Oh Lord, what am I going to wear? Do I have time to do my hair? How's my makeup look? Are these earrings too old-fashioned? Am I dirty from the garden? Do I smell funny? Do I have time for a quick shower? Does my breath smell like wine? Am I overthinking things? Should I just go right over there? Okay, I'll go right over there. Right after I slip into something more... appropriate for the occasion. And a quick scrub down couldn't hurt. Now where did I put that corkscrew? Oh Lord, I'd better hurry. Hold on, Taggie-love, here I come!

TAG

These sheets still smell fresh. When's the last time these sheets have been changed? I feel like it's been a few weeks. I definitely remember sleeping on these sheets with the flower pattern on them for at least a week. Yet they still smell fresh. Hm. Do we have more than one set of sheets with this same kind of flower pattern? Even so, these sheets smell super fresh, like they came out of the laundry this morning. Did Lori wake up early and change the sheets on the bed? Wait, how could she have changed the sheets on the bed if I'm still in the bed? Am I going crazy?

I got to sleep in this morning, but now that I was awake I was afraid to get out of bed. I did get up once when I heard Lori leave, mostly just to make sure she didn't smack Susan in the face with a backhoe right there in the garden before she drove off. Susan was oblivious and ran over to greet her like she always does. I tried to strain my ears to hear what they were saying but I couldn't make any of it out. From the looks of it though, Lori was cordial enough, but I bet that's how she always acts right before a kill. My brain knew she wasn't going to do it right there in the front yard in broad daylight, but I watched the entire exchange with bated breath nevertheless.

After Lori drove off and I was satisfied that she was gone, I slumped back into bed and had no plans to move again until I absolutely had to. I tried to fill my head with all kinds of meaningless chatter to avoid thinking about what I knew I had to eventually think about — hence the deep thought about the bed sheets — but the main issue refused to be ignored for long. Last night I was trying to talk myself out of worrying about whether or not Lori was going to kill our neighbor, now all I could worry about was *when* is Lori going to kill our neighbor. I felt really guilty about it, but I just couldn't shake the feeling that I might not know the woman I love as well as I think I do.

I hadn't yet been able to work up the courage to ask her if she'd killed before. I just wasn't ready to hear the answer — even though I was dying to know. Why was ending a life such an easy thing for her to do? Did she like it? Did she crave the feeling she got when she did the deed? Was helping me just an excuse for her to quench her dark desire? Is she a bad person? Could a good person ever do what she did? Had she ever really been the woman I thought I knew? Did she ever really love me at all? I was beginning to wonder if there were aspects of her that I had misinterpreted. Aspects that my rose-colored view of her wouldn't allow me to see. I remembered things from the past that I'd shrugged off at the time but now I was seeing in a different light.

Like a few years back when we had our apartment on Fairfield, the apartment complex that we lived in threw a New Year's Eve party every year. One year Lori and I struck up a conversation with a new neighbor of ours who had just moved in a few weeks earlier. Despite the festive atmosphere, our new neighbor, I think his name was Frank, was in no mood to celebrate. He tried to put on a brave face for the occasion, but it was obvious that something was wrong when during routine small talk, I began to notice that Frank had started crying. I asked him what was wrong and, unable to keep it in any longer, he launched into this terribly sad story about how last New Year's Eve his wife had been killed by a drunk driver and when he got to the scene she was still alive and she told him one last thing and… I'm getting choked up just thinking about it now.

He was so emotional as he went through every little tragic detail that soon I noticed that without realizing it I'd put a supportive hand on his shoulder and had started to tear up too. After talking it out he felt a little better and he thanked us for listening and I distinctly remember giving this total stranger a big fat bear hug — which I initiated. The story had affected me deeply, as he was talking all I could think about was how I would have felt if that had been Lori in that accident one year ago tonight, and it made me extremely depressed. I turned to Lori and matter-of-factly said something to the effect of, "Wow, that was tough to listen to, you gotta feel for him though."

Lori nodded absently and said, "His hair kind of reminds me of your brother's." I was taken aback. What kind of reaction was that? Who cares about the man's hair, he just cried in front of us at a New Year's Eve Party! It bothered me at first but as the night wore on and we all started to get into the spirit I eventually dismissed it. I guess I must have figured that she wasn't paying much attention, maybe she was distracted by his hair's uncanny resemblance to my brother's.

That excuse was good enough for me at the time, but now

I'm not so sure. I mean, she could have missed a part of a conversation, but how could she have missed a full grown man sobbing right in front of her? No, I think she probably heard the story and… and I don't know what she must have thought. What do people like her think about stories like that? Do they think they're funny? Do they just think, "Hm, well that happened." What would the real Lori think?

I hated myself for allowing these thoughts about Lori into my head, but I was becoming more and more unable to fight them off. I remembered the story Lori's mom told in front of the entire bridal party at our Wedding Rehearsal Dinner. Her mother was one of those histrionic types, always turning every little thing into a national tragedy. She joked about it at parties, but while it was happening nobody thought it was funny. Really it was everybody on that side of the family: Lori's mom and her two sisters (Lori's aunts) would have competitions to see who could overreact the most to whatever situation may arise. I was always proud of Lori for being able to rise above that type of behavior — especially considering it's a trait that usually passes down from generation to generation. Genetics is not an easy thing to overcome.

So Lori's mom is going on about the day her mom (Lori's grandma) died. Apparently the woman just up and passed away one day while knitting a scarf in her antique wooden rocking chair. One minute she was rocking away, the next minute she was gone. She didn't even shut her eyes or anything, she just quietly decided to stop breathing. Lori's Aunt Janice was in the room at the time and it took a few minutes before she even realized that Grammy was dead, but when she realized it, oh did she realize it! She started wailing like a siren, screaming and pounding on the floor, calling out to

Heaven, "Why, God, why?" She called her two sisters up and they came right over to commence the screaming and the pounding as well.

The cousins and the nephews and nieces and the husbands eventually showed up and separated into two camps: the screamers and the pacers. The screamers joined in with the three sisters while the pacers walked back and forth wondering if there was any way they could get the screamers to stop screaming already. Then fourteen year old Lori gets off of school and shows up at Grammy's house. She had just learned that her beloved grandmother had passed away and she was witnessing her mother, aunts, cousins, and big sister sobbing uncontrollably, so I think anyone would understand if she lost it too. But that's not what happened.

Lori immediately took charge. She started barking orders at her older family members: "Tanya, call the ambulance and tell them not to rush… Dad, call the police in case they need to file a report… Christopher and David, lay Grammy on the couch before she slumps over and falls out of her chair… Mom, go grab an outfit we can change Grammy into before they take her… Aunt Janice, snap out of it and set an example, you're the matriarch of this family now…" Lori's mom beamed with pride as she told the story of her little girl acting all grown up and mature before her very eyes, being the strong one when no one else in the family could. I was proud too, she was always the strong one, for her family and then for me. But now I had a different theory.

Maybe Lori took charge because a dead Grammy was no big deal to her, maybe she told everyone what to do because she was sick of hearing them bitch and moan. Maybe that's why she took charge for me when I first found Marcie: not to protect me, but because she was sick of hearing me whine. These thoughts pierced at me like tiny little daggers, I tried to brush them away but the longer I lay in bed the more sense they made, until they eventually became the only possible answer that my mind could fathom. It was the worst morning of my life... and it was about to get even worse.

The first time the doorbell rang it didn't register, I only heard it as a memory. I wasn't even fully aware of it until I heard the second ring moments later. Only then did I stir and pull the bedsheets away from my face. By the third ring I had one foot on the floor and by the fourth I had my pants on. It wasn't until the fifth ring that it dawned on me that this might not be a delivery man or a Jehovah's Witness. They don't ever ring five times, do they? On the sixth ring I was sure it wasn't either of them and I feared it might be who I thought it might be. I pressed my face against the bedroom window to try and get a glimpse of the ringer, but all I could see was a shadow. At the seventh ring I was pretty sure I knew who it was, and as rings eight, nine, and ten came in rapid succession I no longer had any doubt.

I thought about waiting it out in the bedroom, pretending I wasn't home, but a.) she knew damn well I was home, and b.) I wasn't going to be a prisoner in my own home. If I waited it out I'd have to see my ruse through and stay inside the whole day or else be discovered by her omnipresent eye. Forget about going outside, I'd have to stay clear of all the windows too. I'd probably have to wait until she had some errands to run before I could make a run for it, leave, and come back as if I had been gone the whole time. I'd also have to walk to wherever I ended up going to justify the fact that my car is in the driveway. No, too complicated, I'd just have to open the door.

Just see what she wants, be courteous, and get her out of here as fast as possible. I know Lori won't be home for a few hours, but the longer she's here, the harder it will be for me to keep it a secret. Best case scenario, she doesn't set foot in the house at all and I can claim she didn't come over and still be technically correct. That little white lie should only nag at me for a day or two, I can handle that.

By the time I got to the door we were easily twenty rings in, and I could hear her thinking out loud — very loud — about why it was taking so long. I took a deep breath and opened the door. There she was all dressed to the nines and hiding something behind her back. I smiled as warmly as I could and said, "Hi Susan."

"Morning, Tag! Hope I didn't wake you."

"Well as a matter of fact I..."

"I noticed last night that you didn't own a corkscrew," she began as she barged right in and made herself at home. So much for keeping her outside, "And I just can't allow such an egregious homeowner faux pas. No no no, not on my watch! So I went ahead and got you one myself." With that she presented the corkscrew as if it were the Holy Grail.

"Oh, that's very nice of y..."

"Now it's not a housewarming gift per se, let's call it uh... an addendum to the original gift."

"Uh... okay."

"Trust me hon, every American home should have one. I mean, can you imagine being without one in a time of great need?"

Uh... no I guess n..."

"When a cherished guest stops in for a visit with a very expensive Chablis and you can't open it? Well, that sounds like a special kind of hell to me."

"Well I don't know about..."

"I can't even bear to imagine taking a fancy bottle over to someone's house and not being able to open it."

"Didn't that happen last night?"

"At least if you were... what was that, dear?"

"Didn't that happen last night?"

"Didn't what happen last night?"

"Didn't you show up here with a fancy bottle that we weren't able to open?"

"Uh... Well... yes, that's the point. If you would have had this last night, you would have been spared all that embarrassment. So you're welcome!"

"Okay," I said, trying to move things along, "Thank you, Susan, for the uh... for the corkscrew, it's a really nice uh... corkscrew, but now I really have to get back to..."

"Now I don't want to inconvenience you too much," she said, completely ignoring my attempt to get rid of her, "so I'm just gonna put this away mysel..." She stopped in her tracks and looked around in a panic. "Where's your bar?"

"Bar?"

She looked at me in utter horror, "Tag! Don't tell me you don't have a bar." Well, I didn't. "Oh!" she shouted, "What... am... I... gonna do... with you? You absolutely... have... to have... a bar."

This was a rule that I was not aware of. "I do?"

Susan sighed and shook her head, "No matter, that'll have to be for another time and another... well I guess just another time. I'll put this in the kitchen for now."

The plan to get her out of the house had backfired. In fact, now she was moving in the opposite direction. I had to put a stop to it ASAP: “Thank you, Susan, but you've done enough, why don't I take it in the…”

“No no no, hard working man on his day off, you stay put. I'll make my…,” she stopped and looked over at the end table, “well, serendipity indeed.” Oh no, she sees the syrah. Why didn't I move it? Why didn't I move the goddamn syrah? She held up the corkscrew with the phallic end sticking straight up and seductively growled, “There are some things that we as human beings just aren't meant to resist.” Oh… Shit.

She grabbed the wine bottle and sat on the couch, “And there are some appliances that have just got to serve their purpose.” Wait, is she looking at my crotch? She stuck the wine bottle between her legs, straight up *licked* the full length of the corkscrew, and then plunged the corkscrew deep into the top of the bottle. I had to hand it to her, that was pretty sexy. Wait, no! Focus, Tag… on something other than the bottle. Don't focus, Tag!

Once it was open, she took a hefty swig from the bottle, blew me a kiss, and said, “Mmm, I find the taste of rotting grapes so… exhilarating. With a hint of plum and cherry and… hmm, apricot. I love how every time I take a sip I find something new to take into my body. You?”

I had had about enough, the time for civility was long gone. I made a bee-line for the door and said, “Ya know it's been a long… I don't feel so… I really have a full schedule… errands to run… uh…” Apparently the time for tripping over words was not long gone.

“Oh relax, Tag,” she said as she made herself a little more comfortable.

“I just think maybe it's time to… Mrs. Connelly I think you should…”

"Mrs. Connelly!" she said indignantly, "Mrs. Connelly is my mother... in law. Mrs. Connelly is the late mother of my late dead husband Graham. Please, call me Sue."

At this point I was standing halfway out on the porch with the door wide open as Susan continued to not move one inch off of my couch in any direction: "I'm really going to have to insist that you..."

"I hope you don't mind," she interrupted after taking another giant gulp straight from the bottle, "I've always found glasses so formal. Care for a taste?" Gulp. I had to hand it to her again, for an aging widow Susan still had some of the old moves d... Tag, stop it!

I was getting desperate: "Susan, please don't make me call the police."

"The police? I didn't know it was a crime to share a bottle. It's not like I have cooties or anything." She held out the bottle again, "Come on, Tag, what's a little saliva between friends?" The sweat was pouring down my face. I found myself noticing all kinds of things on Susan that I'd never noticed before, like boobs and butts and ankle tattoos.

"I can't," I murmured as she held the bottle out farther.

"You can't, why not? I know you're young but you're not that young."

"No, that's not it, I..."

"What's the problem, baby? It's just wine, it won't bite."

"I can't, it's... childhood trauma. Just looking at it makes me feel sick."

"Childhood trauma? Taggie-love, that's ridiculous."

"It's true!" I said, much louder than I'd intended.

Susan looked at me incredulously for a moment before shrugging and putting down the bottle, "Fine, more for me. It actually works out better this way, I do enjoy another glass... post-coitus as well."

"Run away! Run away!" I yelled. Out loud. It didn't work though, I wasn't running away.

"Come on, Tag, what are you so afraid of?"

"Run away!"

"I'm a woman, you're a man. The math is simple. I should know, I was a Math major for six months."

"Run away!"

"Taggie-love, haven't you ever been curious to know what it feels like to be with a truly experienced woman?"

"Run away!"

"A woman who's had the time to try out lots of crazy things. A woman who knows which crazy things are best suited to drive other people crazy."

"Run away!"

"Have you ever touched a woman knowing that there are literally no boundaries? That anything and everything is on the table?"

"Run away!"

"I can't help but notice that you're not running away, Taggie-Love, so why don't you stop fighting it and come and getcha some?" With that she stood up, took one more big swig from the bottle, slammed it on the table and tore off her gown to reveal some very... elaborate... lingerie... underneath. Oh. Shit. I knew I was powerless to stop myself, my blood was pumping at triple speed, all thoughts of right and wrong and good and bad and should and shouldn't vanished from my head in an instant. I swung the door shut and ran to her.

I kissed her passionately as she wrapped her welcoming arms around me, pulling me with her as she tipped herself back onto the couch into a reclining position. She wrapped her legs around me as we kissed and pawed at each other ferociously. My heart was pounding so fast I could hear it in my head, and my body was quivering in feverish anticipation. Then, just as my hand was reaching for my belt buckle in preparation for phase two, I felt her gently pushing me away. At first I ignored it, but then the pushing became more forceful. Finally, she heaved at me with all her might, causing our lips to disconnect just in time for the vomit to spew all over the couch and the floor. What the…

I recoiled in terror as she dropped to her knees, choking and retching all the way down. What the… She violently pitched forward and contorted wildly on the floor: "Help me… help…" she struggled to say as I stood there frozen. I wanted to help, but my extremities were incapable of even the slightest movement. I couldn't believe my eyes as she coughed and convulsed and died right there in front of me.

What. The. Fuck.

I don't know how long I stood there staring at her corpse in utter disbelief, but it had to have been more than ten minutes. There were no thoughts of the hows and the whys quite yet, in fact there were no thoughts in my head at all. I was beyond catatonic — my mind had completely shut down — Click — lights out. When I finally became aware of my surroundings again, it was as if I was awakening from a years-long coma.

It took a few moments to regain the feeling in my arms and legs, my hands and feet, my fingers and toes. I eased myself onto the couch, still stunned and confused. As I slowly became aware of the reality of the situation, I was surprised at how different it felt than I had envisioned it. A strange numbness enveloped me, shielding me from all fear and sadness and anxiety. I stared at her there on the floor in awe… and that was about it.

Once I became alert enough to try and process what had just happened, my brain immediately began to go through all of the possibilities *except* for the one I knew was true. Many are surprised to learn that not only is heart disease the number one killer of women, but it actually occurs more often in women than in men. So that was a possibility. Or it could have been a stroke, that seems to happen to a lot of older people.

The other day I read about a woman who had surgery on her ankle and three days later she was dead from a blood clot, so I guess there's an outside chance of that. Susan is… uh, was always talking about going to the doctor for this and that, maybe she had a procedure and got a blood clot. It's unlikely she had cancer, something tells me that would have come up during one of our many one-sided conversations — plus I don't think you drop dead from cancer. I hear that happens a lot slower.

Somewhere in the back of my mind, though, the truth about what had happened was lurking, waiting to pounce. I just wasn't ready to consider it yet. That all changed when I regained enough of my motor skills to start walking around. My first act of motion was to search for a phone. I knew my cell had to be out of battery because as usual I had forgotten to take it out of yesterday's pants and put it on the charger (at least yesterday I had a good excuse for it). So the cordless would have to do. Where's the cordless? It's not on the base. Of course it's not on the base. It's never on the base. I headed to the kitchen, and of course it wasn't on the base in there either. What about the counter? Nope. Kitchen table? Nope. The refrigerator? Don't laugh, it's been in there before. I started opening the cabinet drawers and stopped cold at the sight of one object that I hadn't expect to see.

I forgot about the phone immediately as I stared in disbelief at the shiny metal of a brand new corkscrew. Hm. I took the unexpected device with me back into the living room just to make extra sure that I wasn't going crazy, and sure enough there was Susan's corkscrew lying on the floor right where she'd knocked it during her death flail. That's funny, I didn't think we had a corkscrew. Didn't we tell Susan that we didn't have one last night? Yes, that's why she felt the need to bring one over this morning. I didn't think we were lying when we told her that. After all, why would we have a corkscrew? Lori rarely drinks and I never do. No, we definitely don't have a corkscrew. Except now we do. If we don't, how did this one get in our kitchen drawer?

I picked up the spilled wine bottle on the floor and took in the aroma. It did smell kind of funny, but for all I knew that's how wine was supposed to smell. That's when I saw it. I couldn't believe I'd missed it before now. At first I assumed it was still there from last night, but I distinctly remembered wrapping Detective Steiner in it before we put him in the trunk. It must have been there all morning, but I guess I just subconsciously assumed it was the same one, still there protecting the new rug.

I carefully avoided the thin, clear sheet as I sat down on the couch and tried to sort all this out in my head. Could it be? Could Lori have actually… Well, she knew I wasn't going to drink any of it, so…

Oh my God.

I don't know if "the truth hit me like a ton of bricks" is an actual expression or not, but if it is, it describes what happened to me next perfectly. Because suddenly it jumped out from the dark recesses in the back of my mind and everything became crystal clear: all of the things I'd been thinking for the past twelve hours had been completely, 100% wrong. Lori wasn't a cold-blooded killer with a secret life, she was the exact same woman I'd fallen in love with all those years ago. The same woman who I could come to with any issue, who would listen and understand, the only person in the world who really, truly cared about me beyond anything else. She cared about me enough to risk everything in order to save me from myself. Just like always.

Don't get me wrong, I'm still not comfortable with the whole idea of stabbing your problems away — and she was right not to come to me for prior consent because I never would have gone along with it — but it was hard not to be flattered by the lengths in which she was willing to go to help me. She knew from the get-go what Susan had in mind, and she saw my weaknesses more clearly than I'd been able to see them myself. Everything she had kept from me she'd kept from me not to deceive me, but to protect me. And to think that I had doubted her. Shame on me.

I sat there in silence, staring off into the distance, neither happy nor sad, neither tense nor relaxed, neither awake nor asleep, just sitting. Comfortable in my own skin for the first time in a long time. Eventually the memory that there was a real dead body in the room brought me back, but it was a really pleasant trip. If you had asked me a week ago if I could ever be in a room with a real dead body and forget it was there, I would have told you not a chance. I guess it's true that you can get used to literally anything given enough time. For me and real dead bodies, it was about three days.

I looked at Susan and thought to myself that that was probably the first time I'd ever seen her completely still. I hardly recognized her with her mouth not moving. And even though I was getting more comfortable with the dead, I still felt it was only fair to give her a little send-off:

> Hi Susan, don't worry, I'm not here to gloat or tell you that that's what you get. It's true you're less innocent than the first two, but you still didn't deserve this. I sincerely hope you can take some solace in the fact that this whole ordeal wasn't for nought though. You indirectly helped bring two soulmates to an even deeper understanding of each other right at the moment they needed it most. And for that I'll be forever grateful. I know the loss of uh… what was his name again? Your Graham? Yes. I know the loss of your Graham was very tough to deal with, and I hope that if any good can come out of this for you, it's that now you're reunited with him in a much happier place. Sorry about all this, Susan, and I hope you know it was nothing personal. I'll make sure to keep up with the garden until it finds a new owner. It's the least I can do.

I sat there at peace with the world for another few hours — another thing I never thought I could do — until Lori finally got home. When she came in, she saw me sitting quietly in the middle of a crime scene — the wine bottle in front of me, one corkscrew on the floor and one in my hand, and Susan on the floor in a puddle of her own yuck. Lori surveyed her surroundings looking completely unsurprised. She looked at me timidly and said, “I kept my promise. I didn't stab anybody.”

I beamed at her proudly, “How did you know?”

“I didn't,” she replied as she dumped the contents of the bottle into the bathroom sink and dropped it into the trash can, “but it was worth a shot.”

That was good enough for me. I ran over to her and kissed her like they do at the end of old movies as the lights go up and the credits roll. It was as close to a Hollywood ending as we were gonna get. We savored the moment for as long as we could before turning our attention to the small issue of the body getting cold on our floor. Without the advantage of a knife in the back to guide her fall, Susan's crime scene wasn't quite as neat as Detective Steiner's was. In fact she'd missed the mark by several feet and, while the rug was still stain-free, the same couldn't be said for the couch and several other parts of the living room. But this time, I'm proud to say, I didn't go catatonic on her and we cleaned up the scene together. After that we wrapped up the body, bagged the evidence, and loaded up the trunk of the car like a well-oiled machine — teamwork every step of the way.

I even drove this time! Wow, so much had changed in twenty-four short hours. On the ride out to Susan's unmarked shallow grave, I couldn't stop glancing over at Lori lovingly. She'd look back and we'd share a few wonderful moments lost in each other's eyes before she said, “Okay, eyes on the road now, honey.” I couldn't help it, I was riding high, excited about what life might have in store for us next. I felt pretty sure that we could find a way to move forward without any more murders too. I don't know, maybe I could get a therapist or something. But there was plenty of time to talk about that, right now it was time to enjoy the moment.

I mean look at her, sitting here next to me in good times and bad, in sickness and in health, for richer for poorer — I've heard a lot of people recite those vows, but I don't think anyone has ever meant them more than Lori. Really, not since the beginning of time. I'm just glad I get to help her out this time. I feel pretty bad about staying in the car while she did all the work last night, but now I get to redeem myself. I guess you could call that a silver l…

Whoa, that was close. I almost hit that car. I know I keep saying this, but I *really* have to watch where I'm EAkufh;clkmz;…

"Are you okay, honey?"

"Yeah, you?"

"What happened?"

"I think we just got rear-ended."

"I know, but how could he not see my brake lights?"

"He probably could, you just stopped so short that he didn't have time to react."

"Yeah, sorry."

"It's okay, it could have been worse."

"Really? How?"

And with that we watch as the question is answered not by Lori, but by fate itself. Seemingly in slow motion, the trunk of the car pops open, revealing a big surprise to all the rubberneckers and law enforcement officers passing by.

HENDERSON

We were just about to take off when we got the call. It was Maclusky's turn but somehow he got "sick" again so we had to cover a crime scene on a Saturday night. Chambers bitched about Maclusky the whole drive out there. Okay, I admit it, I egged him on a little. I can't help it, it's hilarious to watch him get all wound up.

"Wasn't he sick last week?" I asked innocently.

"Sick in the head if you ask me."

"Last week in the pit he was talking about being burned out."

"That son of a... ya' know some days I get burned out too but ya' don't see me callin' in sick."

"Yeah."

"And ya' know why?"

"Why?"

"Because this is the job. Ya' don't just do it when your fragile sensibilities allow you to, ya' do it every day — because that's what's expected of you, because the public demands it, and because your colleagues demand it."

"Amen to that."

"Fuckin' Macluskey, I tell ya. Ya' know between him and that fuckin' Steiner we're gonna be workin' every goddamn call that comes down."

"Steiner?"

"Fuckin' Steiner!"

"What happened to Steiner?"

"You didn't hear? Walkin' around like Night of the Living Dead motherfucker. Yesterday, that sad sack practically skips in to work whistlin' Dixie, I barely recognized the motherfucker with a smile on his face, then today, he just doesn't show up at all."

"No shit."

"No warning, no call, just up and skips out on us. Like just 'cause he found a case of happy pills hidin' up his ass he can show up whenever he feels like it. Fuckin' Steiner, I tell ya'."

"Fuckin' Steiner," I said, trying hard not to burst into laughter. Fuckin' Chambers.

The scene was an auto accident where the car that got hit had a corpse in the trunk. The victim appeared to be a lot older than the suspects driving the car, and I barely had time to pull out my notepad before Chambers started in with the theories:

> I hope she wasn't one of their mothers, that would be a real shame. I might just have to lose my temper if that's the case. Especially if it's his mother, he looks like one of those Norman Bates types, acting all nervous on the outside but being totally fucked in the head underneath. His single mom raising him alone and being all controlling and inappropriate with him, then he marries this real pretty girl who's not afraid of her and she starts to feel like Bonnie's driving a wedge between

> them. A couple of super uncomfortable, passive-agressive holiday dinners later it becomes clear that Clyde's gotta choose one or the other. It's agonizing for him, but he ultimately realizes he's got a new mama now and this one gives blowjobs, so in the end it's no contest. Only the old mama won't give her golden boy up without a fight, so something's gotta give, and what gives ends up being old mama's heart. Anyway I hope that's not what happened.

Well, to absolutely no one's surprise, that's actually not what happened, although thanks to Chambers we almost never found out what happened. Once we got the suspects back to the station for questioning, this nutjob loses his mind and tries to physically assault the female! And all she did was tell him exactly what I've been wanting to tell him for years. What was the term she used? Chronic incompetence? Ha! Beautiful. I could have kissed her right there in her shackles, but I didn't because I have a thing called impulse control. Ever heard of it, Chambers? Didn't think so.

The shame of it all is that would have probably been enough for a good, long suspension or worse if it wasn't for the fact that Chambers is the single luckiest motherfucker on the face of the planet. This maniac, still fuming from his encounter with the female, decides to go in and take a run at the male! I tell ya', no exaggeration, 999 times out of a thousand that sequence of events ends with Chambers beating the snot out of the male and finding himself in front of the review board first thing Monday morning. But not this time, nope! This time he charges in there with a head full of steam and runs smack dab into a full confession! Gift-wrapped and placed at his feet! What?

By the time he gets through with his version of the story, he's being hoisted up on everybody's shoulders and paraded around the room. I half expected the Chief himself to walk in and give him a commendation. I mean, anybody with even the slightest bit of curiosity could have checked the tapes and seen what really happened, that the guy was ready to confess to literally the first person who walked into the room. I guess nobody around here cares about what really happened though, and why should they? That doesn't make as good of a story. I guess I can't really blame them either, it was a really good story. Man, fuckin' Chambers.

SUNDAY

TAG

I feel naked without my shoe laces. I've never worn flip flops or slip-ons or Crocs or Uggs or cowboy boots or Velcro or any type of shoe without shoe laces. It's not a thing I ever consciously decided, it just worked out that way. But now I know why, because every time I stand up it's like Chinese water torture. It may sound like a small thing, but I'm afraid if I don't get some laces in my shoes pronto I'm gonna freak out or faint or something. I suspect that many of the horror stories about jail are greatly exaggerated, but still, I wouldn't want to pass out in one.

I just don't understand why the first thing they do when you get to jail is take away your shoe laces. If they want to stop you from hanging yourself I guess that might be a reason, but there are literally dozens of other ways you could commit suicide in a jail cell. You could bang your head against the metal cell bars or the concrete walls, you could drown yourself in the toilet water, you could probably even do it with your shoe somehow. But they don't take your shoes, no, they make you take off your shoes, take out your shoe laces, then put your shoes back on without them. I guess the inventor of the prison system considered shoe laces the most dangerous article of clothing imaginable. Hell, I'm wearing a long sleeve shirt right now, I could probably hang myself with this if I was really committed to going out that way. It makes no sense.

So now I have to suffer through jail wearing shoes with no laces in them and it's driving me crazy! Every time I try to take a step I feel my heel pop out and really want to bang my head against the wall. Wouldn't that be ironic? A prisoner ending it all strictly because he has no shoe laces. I know the Constitution says something about cruel and unusual punishment, and for me this is it. Ya' know what? If this really was a free country, every single person would be able to pick a couple of punishments that would be considered cruel and unusual just for them. Then I could demand the immediate return of my shoe laces as an American citizen who is innocent until proven guilty and protected by the rights and freedoms granted me under the Constitution of the United States and whatever that amendment is that says that thing about cruel and unusual punishment. Hey, in jail every creature comfort counts.

My cellmate Dave told me the shoelace thing was also so people wouldn't strangle each other, but that makes even less sense to me. It would be easier to murder somebody by slamming their head into a wall than for somebody to kill themselves that way. If that were really an issue they should put us all in padded rooms. My other cellmate Pete told me people started tying socks to shoe laces and using it as a sort of rudimentary carrier service, tossing contraband from cell to cell, taking out one thing and replacing it with another, and then pulling it back in. I told Pete that sounded ridiculous. Then he tried to fight me.

It's a shame they had to take me out of that cell, Dave was

a nice guy. I hope I remember his phone number if I ever get out of here because I think we could be friends on the outside. He really appreciated the makeshift vision test I gave him, and I appreciated the pointers he gave me on how to fool a Breathalyzer. It turns out he never knew he needed glasses and I never knew how much I could do with a penny. Well come to think of it, he did say he was in on a D.U.I., so maybe his method isn't quite as reliable as he thinks it is. Either way we were having a grand old time until Pete had to come along and ruin it.

I guess the number one reason I enjoyed Dave's company so much, though, is that it took my mind off of Lori. Ever since I confessed I hadn't heard anything about anything from anyone. Apparently they don't exactly feel the need to keep you up to date on the latest news when you're behind bars. Every answer is the bare minimum: “Where am I going?”

“Movin' you.”

“Will I be back?”

“Don't know.”

“How long will I be here?”

“Til we move you again.”

It's kind of dehumanizing, and I might have said something about it — along with the shoe lace thing — but I was so busy being pleasantly surprised with the overall conditions around here that I didn't want to rock the boat too much. Really, the food isn't as bad as I expected, the cot isn't as hard as I expected, the out-in-the-open toilet isn't as humiliating as I expected, and the guards aren't as evil as I expected. I said I suspected the horror stories about jail were probably exaggerated, and that's because as of yet I haven't witnessed any of them. Sure, it's only been about eighteen hours and I'm not in a maximum security penitentiary — not yet anyway — but I have to say I'm pretty flabbergasted that out of all the things you see in gritty prison dramas, not only have none of them happened to me, but they haven't happened to anyone around me either.

The worst thing that's happened to me so far is when I almost got in a fight, and that's only because now I'm stuck in a private cell. If you had asked me before today, I probably would have told you that I'd absolutely prefer my own private prison cell over the alternative of having to share living space with a murderer or a thief of some kind. But before today I had no idea how boring having your own private prison cell could be. Apparently, hours upon hours of solitude strung together has a way of making you long for whatever kind of company you can get. Ask me now and I'll tell you, I'd gladly risk a shanking for the chance to actually have a real, live person in front of me to talk to.

I tried my best to keep busy nonetheless, but my mind would inevitably wander back to thoughts of all the things I didn't know. I didn't know if Lori was still being held in custody, I didn't know if the police bought my story, and I didn't know if Dale Durbin had even been contacted yet. Dale Durbin is our lawyer, an old family friend of Lori's mom. He's about the best there is within our price range I've been told... several times... by Lori's mom. I don't know, he seems like he knows his stuff, but there's just something about him that makes me uncomfortable.

I know as a lawyer you're supposed to keep some things close to the vest and all, but it seems to me like he keeps everything close to the vest. I can't get a read on him. He asks you a question and no matter what the answer, he always has that same droopy, emotionless expression on his face. I'd call it a poker face, but even poker players have tells. This guy is a stone. If he didn't blink I'd think he was dead. And he's always talking like a politician or football coach at a post-game press conference, even in private it's "I take that matter very seriously and I intend to conduct a careful review of all pros and cons concerning all involved entities before making any further comments." I bet when his wife wants to screw him she has to submit a formal affidavit first.

DALE DURBIN

No comment.

TAG

Anyway I was sure he'd be furious that I went ahead and copped to everything before he got here. Not that I'd be able to tell. Maybe he'd feel better if he knew there was nothing he could do to change my mind. I knew I'd made the right decision and that was that. I just hoped with all my heart that Lori was okay. If I had just paid attention to the goddamn road like I'm always telling myself to do, none of this would have happened. It made me sick to think that Lori might have to spend even a minute in jail because of my screw-up. Not after everything she had done for me.

And we had just had a moment! I mean a real, honest-to-goodness, transcendent moment. And I had to go and ruin it. Of course I was going to take the blame, and not only could Dale Durbin not talk me out of it, Lori couldn't talk me out of it either. I just had to talk to them before things spun out of control. What if Lori has the same idea? What if she's already confessed? What if we both confess that we did it alone and then we both get charged with murder *and* perjury? I guess once you're charged with murder the perjury charge doesn't matter so much, but still, I had to talk to them as soon as possible.

By the time Dale Durbin arrived, I'd been in solitary for… well, it felt like days. That's another thing I want to put on my list of cruel and unusual punishments: prison cells don't have clocks in them. Everyone should have a fundamental right to know what time it is. Especially in prison. If somebody gets a ten year sentence, but you put him in a cell with no clock so he doesn't know how long he's in there and it feels like a hundred years, that just seems unfair. Hopefully one day science can find a way to determine exactly how long it feels in solitary confinement with no clock, then that could be figured into a prisoner's punishment.

Wow, that's a great idea. I love that idea. If we could do that we could rehabilitate people in half the time! A life sentence wouldn't have to use up someone's whole life! They could get out afterwards and be re-assimilated as a productive member of society! I have to write that down…

Another one of my cruel and unusual punishments will be depriving me of my basic need for pencils and paper. Unless they're afraid I might stab myself in the eye or something.

So who knows how long I was in solitary, but by the time Dale Durbin arrived, I was going a little stir crazy. As usual he sat down with his ultimate poker face and slowly, methodically opened his briefcase and began setting up a mini-workstation before uttering a word. I didn't have the patience for it today so the moment I saw him the questions just hurled themselves out of me: "Where's Lori? Is she okay? Have you talked to her? Has she said anything? Is she okay? What time is it? Why aren't you saying anything? Are you mad at me? Is Lori okay?"

Dale Durbin took his time and finished setting up without

even a glance in my direction. When he was finally finished he removed his glasses, shut his briefcase, looked at me and said, "Good afternoon, Dr. Taggart," as if I hadn't said anything to him at all.

"Look, I know you don't think I should have confessed before talking to you but..."

"Confessed? You didn't confess."

"Yes, I did."

"Not to my knowledge you didn't."

"Well, now to your knowledge I did because I'm telling you I did."

"That wasn't a confession, you were under extreme duress."

"Yes it w... Where's Lori? Is she okay?"

"Dr. Taggart, would you classify your treatment in this facility as satisfactory, unsatisfactory or undecided?"

"Satisfactory."

"Undecided. Okay." He made a mark on one of his little documents.

"No, I uh... that's not what I said. I said satis..."

"Dr. Taggart, have you or any members of your family ever been known to have manic episodes, or to blackout for extended periods of time with no memory of what happened in the interim?"

"No, uh... never."

"Yes," he said to himself as he made another mark on the document.

"Yes? That's not what I said! I said no! You can't change a no to a yes!"

"Your mother has."

"My mother has? Since when?"

"Since last night when I talked to her."

"She had a manic episode last night?"

"No, but she told me she thinks she's had one in the past, so it's in your family history whether you like it or not."

"What? Don't talk to my mother!"

"Dr. Taggart, have you ever had any previous run-ins with the law? Such as having been arrested for or having been a suspect or person of interest in any felonies, misdemeanors, or the like?"

"No."

"Nothing? Not even a parking ticket?"

"Well, I've had several parking tickets."

"No," he muttered again as he made another mark on the paper.

"Uh, I just told you I've had several…"

"The parking tickets were just for emphasis, they don't count."

"Huh?"

"Thank you Dr. Taggart, I'll be in touch."

"Wait, wait, you didn't…"

He quickly broke down his mini workstation as he said, "Be sure not to speak to anyone in any way, shape, or form about anything until further notice."

"Mr. Durbin I…"

"I am currently the last person you've spoken to. Let's keep it that way for the foreseeable future. Good day." Then he got up and began to walk out.

"Mr. Durbin, I'm taking the blame for this…"

"No, you're not."

"Yes, I am."

"Then you'll plead insanity."

"No I won't, and I'm also going to show them where the other bodies are buried!"

That got his attention. He came back and sat down, once again going through the process of unpacking his briefcase and setting up his workstation. Finally he said, "Dr. Taggart, how long have you been experiencing these…"

"I'm taking them to the other bodies and there's nothing you can say to change my mind. I've already signed the confession…"

"Under extreme duress…"

"…under my own free will and I will take full responsibility as the sole guilty party in these crimes." I waited for Mr. Durbin to respond, but he just kept writing on his forms, so I seized the opportunity, "The only thing I need for you to do is confirm that Lori will be released and will not be investigated any further before I proceed. And I want to see her too."

Mr. Durbin was silent for a long time, scribbling furiously in his notepad, on several documents, and seemingly anything else he could find in that briefcase. Finally with a slight nod he looked up and said, "I'll be in touch." Then he got up and left.

The next few hours alone in that cell could have been five minutes or five days for all I knew. I became so excited every time I heard footsteps, and when the footsteps ended up being just another meal, I'd beg the guard to stop and talk to me for a second. I took to drawing imaginary masterpieces on the wall with my finger. Too bad they were imaginary too, because some of them were actually pretty good.

Finally, I heard several sets of footsteps at once and jumped up in excitement. It was two guards and several unfamiliar faces all ready to take me… somewhere. They led me down a long corridor and through the back entrance of some building, then down another long corridor, and finally into a large room. It wasn't like the other visiting area where I'd first seen Dale Durbin, this was private. It looked like some kind of library with books and stuff, but not enough books to be an actual library.

They opened the door and I immediately saw Dale Durbin and Lori waiting for me inside. Her eyes lit up upon seeing me and I'm sure mine did too. We kissed and hugged and said how much we missed each other and how worried we'd been until the guards finally separated us. Then we all sat down and one of the unfamiliar faces said, "Fifteen minutes," in a stern tone. Dale Durbin nodded at him and then they were gone. We were all alone. Well, alone-ish — I could see that they were standing right outside the door — but it was a thick door.

After the initial euphoria wore off, I could tell that Lori was extremely concerned. "Tag, are you sure you want to do this?"

"Yes," I replied, "I've never been more sure of anything in my life."

"Because you don't have to do this," Lori said, "I did the crime, I can do the…"

"I probably shouldn't be hearing this," Dale Durbin interrupted as he pulled a pair of earplugs from his briefcase. He carefully placed them in his ears and then nodded for us to continue.

"Tag, I want you to think about this, we can…"

"Lori, you've done more for me than I ever expected anyone to do. What kind of a man would I be if I didn't at least try to return the favor?"

"At least let it go to trial, Mr. Durbin is really good, there's always a chance you could..."

"If we let it go to trial and they start poking around, they're going to find out that you were involved. And I can't allow that to happen... to the woman I love." Don't groan, it was from the heart. Lori knew it too, and I could see the tears welling up in her eyes to prove it. Now that's one thing I'd never, ever seen before. She smiled really big on our wedding day, but tears? That was new.

"I love you Thomas Thaddeus Cornelius Taggart," she said, emotion dripping from every word.

"And I love you Lauren Denise McEntire Taggart." Our love for each other was so real we could almost touch it. We lunged at each other and kissed passionately right over the emotionless visage of Dale Durbin. He didn't show it, but I suspect he might have felt a little something too. Either the fifteen minutes were up or the guards don't believe in love, because soon afterward they came in and broke us up. Dale Durbin escorted Lori out and the door shut behind them with a thud. I wrestled free from the guards' tight grip and ran to the door to watch through that small square window as she walked away. Watching her constantly look back for me as she was ushered out, I knew I had made the right decision.

Dale Durbin returned shortly thereafter with several forms for me to sign and to go over the stipulations and other details of the agreement. All I cared about was that Lori was safe. Then along with Dale Durbin, I brought the two guards, the unfamiliar faces, Detectives Chambers and Henderson, and several other policemen out to that empty field where Detective Steiner was buried. The whole tone of the trip changed when they realized that one of the victims was a cop. Detective Chambers actually tried to attack me and had to be physically restrained by Detective Henderson. It was weird, we'd gotten along so well on the ride over.

One of the unfamiliar faces then asked me where the other body was, and for a second I was confused, but then I realized I'd promised to show them two bodies. I apologized for the misunderstanding and told them that technically they'd already found the other body, they just didn't know who killed it... uh, her. I went through my story without a stutter and they bought it hook, line, and sinker. They should have too, I'd had several hours alone to prepare it.

I told them the who, what, when, where, how, and why detail by detail. I stayed as close to the truth as possible so as to avoid inconsistencies, only leaving out the parts about Lori having any idea about what was going on. When we were finished, I thanked Dale Durbin with a firm handshake and bid him goodbye. He told me I was going to regret this in that way that he does and then he was gone and I was alone once again. But now as I sit in my cell and reflect on the events that led up to this moment, I don't feel so alone because I know that Mr. Durbin had that one wrong. I'm never going to regret this. In fact, I think it might be the best thing I've ever done.

Lori was the kind, merciful avenging angel who came down from Heaven and saved me from myself. And this is the least I can do to repay her. It's funny, I never thought a death sentence could be romantic, but I guess there's a first time for everything. If I were more skilled in the finer arts I might rhapsodize her in epic poems and solemn hymns, shout her name out from the rooftops, or discover a star and name it after her. But since I can't do any of those things, this will have to do. It's a small price to pay for the opportunity to experience true love first-hand. And I hope that someday, somehow, some way, you get to experience it too. Just like I did.

ONE YEAR LATER

LORI

Gray is my favorite color. I'm not ashamed of that. I do find it strange however that so many people assign specific feelings to colors. I wonder if they realize that those assignments are arbitrary. I wonder if they realize that if they don't realize that, they're insane. It's strange to me that so many people pick their favorite colors based on the feelings that color is associated with. It's even stranger to me that so many people avoid calling a certain color their favorite just because of the negative feelings associated with it. How else could it be that I've never met anyone who shares my taste in colors? Ever. Is it possible that out of all the people I've ever met, not one of them considers gray their favorite?

On the few occasions that I've mentioned my favorite color to someone (because really, how often does that come up in casual conversation?), their reaction is almost always disappointment. Some people have tried to talk me out of it. Come on, Lori, gray is so drab and depressing, is something wrong? Are you depressed? No, I'm not depressed, and I'm not in denial about being depressed. And I resent the fact that I have to defend myself to you because you attach a feeling to a color. Gray isn't depressing to me. Gray is gray. And I think it's pretty.

If you think about it every color can be depressing if you just base your opinion on certain feelings that are associated with it: Red is bloodshed, blue is sadness, black is death, green is envy and greed, yellow is cowardice, and brown and gray are drab and depressing. Somehow the only one that gets away scot free is white, and we all know the reason for that. I blame my forefathers, and you should too. Of course no one says their favorite color is white, and I think that's because all insane people are miserable. But I'm not miserable.

So no, there's no symbolic reason why gray is my favorite color, but if there was, it wouldn't have anything to do with drabness. It would be because gray is also the color of uncertainty. Some people see the world as black and white: there's a good guy and there's a bad guy, there's right and there's wrong, there's up and there's down, and it's very easy for them to tell which one is which. The people who espouse this world view are known in many circles as idiots. The type of people who would attach a specific feeling to a color. Because anyone who can think knows that everything is painted in different shades of gray. My theory is that the black-and-whiters know it too, they just have to pretend it's not true so their tiny brains don't explode. You know, Plato's Allegory of the Cave and all.

Shades of gray. You can't name me a deed so heinous that there are no circumstances under which that deed is justified. Every deed can be justified under the right circumstances. Well, maybe not rape. But every deed except rape. Check that, I once read that there are many species of animals like ducks, dolphins, and sea otters where one gender forces itself on the other to reproduce. I don't agree with it, and I wouldn't want one of those animals as a pet, but if it's responsible in any way for preventing certain species from going extinct, then I'll begrudgingly accept it.

My point is that looking at the world in terms of black vs. white is absurd. There's always a context, and until you can fully understand the context of a given situation, you have no business making moral judgments about it. That said, I know what I did was wrong, but I'd do it again in a heartbeat. I'd do it ten times out of ten. And I'll tell you why.

You hear it everywhere: in songs on the radio, in TV commercials, in cheesy romantic comedies, there's a constant barrage of platitudes and proclamations of the things people will do for love. "I'd do anything for you... I'd lie for you... I'd cry for you... I'd die for you... I'd beg, borrow, and steal for you... I'd kill for you." But when the time comes to put their money where their mouth is, it's "What's that? Oh honey, I totally would have died for you right there if only I would have known that that's what you needed. We really have to get on the same page, there must be a communication breakdown or something because I was not getting any 'You need to die for me now' vibes. It's crazy too, because I was totally willing to do it."

I don't think people are being disingenuous when they say it either, I think that they think they really mean it. But who really knows how they'd act in a life or death situation until they're actually in one? And most of the time two people will go their whole lives without either one of them having to prove those words true. Maybe in the Middle Ages it came up a lot, but nowadays I don't see a whole lot of "Die for you" opportunities popping up for John and Jane Q. Lover. So I don't blame them for not coming through when one comes up.

What I do blame them for is getting all high and mighty

and judgmental when someone else does come through on their promise. Don't judge because that guy was willing to do anything/lie/cry/die/beg/borrow/steal or kill and you weren't. And it's easy to honor someone who jumps in front of a speeding bullet to protect their soulmate during a stickup or someone who gives a kidney to a dying relative. Those acts have been deemed heroic. Real true love, though? That's when you're willing to help that person out by violating your own principles, moral boundaries, and sense of decency. When you're willing to let everyone look at you in disgust, to allow your reputation to be destroyed, to risk feeling the sting of guilt in your soul for the rest of your life, all for the sake of the one you love. To me, *that's* true love.

I doubt Tag remembers the first time we met because it never happened. I have very vivid memories of it though, because my mom has told me the story hundreds of times. The first time she told me was when I was a recently engaged nineteen year old on the hunt for the proper wedding dress. She had gotten it into her head that she cared about me again because moms are supposed to help their daughters with weddings, so she insisted on driving. The whole way to the bridal shop she reminisced about how her baby was growing up and getting so big and old and how it was so, so hard on her. (My mom always frames things by the way they affect her.) We were sitting at a red light on Bergman Drive next to the park when my mom gasped as if she'd just realized how crazy she was and said, "Lori, look! Remember that tree?" No seriously, she really said that.

Needless to say I did not remember that tree. "No, I don't think so."

"Oh! My baby's growing up so fast! How soon they forget!

But a mother? A mother never forgets." Just that morning she'd forgotten my middle name. My middle name! Which is Denise. Which is my mom's first name.

"Okay mom, what happened at that tree?" I asked with guarded curiosity.

"That tree is where you and Tag first met!"

"Mom..."

"I remember it like it was yesterday..."

"Mom..."

"You were on the playground, you must have been about four or five...

"Mom that's not..."

"Quiet Lori, let me finish! You were swinging away on the playground and this little boy about your age had climbed up in that tree and was afraid to get down..."

"Mom that's not..."

"Lori, I am trying to tell a story here."

"Okay," I gave in. Tell your made-up story, mom:

> His parents were worried sick, they tried everything to get him to come down: coaxing, begging, bribing, the dad tried to climb up and get him but he had a bad back, it was terrifying! A crowd had gathered around the tree and they were trying their best to help — one guy even offered to go home and get an old mattress to put under the tree. The whole time the poor boy just kept saying, "I can't, I'm scared, I can't, I don't wanna!" It was heartbreaking!
>
> Then all of a sudden the crowd parted and a little voice chimed in from the back: "If you come down I'll

> give you a kiss." It was the most adorable thing I'd ever seen! You standing there looking up at the boy all sweet and innocent, him looking down at you like it was his lucky day. Imagine that, not two minutes before, it was the worst day of his life — stuck up there in that tree with the whole town watching. Then you came along and gave him the motivation he needed.
>
> Well, he came right on down and collected his kiss on the cheek and said, "My name's Tag."
>
> You said, "I'm Lori," then you two held hands, the whole crowd burst into applause, and you've been inseparable ever since!

She searched my face for a spark of recognition, but saw none. "Are you sure you don't remember, Lori? I can't believe you wouldn't remember that tree." She kept pointing in the same direction even though the light had long turned green and we were well past the tree.

"Oh yeah, that's right," I lied.

"See? Now what would you do without your mother?" I smiled at her and let her have her fake memory. The truth is I remembered the event well, only the boy wasn't Tag and it wasn't that tree. His name was Eric and I went to school with him for three years before his family moved away when his dad got transferred, the tree was in Kallenbach Park which is much closer to our house than Bergman is, and I never actually kissed him. I offered to kiss him if he'd come down, but he just made that Ick-face that boys make at girls before puberty hits and ignored the offer. I do remember the crowd cheering when eventually the park's maintenance man showed up with a ladder to get him down though.

It was strange to me at the time how my mom had completely convinced herself that that highly romanticized version of the story was true, and she still tells it to this day. Why do people have to lie to themselves to get through life? Why is dealing with the truth such a scary thing? And why do people like my mom not only polish up the bad memories, but add on to the good ones too? Why can't some people leave the Cave even when it's sunny outside?

In reality I'm not sure when I first met Tag because he was just always there. I don't really remember a time when he wasn't. We weren't always as close as we eventually got, but he was always around. In high school he'd come sit next to me in the library while I was studying and exhale really loudly until I asked him what was wrong. I do remember finding it annoying at first, but over time I grew to feel honored that this kid chose me to unload all of his problems on. He didn't say a word to most people, but he told me everything.

The best part was that he made it so easy to listen. He didn't expect me to fix anything or even respond to him at all sometimes. I could zone out and think about other stuff as long as I periodically looked up and nodded. I wasn't trying to deceive him — if he ever asked me if I was paying attention I would have told him when I wasn't, but he never asked. As time marched on I listened more and more though. How could I not? The way his mind worked was fascinating. He would create these elaborate fantasies out of whole cloth seemingly for the sole purpose of having something to worry about, then he would worry about them. It was impressive how creative he could get to come up with them too, even if in the end it worked to his detriment.

I remember during one of his sighing sessions he shared with me how he was worried about his locker. Our school set up its locker system as a serious of double decker rows of lockers against the hall walls on either side of each floor in the building, so every student would have either a top locker or a bottom locker. Tag got it in his head that one day he might forget to close the door to his locker when he crouched down to unpack his bag, then if he were to spring up he'd suffer massive brain trauma as he slammed his head into the bottom of the locker door.

On this particular occasion I felt compelled to say something. I asked him why he didn't just unpack his bag in some place other than directly under his locker door. He said he usually does, but one day he might forget. I asked him if it seems so easy to do, how come it's never happened before, not just here but anywhere. He muttered something about schools keeping it quiet to avoid the expense of replacing all the lockers. I asked him how fast he normally stood up from a crouching position. He said he'd never measured. I thought about it all for a second, then I placed a hand on his shoulder and nonchalantly said, "I'm sure you'll figure it out."

It's not like I didn't believe what I said — I did — but it was funny how he took such solace in such a benign sentiment. The moment I said it his face lit up like some immense burden had been lifted off his chest. "Thanks," he said optimistically before practically skipping away. I don't think it's what I said that made him feel better either, I literally offered zero answers to any of his issues. I just think he appreciated being able to tell somebody that crazy stuff and not be treated like he was a crazy person. And I was happy to help.

He was the only person I ever knew who didn't need me to

tell him how I was all the time. He didn't need me to be okay, I could just be whatever I was. Everyone else was constantly telling me I was too quiet, that I looked like I was always down, "Why the long face, Lori?" was my dad's way of saying hi to me. No matter how much I insisted that I was fine, they would always hear it as a cry for help. They thought I was in denial, but I wasn't in denial, they were in denial. They thought that if they smiled and laughed enough on the outside they could fool their insides into joining in on the fun, but deep down they all knew they were miserable. I was the only one comfortable in my own skin, who didn't need to hide behind a smile. It's not like I never smiled, but I didn't feel the need to force one on to convince myself I was okay. Forcing a smile takes so much effort. Just let my face be, it's fine the way it is.

I became so appreciative of Tag's low expectations that he quickly became my best friend. I actually looked forward to his sigh sessions, although I was careful not to appear too excited lest I put a damper on his misery. After I listened and he felt better, then we both got to be excited together! It was worth the wait.

Throughout all of this I never once thought of Tag in a romantic light, his friendship meant too much to me. I would have been perfectly happy growing into a crazy old cat lady as long as I had him popping in for a visit every once in a while, exhaling loudly until I asked him what was wrong. But then after high school Tag went away to college while I stayed home and, well, you know what they say about absence making the heart grow fonder, and then I had a decision to make. I knew that we got along well together, that we enjoyed each other's company, and that with him there would be no undue pressure. Plus, in my crazy cat lady scenario there was always the possibility that Tag's eventual wife would get jealous and make our friendship an issue — and I didn't want that. So I went ahead and married him.

After we got together, nothing changed in the way I treated him, but I slowly began to realize that he was putting all kinds of extra pressure on himself. He was just so afraid that he would let me down now that I was someone who he *could* let down.And in Tag's mind, the way he would end up letting me down was by being unfaithful. In fact, the whole "not cheating" thing was so important to him that even when I tried to tell him he was being too hard on himself, he dismissed it wholeheartedly. He wanted to be monogamous for his sake as much as for mine, and I know better than to try and talk someone out of something after they've already made up their mind. I just tried to encourage him whenever I could.

I guess I wasn't fully aware of the extent to which he was struggling, though, until the day he came home and told me about Marcie. He was a nervous, sweaty mess as he desperately grasped for the right words to use to inform me of his plight. I tried to calm him down, and it worked well enough that first night, but I know Tag and my real worry was this: what if he eventually broke down and slept with her? I could forgive him all day and night, tell him that he hadn't let me down at all, that my feelings about him were the same, but I would never be able to get him to forgive himself.

The last straw for me was later that night when I found Marcie's torn up business card in Tag's trash can. No, I wasn't snooping, I was concerned. And sometimes I don't get around to emptying out the trash cans until really late at night anyway. And sometimes I... Well what was I supposed to do? He had just poured his heart out to me a few hours earlier and now I was being shaken out of a peaceful sleep by a sweating, guilt-ridden ball of emotions who was violently tossing and turning and mumbling unintelligibly. I had to do something.

So I found a few items that appeared to be clues, and over the course of the next several hours I literally pieced them together — which was even more difficult than it sounds. I mean, he really went at that thing with a vengeance. Some of the pieces were so tiny I had to pull out a magnifying glass to see them. Then I had to take the magnifying glass back to the trash can to find all the tiny pieces I'd missed!

As I began to realize exactly what it was that I was reassembling, my thoughts became more and more conflicted. I asked myself why I was doing this. What am I gonna' do when I find out Marcie's info? Am I gonna' go talk to her? What am I gonna' say? "Would you please try and look uglier when you're with my husband?" Am I gonna' threaten her? Tell her to come up with some excuse and quit or else?

No, there was only one way to ensure Tag's piece of mind, but as of yet I hadn't allowed myself to think about it. Then, as I gradually let the thought peek out from behind the shadows in the dark recesses of my mind, I was shocked at how little distress it caused me. I'd never even thought about murder before. I had no reason to. But now that I had a reason and I was allowing myself to think about it, I was fascinated and a little bit frightened by how reasonable it sounded.

But would it really solve the problem? Who's to say another sexy temp wouldn't replace her and get him hot and bothered all over again? Well, I'd cross that bridge when I came to it, but for now the idea of going full tilt to protect my soulmate was starting to sound like the ultimate romantic gesture. I have to admit it, after thinking about it that way I couldn't resist. After a while the “Am I really thinking about this?” in my head became an “Am I really going to do this?” which then turned into a “Why wouldn't I do this?” and finally a “*How* am I going to do this?” Eventually even my initial disturbance about how non-disturbing the whole idea felt was gone.

After I was finally able to piece the card back together well enough to make out all the numbers, my eyes were red, my vision was blurry, and I had a massive headache. The temptation to go back to bed was strong, but I knew if I didn't act fast I could miss my chance altogether. I asked myself one last time if I really wanted to take it this far. I knew the stakes, but I also knew that Tag was worth it and that I was willing to accept the consequences. I checked the clock to make sure I had enough time: 4 AM. Tag wouldn't be up until around 7:30. Okay, this is doable. Just a few quick preparations, then I was off to do my first murder.

On the way over I decided that I wouldn't be doing Tag any favors by telling him about this. It would just get him worried and bent out of shape all over again. The protective thing to do would be to protect him from this burden too. If circumstances led to it, I'd tell him later, but only if I had to. Besides, I knew what I was doing — I have the Internet — so I wasn't planning on leaving any evidence behind. The only thing that could possibly go wrong was if the police suspected Tag and he had to lie to them, because he's worse at lying than he is at driving. And he's terrible at driving. Yes, definitely better to keep him in the dark. For his own protection of course.

When I got to Beachwood I parked two blocks down and hoofed it. I wore exercise gear over my all-black clothing to appear like an early morning jogger on the walk over — because the best place to hide is in plain sight. When I got to her house I crouched in the alleyway, tore off the yoga pants and windbreaker, placed them in my gym/murder bag, and became one with the shadows.

One lock pick later and I was inside the house. Marcie was asleep on the couch, resting beneath a sea of used tissues, an empty quart of Butter Pecan ice cream by her side. This was bad. I started to feel a little better about the situation, thinking I might actually be doing her a favor. Still, she didn't deserve to be remembered this way. I stealthily picked up the tissues and the empty quart, disposed of them in the kitchen, and grabbed a kitchen knife while I was in there. Okay, quick and painless. Surgical precision. I closed my eyes and remembered what I read on the Internet about the carotid artery. One, two, three...

I dropped the knife and was out of there before the body hit the floor. No need to check, I knew the score. I zipped back to the car and was back in bed by five. I had to hand it to myself, I had a gift. Maybe in another life I could have been an international hit woman, where no one knows my face, they only know me by the name Tigerlily. That might be fun — in another life — but right now I'm happy with my own. I was amazed at how normal I felt about the whole thing, I wondered if I was some kind of monster. No, I concluded, a monster would feel this way all the time, I don't think I'm capable of doing this except for the most noble of reasons.

I was a bit wired so I couldn't sleep and I decided to get up and make breakfast. When Tag came into the kitchen he was still riding high from the previous night. I love how such a small gesture can make his week, if only he knew about the bigger gesture. Too bad I couldn't tell him. I so badly wanted to though. That was the big catch to this whole ordeal: going above and beyond for the one you love doesn't taste quite as sweet when you know he'll probably never know about it. Part of me wanted him to find out, but I knew I couldn't let that happen… for his own protection.

By the time I was off to work myself it was all sort of a distant memory. I wasn't thinking too hard about what might happen when Tag found out about Marcie, I figured he'd be bummed out for a day or two and feel better after he shared it with me. I never expected his capacity for feeling guilt would drive him to make a trip to her house. That one was a surprise. I wrapped up the open house early, it looked like we had a few interested parties already anyway. The sellers wanted to get out of town fast and the price was a steal so I wasn't worried about it. Selling houses is like anything else: what price are you willing to pay? What price are you willing to give? It's not exactly that simple, but nothing ever is. Shades of gray.

I enjoy my job and dealing with people, but most of all I like the flexible hours it affords me. I love being able to be there to kiss Tag goodbye in the morning and kiss him hello in the evening without having to sit at home or go shopping all day in between. I know it's important to Tag too, even though he would never say it. It's one of the things that I thought I'd never want to have to do when I was young and skeptical about marriage, and if I had to do it I probably would have hated it. But when you want to do it, it's kinda' nice.

It wasn't kinda' nice that day, though. The moment I heard the screeching of tires and the thump of the garbage cans bouncing off the car and onto the lawn, I knew something had gone very, very wrong. A mad man came tearing through the door as if the law was hot on his tail at that very moment, but that's not possible, right? Right? Seeing that he was in distress, I held my tongue as he destroyed the brand new rug — I know it's just a rug, but I'd like to keep it clean for at least the first month — and almost took out the coffee table too. As soon as he caught his breath, he proceeded to tell me how he went to check on Marcie when she didn't show up for work — for business purposes only — and was subsequently the first one to find her body. It wasn't until much later that I'd find out about the voicemails, which didn't help, but he was doing his best and that's what counts.

So Tag had stumbled onto the scene of a crime for which he could reasonably be considered a suspect. Now I'd have to coach him through a cover up. I wished I could just go back alone and clean up the scene myself, but A.) I didn't know what he'd touched and where he'd been in the house, B.) I needed a lookout, and Tag's nerves would have almost definitely given him an itchy horn finger, and C.) As far as Tag knew I'd never been in the house before and he had.

Nope, he'd have to be the one to go in, I'd just have to very carefully explain to him the importance of being thorough. So I played lookout and Tag went in, and minus making way too much noise and breaking a light bulb and losing his hairnet and having to go back in and tripling our risk of being caught, he did okay. I was proud of him, and I told him so.

I should have been relieved, but something nagged at me, telling me we hadn't dotted all our I's and crossed all our T's. I couldn't put my finger on what it was, but somehow I knew it wasn't over. Oh well, I thought, can't cry over water under the bridge… or something like that. The best I could do was to have the serenity to accept what I couldn't change, change what I could, and the wisdom to know the difference. I sincerely thought about praying at that moment, but I figured that would be pushing my luck. There are some things you just don't ask God for, and one of them is help getting away with murder. It would have been disingenuous anyway, nobody's gonna answer a prayer that starts off "Dear God, on the off chance that you exist I'd like to ask for your help..." I was on my own on this one, but I was pretty sure I had enough serenity to pull it off anyway.

So I made a to-do list in my head of steps I could take that would minimize the chances of more trouble:

1. Convince Tag that he possesses the ability to answer questions from the police without crying.

2. Don't let Tag know any more of the truth than he already knows. At least not until it all blows over.

3. Make sure Tag goes about his daily routine as if nothing happened.

4. Get Tag's mind off of this as much as possible.

5. Be prepared for anything.

The next day I put my plan into action, gently coaxing Tag into the proper frame of mind. Showing him rather than telling him not to act like he already knows Marcie is dead or that he's got something to hide. It took him a second to catch on but he was an eager learner and got up to speed quickly. I had to call him once during the day to remind him that a person who didn't know Marcie was dead would probably call her agency and ask what the problem is, but overall I felt that he was well-prepared.

Now all that was left to do was to wait until the police investigation brought some detective out to the victim's last place of employment. There was no way to know if Tag would be a suspect when they talked to him or not, it all depended on the hunches the investigator chose to follow and whether or not Marcie told anyone that Tag had fired her that day. And also whether or not he discovered those voicemails that I hadn't found out about yet.

But I had the wisdom to know that I couldn't change any of that, what I could influence was Tag's response to being questioned. It was a tricky situation because I didn't want to come on too strong in emphasizing the importance of his performance — that would just make him nervous and more likely to crack under pressure. What I needed to do was delicately communicate to him that if he handled those questions properly, we'd be guaranteed to make it through this intact. *If* he handled those questions properly, or even adequately, or even semi-suspiciously, but that's not quite how it turned out. I guess I should have communicated it a little less delicately.

I tried to keep him calm when he came home later that day, but the truth is I was a bit concerned myself. He had obviously botched the interview in a spectacular way, and now this detective was a problem that was going to have to be dealt with. I didn't know how just yet, but something had to give. For the moment I'd talked Tag off the ledge once again, but the whole "You didn't do it, so what's the big deal?" act was only going to keep him calm for so long. The moment he felt under pressure again he'd explode. I feared that telling him that both of our fates depended almost solely on him keeping it together would send him spiraling and make it even worse, but I was beginning to think that now I had no choice, I'd have to risk it... tomorrow. He needs his sleep right now.

I went upstairs to get ready for bed myself, but the moment I walked into our bedroom I saw the top drawer of my nightstand partially open. To my initial delight I saw that Tag had left a beautiful poem for me in there:

Dearest Lori-Bear,

Hey.

Throughout all the tough times
and all the hard days,
You're special to me in so many
great ways.

You wipe off my tears when I'm
down and depressed,
You sew up my buttons when
I can't get dressed.

But the greatest of all of your
numerous sides,
Is how you can find me when I
want to hide.

You bring me the truth when I
need it the most,
And that's even sweeter than
your sweet French toast.

I want you to know that no matter
the year,
I'll always adore you and love you
my dear,

Love,
Taggy-Bear

Aww, that big softie! I immediately sat down and composed a reply:

Dearest Taggy-Bear,

Hey.

You're worth every dollop of
syrup each morn
You're worth every tear when
you're feeling forlorn

But the reason I love you a whole
whole whole lot
Is all of the strength you don't
know that you've got

You can stand up to mountains
and come out on top
You can vanquish ten ninjas
with only one chop

You can make me feel like I'm
afloat on a cloud
You're the best man I know
darling you make me proud.

Subtle? Maybe not, but I knew I'd have to get even less subtle in the morning. I folded up the poem and placed it in his nightstand drawer and... what's this? No... but it is. Oh no! I left the taped-up card in my top drawer! He must have found it when he put the poem in my... How could I be so stupid? After all the care I took to leave no evidence at the scene of the crime, I go and do a stupid thing like leaving Marcie's taped-up business card right in my top drawer! Why did I do that? Tag has even left me notes in there before! How could I be so reckless? Wait... does this mean I'm not as careful as I think I am? Does this mean I may have left clues back at the scene? Could Tag have buckled under the force of the police's questions because they really do have something?

No, Lori, quit catastrophizing. I was a stone cold ghost at the crime scene, and it's not like I forgot where I put the card. I distinctly remember putting it in the top drawer, easily brushing away any nagging voice in my head telling me not to. I guess maybe part of me felt bad about keeping Tag out of the loop, no matter how wise a decision that may have actually been. I think part of me deep down wanted Tag to find out, I just knew it wasn't a smart idea and I wouldn't consciously let myself tell him. Thanks a lot, subconscious mind.

I quickly replaced the card in his drawer and got into bed. I knew that now there was going to have to be a slight change of plans. Now I was going to have to tell Tag the truth. Maybe it would be better this way, I desperately tried to convince myself, if Tag knew that I was in more danger than he was maybe he'd try harder to keep it together with the police. But would he ever look at me the same? His lovely little Lori-bear? Capable of ripping the life out of someone?

I'd have to make him understand that it was all for him, but I couldn't put it in a way that made it sound like I was trying to shift the blame. That was gonna' be tough, but I could make him understand, right? I could explain to him that the reason I didn't tell him was because I wanted to protect him without making him feel like he was indirectly responsible for a crime, couldn't I? Yeah, that could work. Maybe. Forty percent chance, ya' think? That's pretty good under the circumstances, isn't it?

I knew I had to prepare myself for a long cooling off period though. I had to be willing to give Tag time to adjust to this new reality. I couldn't give up hope if he initially told me hated me and wanted a divorce. After all that's a fairly reasonable reaction to finding out that the person in your life that you're closest to is capable of premeditated murder. If he needed time, I'd have to give it to him. He'd eventually come around. He'd have to. We're soulmates.

I had my whole strategy planned out for the next morning, but when I woke up Tag was already gone. I checked the closets in a panic. Nope, nothing packed, he didn't move out, he must have just left for work early. He does that sometimes. Nothing to worry about. Don't catastrophize, Lori, you knew you might have to give him some time. But how much time? And what will I do with myself while I'm waiting? I just have to keep busy, that's all. Get going on some of those projects I keep putting off. Hopefully there's a big hassle with the offer on the place on Old Mill Road. That could keep me at work all day! Fingers crossed.

Of course that's not what happened. The offer was accepted immediately and I was home before two. Maybe I should pick up a heavier workload. If I end up divorced I'm going to need the extra income, plus I'll have a lot more time to kill. Actually there's always the possibility I could end up in prison — then I'd have lots of time to kill. No, Tag would never take it that far, even if he wanted to I'm fairly certain I could talk him out of it. Unless he's telling the police now… Maybe I should call the mall and make sure he's… Lori, stop it, your marriage is based on mutual trust and respect and you're not gonna go around checking up on him. Relax.

That's when the doorbell rang. Tag? No. Why would it be Tag? He doesn't ring the doorbell. Unless he doesn't consider himself a resident of this house anymore. Why did my mind go there? It's probably just Susan trying to recruit me for the Unofficial Neighborhood Welcoming Committee again.

I looked out the door and saw a stranger. Hm, is he police? A divorce attorney? Jehovah's Witness? Oh, I know I've never said this before but please be a Jehovah's Witness. "Yes, who is it?"

"Wayne Steiner, ma'am, Detective Wayne Steiner, homicide."

"Oh my gosh, did something happen? Is my mother okay?" These cops always like the damsel in distress role, so I try to give them what they want.

"No ma'am, your mother is fine. Well, actually I have no idea how your mother is doing, that's not why I'm here."

"Oh my gosh, should I be worried?"

"Ma'am could you just open the door, I have some rather sensitive information. I'd prefer not to yell it on your front porch."

"Oh my gosh, um, okay, just a second, I have to get dressed."

"Take your time ma'am." I was hoping I wouldn't have to do anything drastic, but Rule 5: Be prepared for anything, so just in case I pulled out the plastic covering for the brand new rug (sometimes it pays to never throw anything away) and covered that thing right up. The rest of the furniture was old and frankly I wouldn't mind having an excuse to replace it, but I was not gonna' let any blood stains get on my new rug. I couldn't find anything I liked in three stores before I found that pattern and I didn't want to go through that again.

I opened the door and greeted the detective — he appeared to be in a really good mood — and sat him on the couch in *just* the right spot.

"So Detective, uh… Steiner, is it?"

"Wayne."

"Wayne, I like that name. It sounds very rustic."

"Rustic?"

"Like a cowboy."

"Oh, well thank you, I guess I never thought of it that way, Mrs. Taggart…"

"Lori."

"Lori. Okay, Lori I'm here about your husband, Mr. Taggart."

I gasped, "Oh my gosh, is Tag okay?"

"Yes, yes, he's fine. Tag's fine."

"Oh! That's a relief. So what happened? Did Tag kill somebody again?" Wayne stared at me like a deer in headlights. I let the tension build for about five seconds before bursting into obnoxious laughter, and soon enough Wayne caught on and joined in.

"You are… you are a kick, Mrs. Taggart."

"Lori."

"Yes, Lori, but to get down to business I've got a few…"

"Yes! Please, get down to business, I know you're a busy man, and the last thing I want to do is take up too much of your time, as much as I'm enjoying your company I know that…"

"Lori, how well do you know your husband?" He gets to the point, I'll give him that.

"I'd say pretty well, I've known him just about all my life. You could call us high school sweethearts, although you'd be technically incorrect because we didn't make it official until we were freshmen in college. But I still like to say we were…"

"College? What college?"

"Mine or his?"

"You didn't go to the same college?"

"No…"

"That's funny, you were college sweethearts but you didn't go to the same college."

I stared at him for a moment, then I burst out laughing and said, "You know what? I never thought of it that way! You're right, that is funny!"

Now we were both laughing and having a grand old time. "That's… that's great," Wayne said, "so which college did you go to?"

"Yeah, I stayed in town."

"So Ashman then?"

"Yep."

"That's out near Beachwood, right?" Oh, now I see where's he's going with this.

"Yeah, I think so."

"Did you live in that area?"

"No, I'm local, so I lived with my parents."

"Oh, okay."

"But I know the area, it's beautiful. Why?"

"Well Mrs. Taggart…"

"Lori."

"Yes, well Lori…"

"Oh my gosh!"

"What?"

"I am so rude, I did not ask you if you wanted a drink. I apologize."

"That's okay, I…"

"No no no no no! Here you are, a guest in my house and I violate the first rule of hostessing. Oh! What would my Grammy think? God rest her soul."

"It's really okay, I just wanted to stop by for a…"

"Now let's see, I have water, lemonade, I may have some Diet Coke unless Tag finished it off last night. Oh! Men and their kitchen habits! Always finishing things and not telling anyone."

"Lori, I…"

"Then they have the audacity to complain when they go back to the kitchen and find an empty jug!"

"Mrs. Taggart, I…"

"I bet Mrs. Steiner never has to… I'm sorry, is there a Mrs.

Steiner?"

"Uh, yes there is, but…"

"I bet Mrs. Steiner never has to deal with that kind of thing from you, does she?"

"Well, I do my best, but…"

"And that's all that the good Lord expects, right?"

"Well, that and a check in the collection box every Sunday," he said, a faint smile creeping up from the ends of his mouth. I took his cue and we busted out laughing simultaneously.

"You are… you are a trip, Wayne," I said, desperate to get out of the room and regroup before he had a chance to bring it back to Marcie again. So I pushed the issue, "So what'll it be? Water, lemonade…"

"Oh no, I really shouldn't…"

"Please, I insist."

"But I…"

"Pretty please?"

"Uh, okay. Water's fine."

"One water, comin' up! Back in a flash!" I disappeared into the kitchen and thought about my next move. He wouldn't have come here if he didn't consider Tag a fairly strong suspect, but I needed to find out why he suspected him. And I needed to find out without tipping him off that I knew… well, anything. It wouldn't be easy, but the niceties had already been exchanged and he seemed to like me well enough so hopefully I could… was that the door?

"Lori! Lori! Come on Lori, we gotta go!" Okay, Tag's home early, that's a new wrinkle. I peeked through the crack in the door and saw a horrifically stressed out Tag talking away our freedom. No time to think, quick! Get the water and get back out there now! Just act natural, try to put Tag at ease, don't let

Wayne smell a rat, easy. Well, easy-ish.

“Well, hello again Mrs. Taggart,” Wayne said as I returned to the living room.

“Here you go, and please call me Lori.”

“Thank you so much, Lori.”

“Honey, what's the Detective doing here?”

“Tag, you never told me Wayne was so funny!”

“Wayne?”

“That's me. Most detectives also have first names.”

“Well whatever Wayne said to you, it's…”

“Oh, don't worry,” I said, “It's all been good. So far.” This time Wayne took my cue and we busted out laughing again. I made a face at Tag trying to get him to join in, but it was a lost cause. He was imploding in front of us.

“Yeah,” Wayne said, “I was just getting to the part about the voicemails you left on Ms. Tucker's phone. But before I go on, is there anything you'd like to talk about privately, Tag?” What's this? Tag left voicemails on Marcie's phone? I didn't remember him mentioning that — maybe it slipped his mind. Well, he did say, “When she didn't return my calls…” he went over to her house, so maybe it was my fault for assuming he wouldn't say anything more than “Call me back.” I wonder what he said to her — something incriminating no doubt. At least now I knew for sure what I had to do.

And lucky for me, Wayne gave me the perfect out so I didn't have to come up with another excuse. I smiled and broke the silence: “Nope, you don't even have to say it, I know guy talk when I hear it, I'm gonna' go…”

“No!” Come on, Tag, let me go, “No secrets between us, I don't mind if she stays.”

“It's alright,” I said, “I have a feeling I'm not gonna' want to hear what this is about anyway. Especially if what's on those voicemails is of a… sexual nature." That should get Tag to back down.

"What? That's ridiculous!" Tag replied, "Come on honey, stick around, it's the twenty-first century, we don't send the women away like they did in the old days." Nope! It sure didn't.

Thankfully, Wayne bailed me out once again: "Ya' know, Tag, maybe it would be in your best interest to talk to me alone for a minute." Thank you, Wayne.

"Wayne's right, Tag, this is between you two. And don't worry, I don't feel discriminated against." I watched Tag look at me like, "Why are you leaving me alone with this guy? You know I'll blow it!" I tried to make my face say, "Just give me a minute and I'll handle this," but I don't think the message came across. I hurried into the kitchen to pick out a proper knife. It had to be able to get the job done, but it also had to be one that I was willing to part with. I wouldn't want to dice tomatoes with a kitchen utensil that had been inside of a man's still-beating heart. I made my selection and tried to fight back the last minute doubts.

Are you sure you want to do this, Lori? This is a bridge you can't uncross. Tag will not only know the truth, but he will have seen it in action, up close and personal. He may not be able to look get past that. Well, first of all, I have no choice, it's either this or prison for one or both of us. Second, he most likely already knows about Marcie, so I'm going to have to deal with that anyway. Third, I love him enough to risk everything to protect him, even his love for me.

Now that I was good and convinced, I stealthily snuck up behind Wayne and did it. Thwap! Quick and easy, painless.

Now fall onto the plastic. Good. I don't think he even made a sound, and the mess was mostly kept off the furniture. I was getting pretty good at this. The next step was to look up, which I was afraid to do, knowing the look on Tag's face wouldn't be one I'd remember fondly. And it wasn't. I tried to explain it to him, but it didn't go very well. I was right when I figured he'd need some time. Hopefully time would be enough. He curled up, shocked and petrified, and retreated into his shell.

His mind was welcome to take its time, but I still needed his body to help me move Wayne's. I cleaned up and packed the evidence and the supplies we would need out at the site: jumbo trash bags, matches, lighter fluid, both shovels from the shed in the backyard that Tag never goes into, and antibacterial wipes. Then Tag helped me get Wayne into the trunk. His movements were robotic, zombie-like, he was hanging on by a thread. Come on, Tag, stay with me, we just have to get rid of all the evidence then you can zip up your cocoon and process away.

On the road I kept looking worriedly at Tag. Well, I was looking at part of him. The rest of him seemed to be a thousand miles away. We never had a problem with uncomfortable silences — we could sit silently in a room together for hours without it getting awkward — but this was different. The silence was so suffocating for me that I had to start talking or I would have gone crazy too. I didn't know if he'd hear me, but I tried to explain nevertheless.

"I really wanted to tell you, but I just couldn't. I was afraid it might upset you even more, and you already had so many things on your plate to stress out about. I thought it might cause you to have a nervous breakdown, and it looks like I was right. I mean, look at the way you're acting now. But it had to be done, Tag, it had to be done. It always hurts worse when you rip the Band Aid off quick, but the pain doesn't last as long. Believe me, you'll feel better, you just need a little time. Just imagine what would have happened if I didn't nip this in the bud tonight. Then that Band Aid would have come off real slow over a period of 25 to life. I know you're angry and confused, you probably feel deceived and disoriented, and I understand, I really do. This may be hard for you to comprehend right now, but all I wanted to do was make everything better. I don't expect you to see it my way, or even to forgive me for what I've done. I just hope you understand why I did it. I told you we're in this together, and I meant it from the bottom of my heart."

I searched Tag's face for any evidence of a reaction, but I couldn't find one. I assumed my speech had fallen on deaf ears, but it still made me feel a little better to get it out there. Maybe one day in his subconscious mind he'd remember it and smile a little... or something. Maybe one day at the institution he'd be sitting there with Jello running down his face and a little piece of it would get him through the day. A piece of the speech, not the Jello. I know, I shouldn't be thinking like that, Tag is going to be fine, he'll snap out of it. His brain is just using all of its manpower on double-timing the healing process, that's all. Once he works it all out he'll be fine. I hope.

Once I found a nice, secluded area I parked the car and looked at my frozen husband long and hard. I was tempted to wave my hand in front of his face or snap or do something to try and get his attention, but I read somewhere that you're not supposed to wake a sleepwalker and for some reason this situation felt comparable. I just let him be and got busy. I can't say I enjoyed dragging the body and digging and filling the hole all by myself, but I will say I more than made up for skipping Pilates that week. Once all the flammable evidence was burned and buried it was back in the car and on the road again.

Tag still hadn't budged though, and I was getting more and more concerned as the minutes ticked by and he continued to be part vegetable. I figured I should keep talking to him, at least that's what they do when a person is in a coma. It was funny, I'd helped Tag out of a jam hundreds of times in the past, but I'd never had to use so many words before.

"I'm not angry that you didn't help back there," I said, "I realize this is a lot for you to handle, and I want you to know that I'll be here for you as you try to get through it." It wasn't an overly generous gesture, but I guess it pushed the right button, because all of a sudden Tag turned his head toward me and softly said, "Thanks." Now I'm not sure if I've ever cried before — I'm talking about the kind with real tears, crumpled faces, and the like — but I sure came close at that moment. That one tiny word gave me hope that no matter how bad things were, there was always a chance that they could get better.

By the time we got inside the house, Tag had started talking almost normal again, and he made me promise not to "stab his problems away" anymore. It was a fair trade to have him back on my side. I only hoped he didn't bring this up every time we got in a fight: "And what if I don't wash the dishes? Are you gonna murder me?" Or whenever I wanted to do some healthy, behind-the-back girl-gossip: "Christy said what? You should totally kill her." Well, we'd get our first real test in 3… 2… 1…

Ding dong.

Who could that be? Oh, only Susan from next door with the single worst timing in all of recorded history. I was still a filthy mess from handling all the grunt work out at our makeshift graveyard, and now I was going to have to entertain! One thing I wasn't going to have to do was think of much to say, though, because Susan usually took care of that part all by herself. They say you can't teach an old dog new tricks — and maybe you can't — but those old tricks can certainly get more obnoxious over time. I don't know what kind of fire was lit under that feisty widow's skirt, but she took her typical innocent flirting with Tag and brought it to a whole new zip code.

Her purpose for coming over was ostensibly to drop off our long overdue housewarming gift, but I suspect the real reason was to passive-aggressively insult every aspect of our home while disrespecting me and embarrassing poor Tag. It was not her finest hour. I admit it was fun breaking it to her that wine wasn't the best gift for me, a seldom drinker, and Tag, a never-drinker, but I did feel kind of bad about snapping at her. Well, it did get her to leave, so I couldn't feel that bad.

After I closed the door behind her and turned back to Tag, I was taken aback by the accusatory look on his face. "No," he said to me in a tone somewhere between pleading and demanding. No what? Oh… that. So I guess I had my answer — it was gonna' come up a lot. Now up to that point I honestly hadn't thought about doing anything to the poor woman — she was annoying but ultimately harmless. I didn't blame Tag for thinking it was a possibility, but I couldn't help but feel a little disappointed that he didn't see the difference between what I'd done and what he'd gotten in his head that I might do. I found myself trying to talk him down from the ledge all over again. He seemed to calm down after I said my piece, but this time I was sure he wasn't completely convinced. He'd lost some of his faith in me, and I probably deserved it.

I watched him toss and turn in bed all night knowing that probably for the first time ever, I was the cause of his worry. It broke my heart a little, but I kept reminding myself that he'd had a rough day and his reactions in this raw state were mostly emotion-based. If he'd been capable of using his head I knew that he'd see my intentions much more clearly. And that gave me hope because I knew his head would be back to normal after a few days.

Of course in the meantime he was in the same vulnerable state that I'd been trying so hard to help him stay out of all week. It would be a shame if after all that hard work Tag's fragile mental state caused him to give in to his lustful passions anyway. Then not only would he have failed to stay faithful, but I would have failed to protect him, and two people would have died in vain. I couldn't let that happen, it wouldn't be fair to any of us.

I knew how Tag got when he was stressed out, and I knew how he was about taboo things as well. Everyone has an innate instinct to want to disobey when someone says, "Don't touch that button!" I guess most people call it curiosity. Why don't they want me to touch that button? What happens if I touch that button? Who are they to tell me not to touch that button? I want to touch that button! Most people are able to resist the urge and avoid touching the button, the ones who can't are called... well I don't know what they're called. Children, maybe? Tag is a child, but in the best sense of the word. It's interesting that there's such a gulf of meaning between the words "childish" and "childlike." I heard someone talking about it on TV once… I wonder if he was a psychologist. Even if he wasn't I think he was right. Tag falls squarely into the "childlike" category, and I wouldn't have it any other way. But…

One of the unfortunate side effects of his condition is that he has got to touch that button. He's got to press it, and if nothing happens he's got to press it again. And again. And again and again. If nothing happens still, he'll wonder if he's not pressing hard enough or long enough or fast enough or short enough. He'll keep pressing until something happens, even if that something is utter self-destruction.

I could tell that while he was tossing and turning in bed he was telling himself not to touch that button, and in this case that button was Susan. But what could I do? I definitely couldn't kill her, especially after I just got through chiding Tag in my head for thinking that that's something I would do. And there's also that thing about promising not to stab anybody else. Ugh. It was gonna be a long night, not that I could have slept either way with all the tossing and turning coming from that side of the bed.

At around 5:30 I woke up with a start. I'd fallen asleep and had a nightmare that the worst case scenario had played out in every possible area. The worst part about it was that that's all I could remember, the details escaped me. You'd think if the human mind were anywhere near as efficient as we believe it to be, the subconscious part would think up a better way to communicate with the conscious part than in dreams. Their cryptic, vague, often terrifying, but still apparently very forgettable. It's like if the military transmitted their orders using bad European art house films. But I'm a firm believer in determining my own fate, so whatever that worst case scenario was, I wasn't going to let it happen. I brushed off the cobwebs, sat up in bed, and thought up a plan.

I looked over at Tag — he definitely wasn't having a nightmare. He was sleeping like he was dead. I checked just to make sure… okay good. If I was gonna' do this I'd have to do it now, the sun was just peeking up over the horizon and pretty soon I'd be under Tag's suspicious eye again. I slipped on some jeans and headed for Howard's Big Buy.

On the way there I thought about poison. I didn't want to do any research on it for fear that if everything went bad they could seize my computer and use it as evidence. Forget erasing histories and cookies and hard drives, it's scary what those hackers can do with just ten fingers and some time on their hands. I wasn't prepared to take that risk, so I'd have to do it from memory. The good thing was I wasn't planning on the body ever being found so I wouldn't have to worry about anything showing up in any autopsies. But still, better safe than sorry, so if I could find an undetectable one that would be ideal.

First thing's first though, what do I know about poison? Hm. I know some names. There's strychnine, arsenic, hemlock, cyanide, belladonna, nightshade… wait, those two might be the same thing. I don't know. I know arsenic is one of the elements on the periodic table, but I don't see how that could help. I know hemlock is some kind of plant, but I don't know what it looks like or why they'd sell it at Howard's Big Buy. I know strychnine is used in a lot of pesticides and rat poison… ooh! Rat poison! That'll be at Howard's Big Buy. But I don't know, what if it has a funny taste to it and she doesn't drink enough of it? How much rat poison does a person need to… Wait! I remember seeing a thing on TV warning you to be careful because there's cyanide in the seeds of fruits like apples, peaches, apricots, cherries, and... plums! The label on that wine bottle Susan brought over mentioned a "rich plum flavoring" or however they put it. I bet a few crushed plum seeds would blend right in and do the trick just fine, maybe a hefty amount of crushed plum seeds. Yes, that's it! Plums it is! Better get a little rat poison too just in case I'm remembering that wrong.

I'd never been to Howard's Big Buy that early in the morning before. I'd been there really late, but it's amazing how much of a difference there can be between really late and really early, especially since they're only about an hour or two apart. The biggest difference seemed to be the amount of elderly people browsing the shelves. It occurred to me that I should be extra careful due to the very real possibility that I might actually run into Susan while I was there. She would be the type to get up at 4 AM and have all her grocery shopping done before the sun rises.

I quickly got my supplies and headed for the checkout. The produce section was running low on plums so I get apricots instead, but that should blend in well enough. Actually it sounds like a pretty yummy combination if you ask me. No harm in making her last sip a bit more enjoyable, I thought — you know, to show it isn't personal.

As I stood in line behind an elderly woman who from the looks of it had done her grocery shopping for the entire month, I stared at my items: a dozen fresh apricots, a jumbo pack of heavy duty black trash bags, a 9 foot roll of clear painter's plastic, a small bottle of odorless liquid ant killer, and one corkscrew. I suspected there was a small chance that my purchases might strike the cashier as rather... well, if not odd at least memorable. I got out of line and returned to the store. I loaded up my basket with as many normal-looking items as I could find: 2-liter sodas, chocolate chip cookies, a gallon of milk, Neapolitan ice cream, a bottle of dish soap, baking soda, and a Cosmo magazine. That should do. I paid in cash and headed for the door, grateful that Susan's piercing shriek hadn't greeted me around any corners.

I rushed back home and headed upstairs to check on Tag — still asleep. What time is it? 6:45, better hurry. I carefully and quickly made my preparations: cover the rug, poison the wine, put everything back where you found it, put the other supplies away — check, check, check, check. Getting the cork back into the wine bottle proved to be especially challenging, but I think I managed to do a pretty convincing job. It wasn't gonna have to pass a thorough inspection, just the glance test, so I was confident in my handiwork.

At 7:25 I slid back into bed and closed my eyes. It was Tag's day off and I knew he was sleeping in today, but how many times does someone instinctively wake up early on a Saturday? I was glad I'd gotten it all done in time because after 7:30 I'd be playing with fire. Not today though. Today he slept right on through 9 A.M. when I had to get ready to go to work myself. I looked over at him worriedly as I got dressed. They say one of the signs of major depression is an unwillingness to want to get out of bed, and Tag rarely slept past 10. Of course I reminded myself that he had just witnessed his beloved soulmate off a guy less than 24 hours before, so perhaps today there were extenuating circumstances.

I thought over the wisdom of my plan as I watched him sleep. I wasn't killing anybody per se, he'd have to understand that. I was merely providing someone with the opportunity to unwittingly kill themselves if and only if they crossed the line. But would she cross the line? I honestly didn't know, but if she did I couldn't let her destroy Tag's slowly rehabilitating self-esteem. I just couldn't let that happen. Hopefully he would understand that I exploited this loophole only for the noblest of reasons.

The one thing I definitely wasn't afraid of was that Tag would drink any of the wine. I'd heard him talk about his childhood trauma enough times to know that even an errant whiff of the stuff would bring back terrible memories. He wouldn't even drink a celebratory glass at our wedding. Everyone else toasted with champagne, he toasted with apple juice. Even the non-alcoholic bubbly apple cider was too close for his comfort. My mom told me I shouldn't trust a man who couldn't hold his liquor, then I asked her if that meant she trusted dad. That was the end of the conversation.

So I left the house with Tag still sleeping it off and prepared myself mentally for the daily barrage of words from our kindly gardening neighbor Sus…

"Lori! Good morning!"

"Good morning, Susan."

"Isn't it? Listen, about last night…" she said before launching into the longest, most meandering apology I've ever heard. I told her not to worry about it, she apologized some more, I told her it was no big deal, she apologized some more, I told her to forget it, she apologized some more. When she was finally out of either apologies or shame — or both — she moved on: "And I hope you don't mind, but I just so happened to be in Howard's this morning and… well, what's a good bottle of wine if you can't open it, right?"

"Right," I said. Oh my gosh, I must have just missed her. I

knew she was the type to go shopping at four in the morning.

"So I was in the store," she continued, "and I picked you up a corkscrew. Actually, it's a combination corkscrew, can opener, and bottle opener — it's top of the line stainless steel, the whole shebang!"

"Susan, you're very kind, and I can't thank you enough, but…"

"It's right inside if you want to come and grab it."

"I really have to get to work so…"

"Work?" Susan barked in horror, "Lori, I didn't know you had a job!"

"Yes, I have a job," I said, trying not to sound too annoyed. "I'm in real estate."

"Oh! That is so cute! Housewife, housekeeper, house seller, is there anything you can't do?" I can't get out of this conversation. "Lori, you are a doll!"

"Uh… okay." I mean, what do you say to that?

"Okay then I won't keep you, I'll just bring it over later. I see Tag's car there, is he home?" Careful, Susan.

"Yes, he's off today so…"

"Perfect! I'll just bring it over later then. You go on, dear, go on to 'work,'" she said. And yes, she really made air quotes when she said "work." So I felt a little better about killing her now. I'm kidding of course?

I bid Susan goodbye and drove off, wondering exactly what I was going to come home to later. I still considered the odds to be against Susan trying anything — and my preparations just a precautionary measure — but she did come on stronger last night than usual. And she did go to the store this morning and buy an excuse to go see him. Should I have just taken her up on her offer and gone over to pick it up myself?

Why didn't I do that? It would have been easy enough. Does part of me hope that she does come over and make a move? No, that doesn't sound like me.

And if she has decided to come over, me picking up the corkscrew wouldn't stop her. She would have come over to check on how we like our new corkscrew or if the wine's too tart or if Tag's got his doctor's pants on. Any old excuse would do. Regardless, it was definitely strange that despite how talkative she's always been with us, yesterday was the first time she ever knocked on our door — and now she was planning to do it for a second day in a row.

Eventually I knew I would have to deal with the twin elephants in the room: 1.) What if Susan goes over with innocent intentions and ends up partaking of the wine, and 2.) What if she goes over with seductive intentions and *doesn't* end up partaking? Well, first of all, the plan wasn't perfect. I was trying to make the best of an unfortunate situation, plus I was working with one hand tied behind my back. If Tag hadn't made me promise not to stab anybody, I could have just waited in the closet for some definitive evidence of Susan's intentions before pouncing. That said, let's be real, Susan's not stepping over that threshold unless it's with indecent intentions. Innocent Susan would drop off the gift and go right back home, and naughty Susan would have to force her way in because there's no way Tag's inviting her — she's the last person he wants to see right now. There's also no way Tag offers her any wine, she'll have to help herself, and since she chose to bring us our very own corkscrew this morning, I suspect she probably will.

Still, the seeds of doubt swirled through my head all morning. I was barely present at the open house I was supposed to be helping put on, and I could hardly bring myself to care. I asked myself if I had done all I could to prevent the worst from happening, and the voice in my head said yes, but the feeling in the pit of my stomach said no. Well, there was nothing I could do about it now, I'd just have to wait and see. It was the longest day of my life, I'm still not sure how I got through it, and it was only four hours. So I guess that means it was the longest half-day of my life.

As I drove back I was finally able to admit to myself that I'd be a little disappointed if I went home and didn't find a dead body waiting for me inside. Then what? Would I be satisfied that Susan wasn't trying to be a homewrecker and that Tag was safe from further mental anguish? Unlikely. It would probably mean we'd all have to start back at square one and do this whole dance all over again tomorrow. What would our end game be if Susan was still alive upon my return? I couldn't answer that question, but hopefully it would be answered for me once I got there.

I pulled into the driveway anxiously, looking for clues as to the fate that awaited me inside. No sign of Susan, but that's not out of the ordinary, she's rarely outside in the mid-afternoon. It felt awfully quiet, but I didn't want to let myself get my hopes up just yet. As I opened the door to the house, despite the fact that I was expecting it, I still couldn't help but be a little shocked that yes, Susan had indeed come over and died on our living room floor. I tried to hide my glee and look somewhat pensive, but I could feel the smile trying desperately to move the corners of my mouth in an upward direction. I braced myself for Tag's reaction, but all I could see in his face was gratitude.

"How did you know?" He asked in amazement.

"I didn't," I confessed as I dumped the rest of the poisoned bottle, "but it was worth a shot." After that he couldn't contain himself. He ran over and kissed me the way he did on our wedding day. Could it be that in less than a day I had already gotten my old Tag back? That he understood me so well that there was no need for an explanation? That moment in time cemented for me once and for all the fact that Tag and I are the rarest kind of soulmates — the kind you don't see every day, the kind you sometimes don't see for a whole generation, the kind whose love can withstand anything: temptation, lust, doubt, the police, murder, incarceration, and yes, even death.

I suppose you already know what happened next, it was on every news channel for heaven's sake. Tag's driving skills ended up being our undoing and we got busted. I don't blame him, though. I knew what I was getting into and the risks involved, and I accepted them happily. So why did I let him take the fall? Because it was the right thing to do. I would have loved nothing more than to take the rap for both of us, but that would have been selfish. In his eyes I'd already done so much for him, and he had done nothing for me in return. In his eyes. I tried to talk him out of it, and I suppose I could have forced the issue, but that would have defeated the purpose of this whole ordeal.

All his life Tag felt unspecial. He felt like he never made a difference to anybody for any reason. The only reason we became so close is because it happened while he was worried about other things. If he'd been paying attention he wouldn't have been able to allow himself to get that close to me. Once we made it official he felt like he did all the taking and I did all the giving. That wasn't true of course, but as I've already said you can't talk someone out of something they don't want to be talked out of. And try as I might, I couldn't make him see what I saw in him.

When he announced his intentions after we got caught, I saw a determination in his eyes that I'd never seen before — that I didn't even know he was capable of. But that's not all I saw, and it took me a little while to figure out what that other thing was because I don't think I'd ever seen it in his face before. It was pride — pride in himself that he could finally do something for me that he felt was on par with the things I'd done for him. So yes, I guess I could have yelled and screamed and gotten him to relent if I wanted to, but I wouldn't have taken that pride away from him for the world. I didn't enjoy the prospect of moving forward without Tag in my daily life, but sometimes, as the saying goes, when you love someone you have to set them free.

He wouldn't let us fight the charges in any way because he didn't want the authorities to investigate and find out that I was involved. He wouldn't cut any deals, he wouldn't mount a case, and he wouldn't speak at the sentencing hearing. He took the full rap for three murders, one of them being a cop. I pretended to cry when they gave him his sentence, but in reality I'd never been more proud of him in my entire life. And standing in that courtroom as it was announced, he looked so brave and confident and... happy... yes, he looked truly happy for the first time in a long time. No, I couldn't take that from him.

If that makes me a terrible person, then I'm a terrible person. I'll take on that burden for him. Believe what you want, I'm not here to change anyone's mind. Tag always loved the story my mom told about me at our rehearsal dinner. He thought the way I handled my hysterical family when my grandmother died showed an amazing ability to rise above my circumstances and do what was necessary. He was so impressed with how I rejected the terrible example set by my self-centered mom and the rest of my self-centered family and followed my more altruistic instincts. And hearing my mom tell the story I don't blame him — but that's not the way I tell it.

The way I tell it is this: I was definitely sixteen, don't let anybody tell you otherwise, I remember because when I got to Grammy's house I was already fuming because I knew my mom wasn't gonna let me order the expensive senior class ring like everybody else in my class. I walked in to the symphony of tears that was my mom and my aunts freaking out over Grammy, who was apparently dead in the chair in the front room. The men didn't know how to handle it, the kids were confused and scared, my sister was in shock, and the three daughters were trying desperately to one-up each other in a game of who can cry the loudest.

I surveyed the scene for a moment and became physically sick to my stomach. The one thing nobody was doing was paying any attention to Grammy in the chair. I walked over to the chair and silently kissed Grammy on the cheek, and for some reason that got everyone silent. My mom and my aunts were staring at me like, "Ew, you just touched a dead thing." I walked over to the front door, turned around, and said, "You guys are all insane." Then I walked out. I had no intention of getting any of them to do anything, but apparently that one little comment caused them all to decide to shape up and get down to business. There was no taking charge of anything— I expressed my disgust and left. But that doesn't make a very good story, so it got spruced up a bit over the years.

The first time my mom told that story publicly was the

night before my wedding in front of a crowd full of family and friends. I think my mom practically had an orgasm when a loud "Awwwww" emitted from the crowd at the end. Then she turned to me, held up her glass of champagne, and said the words that haunt me to this day: "That's when I knew I raised my girl right." That's right, mom, make it all about you. Another "Awwwww" from the crowd and I smiled for the cameras and hugged and kissed my mom. I have no doubt that she believes that her version is the way it happened too. I bet she believes it with every fiber of her being. I bet if someone magically unearthed a video of the occasion it still wouldn't change her mind.

For everyone else the point of that story was that I was some kind of wunderkind golden child who was capable of working miracles with my own bare hands. The point for me, though, was that people believe what they want to believe, they think what they want to think, they see what they want to see, and they remember what they want to remember. And they use it all to support their particular worldview regardless of the true meaning of any of it. For my mom that means fashioning every memory to remind her that despite all her faults and failings, she's still a good person who is constantly being wronged by others for no good reason. For Tag it means fashioning every memory to confirm his belief that he's not that special and is incapable of doing anything that truly matters.

Me? I know it's not that simple. I know the answer is always a combination of the good and the bad. I know my memories often deceive me and I have to try to be as objective as possible. I know there's no excuse for the wrongs I've done in my life and I know I deserve all the consequences. I make many mistakes but no apologies. The shades of gray are not just part of the fabric that makes up my life, they *are* my life.

So it didn't bother me that the others in the viewing booth were staring as I beamed with pride at the man being led out in shackles toward a cold, hard, metal bed with leather straps. They didn't understand why I was crying tears of joy as I waved and blew kisses at him. They didn't understand the excitement I felt when I saw his face light up as he realized that the wildly flailing crazy woman on the other side of the two-way mirror was me. They didn't understand why a man in his situation would feel the need to ecstatically wave his shackled hands and blow kisses back. And they definitely didn't understand why I didn't care that they didn't understand.

As they strapped him into that metal bed all I saw was a man finally at peace with himself. A man bursting with pride that for the first time in his life, he felt like he was doing something worthwhile, something that mattered, something great. Sure it was bittersweet, but I couldn't feel too sad about it, after all Tag was about to do what every single human being on this planet hopes they get the chance to do one day — he was going to die with a smile on his face.

Nowadays as I sit on the couch in the late afternoon, Tag is still beside me. He's beside me in spirit and in the urn that decorates the table above the now not-so-brand-new rug. I still have regular conversations with him in my head, only they go a little bit different now:

"Hey."

"Hey."

"Something wrong?"

"No, everything's perfect."

"Oh?"

"Yeah."

Then I smile and relax, taking comfort in the fact that we're still together. Just like always.

Acknowledgments

This book wouldn't exist without the dedicated help and/or support of several people. I'd most like to thank Tierza, Natty, and Chloe for their patience and encouragement throughout this process. Lynae Leblanc, Jay Tombstone, Todd Berger, Michael Messonnier, and Marsha Philips also helped in various ways during the writing and editing of this book and I'm grateful for their contributions, both large and small. I'd also like to thank Janet, Barbara, Kim, Jeff, and the Guggenheimer and Wall families. Finally, to my publisher and my entire behind the scenes team for their hours of dedication, you went above and beyond the call of duty, and I am very grateful.

www.ingramcontent.com/pod-product-compliance
Lightning Source LLC
Chambersburg PA
CBHW020936310726
48980CB00007B/790/J

* 9 7 8 0 9 8 6 4 1 7 8 0 1 *